MRS. JEFFRIES
and the
Midwinter Murders

MRS. JEFFRIES
and the
Midwinter Murders

Emily Brightwell

BERKLEY PRIME CRIME
NEW YORK

BERKLEY PRIME CRIME
Published by Berkley
An imprint of Penguin Random House LLC
penguinrandomhouse.com

Library of Congress Cataloging-in-Publication Data

Names: Brightwell, Emily, author.
Title: Mrs. Jeffries and the midwinter murders / Emily Brightwell.
Description: First edition. | New York: Berkley Prime Crime, 2021. |
Series: A Victorian mystery; 40
Identifiers: LCCN 2021022238 (print) | LCCN 2021022239 (ebook) |
ISBN 9780593101087 (hardcover) | ISBN 9780593101094 (ebook)
Subjects: GSAFD: Mystery fiction.
Classification: LCC PS3552.R46443 M635 2021 (print) |
LCC PS3552.R46443 (ebook) | DDC 813/.54—dc23
LC record available at https://lccn.loc.gov/2021022238
LC ebook record available at https://lccn.loc.gov/2021022239

Printed in the United States of America
1 3 5 7 9 10 8 6 4 2

*This book is dedicated to the Very Reverend Jeffery
Paul with thanks and gratitude for all his help,
and to St. Peter's Episcopal Church,
Carson City, Nevada*

CHAPTER 1

"How much longer is your wife going to keep us waiting?" Ellen Swineburn glared at the empty chair opposite her father before turning her attention to the others around the elegantly set table. Percy, her brother, drummed his fingers on the top of the silver napkin ring around his serviette. Next to him, Marcella Blakstone, their houseguest, took another sip from the aperitif she'd carried in from the drawing room.

Ellen pursed her lips in disapproval. Marcella was her stepmother's friend and, like her stepmother, was immune to the subtle nuances that separated the genuinely well bred from upstart pretenders. The frown disappeared off her thin, horsey face as her gaze met that of the Reverend Daniel Wheeler, the handsome nephew of the very same stepmother who was keeping everyone waiting for their dinner.

"Be a bit patient, Ellen," Jacob Andover, her father, replied. "I'm sure Harriet's on her way down. She wouldn't deliberately keep everyone waiting."

"You said that ten minutes ago," Percy interjected. He pushed his spectacles up his thin nose. "I'm hungry and we've waited long enough. I say you tell Mrs. Barnard to start serving."

Jacob sighed and reached for the small bell at the side of his plate. Picking it up, he rang it, and a moment later, the housekeeper, who was waiting in the adjoining butler's pantry with the serving maid, stepped through the door and stopped just inside the huge dining room. "Ah, Mrs. Barnard, send one of the maids upstairs to see what's keeping Mrs. Andover."

"She's not upstairs, sir. I don't think Mrs. Andover has come out of the conservatory as yet," Mrs. Barnard replied.

"Then send the maid to the conservatory and tell her we're waiting," he instructed.

"Right away, sir." Mrs. Barnard disappeared.

"Thank you, Father," Ellen said before looking again at Daniel Wheeler. The good reverend was tall, well proportioned, and youthful looking for someone she knew to be forty-one. Brown haired with just a sprinkling of distinguished-looking gray at his temples, he had a lean, attractive face, his complexion was smooth, and his deep-set eyes were a warm brown. She found it difficult to believe that someone as refined, well educated, and intelligent was a blood relative of her very common stepmother. "One hates to be insistent, but we do have guests and we can't keep them waiting for their suppers." She gave Daniel a bright smile as she spoke.

"Please, Ellen, don't be concerned on my account," Daniel

said quickly. "I'm sure Aunt Harriet will be here soon and then we can all enjoy a lovely meal together."

"You were late getting home today." Ellen slipped her serviette out of her napkin ring. "Did you find something interesting in your research?"

"I did indeed. There isn't much known about the real life of Saint Matthew, but I find that reading the history of Israel from that time period provides fascinating details on how he must have lived and what he had to endure to be a follower of our Lord."

"Do you enjoy doing research?" Marcella Blakstone asked.

"Very much." He took a sip of water.

"Of course he does," Ellen cut in, annoyed that Marcella was trying to interject herself into their conversation. She shot the attractive, blonde-haired widow a stern frown. "He'd hardly have come here all the way from America if he didn't."

"Well, I, for one, find mucking about in libraries very tedious," Percy said. "I like being outdoors and breathing fresh air."

"As do I." Daniel grinned. "But I also like mucking about in libraries, and the Reading Room of the British Museum is wonderful."

"But I'm sure there must be some wonderful libraries in California." Marcella smiled again. "I've always wanted to visit San Francisco. It sounds like such a colorful city."

Mrs. Barnard reappeared, her broad face creased with concern. "Excuse me, sir, but the conservatory door is locked and there's no answer. I've sent Marlene down to the kitchen to get the other key."

"It isn't like Mrs. Andover to be late for dinner." Jacob rose to his feet and moved toward the hallway. "I'll go and see what's happened. She might have fallen asleep."

"Well, do hurry it up, we're all hungry," Ellen called after him.

Jacob stepped into the hall, his footsteps making no sound on the new, thick carpeting Harriet had just had installed. Mrs. Barnard was right behind him, but he walked so fast, it was hard for her to keep up with him.

They reached the end of the long hall. The conservatory door was directly opposite the servants' stairs leading to the kitchen. Jacob raised his fist and banged lightly against the wood. "Harriet, Harriet, are you alright? Have you fallen asleep?" He paused, listening for a reply, but heard nothing. He banged again, this time hard enough to rattle the sconces halfway down the corridor, and then again before putting his ear to the wood. There was still nothing but silence. "Are you certain she's not upstairs?" he asked the housekeeper.

"I'm certain, sir," Mrs. Barnard replied. "Right before I brought the trolley up with the first course, the upstairs maid told me she'd taken some extra blankets into Mrs. Andover's room and she wasn't there nor was she in her study."

"What about the library or the little drawing room?"

"She isn't in any of those places, sir. I've looked. Oh good, here's Marlene with the key."

The maid bobbed a quick curtsy and then handed the key to the housekeeper. But before she could move, Jacob grabbed it, shoved it into the keyhole, and unlocked the door.

He stepped inside, followed by Mrs. Barnard and the housemaid. Alarmed now, he rushed past the two huge ferns standing either side of the door, irritably brushing a dangling frond out of his way. "Harriet, Harriet, are you in here? For God's sake, we've been waiting for fifteen minutes."

The short corridor opened into an oblong-shaped room. The floor was cream-and-white tile, which contrasted beautifully with the green metal of the conservatory skeleton and the heavy glass of the walls. On the far side there was an outside door flanked by two polished brass urns overflowing with massive blossoms of white jasmine. Barrels with blooming red and pink geraniums, begonias, African violets, and Christmas cactus were placed around the perimeter. Interspersed among them were colorful ceramic pots, plant stands filled with exotic greenery, and urns with vibrant blooms from all over the world.

A set of white wicker furniture with red upholstered cushions and two matching chairs stood next to a round table with three straight-backed chairs. One of the chairs had overturned.

"Oh my God, Harriet." Jacob broke into a run as he saw his wife lying on the floor next to the upended chair. Mrs. Barnard gasped and Marlene screamed as she saw her mistress sprawled on the floor.

Harriet Andover lay on her back, her attention focused on the ceiling. Tendrils of hair had slipped out of her chignon, her eyes were open, her tongue protruded, and there was a snakelike red-and-black sash wound around her neck.

Jacob dropped to his knees. "Oh my God, Harriet, Harriet, what's happened to you?" He grabbed his wife by the shoulders and began to shake her gently. "Harriet, Harriet, for God's sake, speak to me."

The others, alerted by the maid's scream, came racing

inside. "My Lord, what's all the fuss about?" Percy demanded. He skidded to a halt, causing his sister to stumble into his back and Marcella Blakstone to dodge to one side to avoid crashing into both of them. Daniel Wheeler came in last.

For a long moment, no one said anything; they simply stared at the fallen woman. Marcella Blakstone's hand flew to her mouth. "Oh Lord, what's wrong with her? Has she had a stroke or a heart attack?"

"Harriet, Harriet, wake up." Jacob shook her again. "For God's sake, speak to me."

"Goodness, I hope she's alright," Marcella cried. "Why isn't she waking up? Why isn't she saying anything?"

"Of course she's going to be alright," Ellen snapped. But then her voice trailed off as Daniel Wheeler shoved past her and the others, dodged around Jacob, and knelt down on the other side of his aunt.

He stared at her, his gaze moving quickly over her face and body before fixing on her neck. Then he put a finger under her nose and grasped her wrist with his other hand.

"What are you doing?" Jacob demanded, but Daniel ignored him and merely raised his other hand for silence.

"Don't raise your hand to me, I asked what you're doing," Jacob barked.

"Please, Jacob, I've some experience in these matters. I'm trying to find her pulse."

"Find her pulse?" Jacob repeated. "That's ridiculous, she's merely fainted or had some sort of attack or some such thing."

But Daniel ignored him, dropping her wrist and reaching toward her neck. He pushed the length of fabric to one side and shoved his fingers against her skin. After a few moments, he leaned back and studied her, his attention focused on the red-and-black-plaid cloth and her chest. Then he looked at Jacob. "She's no pulse and she's not breathing. She's gone."

"How do you know that? You're not a doctor." Jacob eased his wife's shoulders onto the floor. "She's merely unconscious."

"Jacob, I'm so very sorry, but as I said, I've had some experience in this area. I'm familiar with both illness and death. I helped the doctors at my parish in Carson City as well as the mission houses in San Francisco and Sacramento. My dear aunt is gone. She's been called home to the Lord."

"She can't be gone, she can't be," Jacob insisted. "We'll call the doctor. Yes, that's right, we'll get the doctor."

"I'm afraid you're going to have to call the police." Leaning over, he pulled the red-and-black sash to one side and showed them the deep indention on her neck. "Someone has strangled her."

"We sent for you as soon as we saw the ligature around the poor woman's neck," Griffiths said to Inspector Witherspoon as he led the way down the corridor to the conservatory.

"Has the body been moved?" Witherspoon asked as they stepped inside.

"Yes, but not by much. Mr. Andover, the victim's husband, didn't realize she was dead and moved her about." Griffiths pointed to the center of the room. "She's over there, sir. I've had the family wait in the drawing room. They're all very upset."

"Thank you, Constable." Gerald Witherspoon was a man of medium height with a pale, bony face, spectacles, and thinning brown hair. "Has the police surgeon been notified?" His steps slowed as he spotted the body. He didn't like corpses, the truth was he was dreadfully squeamish, but he knew his duty.

"Yes, sir, it's Dr. Procash. He should be here soon."

The inspector steeled himself and knelt down by the dead woman. Constable Griffiths knelt down on the other side. Witherspoon gently moved what looked like a thick, dressing gown sash to one side and stared at her neck. "She was strangled."

"It looks like it, sir," Griffiths said.

"Her name is Harriet Andover?" Witherspoon clarified. "And I take it she's mistress here."

"Yes, sir. Her husband is Jacob Andover. They found her body when she didn't come in for dinner."

"Do we know what this is?" Witherspoon pointed at the length of flannel wound loosely around her neck.

Griffiths glanced over his shoulder toward the door. "No one has said, sir, but when I came in, I overheard one of the maids say it looked like the sash to Mr. Andover's dressing gown."

"I see." The inspector ran his hands along her sides, brushing lightly against the blue material of her dress. Finding a pocket, he wiggled his hand inside, trying his best to be both thorough and respectful simultaneously. His fingers closed around a metal object and he pulled it out. "It's a key," he murmured as he handed it to Constable Griffiths. "Take this into evidence."

"The housekeeper said the door was locked, sir." Griffiths nodded toward the inside door leading to the house proper. "They had to send down to the kitchen to get the maid to unlock the door."

"She was locked in here?" Witherspoon found the pocket on the other side and pulled out a neatly folded dainty white handkerchief.

"She locked herself in to work; at least that's what we've been told, sir. But we didn't take comprehensive statements as yet," Griffiths explained.

"Understood, Constable. That makes sense if all she had in her pockets is a handkerchief and the key." Witherspoon rose to his feet. He took a long, hard look at the body, forcing himself to notice each and every little detail. He wasn't certain this was doing any good whatsoever; after all, the body had been moved about. Nonetheless, he'd learned to trust his methods. "Right then, as soon as the police surgeon arrives, we'll take statements."

"What time is Inspector Witherspoon due home tonight?" Phyllis, the housemaid, asked. She put the platter of roast beef and potatoes in the center of the table and took her seat. She was a lovely, slender young woman with dark blonde hair, a porcelain complexion, and sapphire blue eyes.

"He's on duty until ten," Mrs. Jeffries, the housekeeper, replied. "But he left instructions that no one is to wait up for him and we're not to bother with his supper. He said he'd eat at the station."

"Humph," Mrs. Goodge, the white-haired cook, snorted. "There's no canteen there, which means he'll get one of those miserable meals from that café across the road, and their food isn't fit to eat. I don't see why someone of his stature has to do night duty anyway."

"He's only there tonight because Inspector Tarrant came down with shingles," the housekeeper reminded them. She was a woman of late middle age, with dozens of freckles sprinkled over her nose, brown eyes, and auburn hair liberally streaked with gray. She glanced toward the corridor as she heard the back door open. "Wiggins is here now so we needn't wait. Go ahead and serve yourselves."

"It smells so good in 'ere." Wiggins, the footman, hurried into the kitchen. He was a handsome, dark-haired young man in his early twenties. Taking off his cap as he walked, he put it on a peg of the coat tree, slipped out of his jacket, and hung it on the peg beneath it. "Cor blimey, I was afraid Mr. Mulligan wasn't ever goin' to stop talkin'."

"So it's Mr. Mulligan's fault you're late for supper?" the cook teased.

"In a way." He took his seat next to her. "I didn't like to be rude, but I asked him a simple question about how to fix that latch on the dry larder cupboard and he went on about it for ages."

"Does that mean you can fix that latch now?" Phyllis helped herself to a slice of roast beef and then added a generous amount of potatoes.

"I could fix it before he started chattin' about it," Wiggins insisted. "I only asked him about which sort of screw would be best to use on that old wood."

"I still don't like the idea of our inspector eating that dreadful food from the café," the cook continued. She motioned for Wiggins to hand her his plate, and when he did, she plopped a huge slice of beef on it and then a large scoop of potatoes. "What if we get us a murder?"

"Don't say that," Mrs. Jeffries exclaimed. "It seems to happen every year, but I want us to enjoy this Christmas."

"Ta, Mrs. Goodge," Wiggins said as he took his food. He picked up his knife and fork. "But even with all the other murders, we've enjoyed Christmas. We've not had one for months now."

The household wasn't just talking to hear the sound of their own voices. Inspector Gerald Witherspoon had solved more murders than anyone in the history of the Metropolitan Police Force, and one of the main reasons he held such an exemplary record was because of his devoted household. They helped him. Of course, he was unaware of their assistance, and they were determined to keep it that way. All of them, as well as some of their trusted friends, contributed to the investigations in their own way.

Mrs. Goodge contributed her share without leaving her kitchen. Before coming to work for the inspector, the cook had spent her entire career working in the houses of the rich, the well connected, and even an aristocrat or two. More important, she stayed in contact with many of her former colleagues who were scattered all over England, and many of them were right in London. In her experience, gossip, whether true or not, always contained information of some sort, and she was very good at getting old friends to chat about what they'd seen or heard. Additionally, she kept every tradesman, workman, laundry boy, and deliveryman who came to her kitchen plied with tea and treats. Strawberry tarts, seed cake, currant scones, and sponge cake kept them at her table and, more important, kept them talking. It was amazing how much information one could gather just by being hospitable and listening to the bits and pieces they'd picked up.

Wiggins, being a natural sympathetic sort, was excellent at getting people to talk. Once they had a crime to investigate, he'd cozy up to a housemaid or a footman and find out all sorts of useful information.

Mrs. Jeffries had come to London after the death of her husband, a village policeman in Yorkshire. But once she started working for Inspector Witherspoon, she knew her true talent lay not in being a good housekeeper, though she was, but in having the ability to put together clues, gossip, and miscellaneous information to come up with the solution to every murder they'd investigated.

"Still, it would be nice to have one Christmas where all we had to worry about was buying presents and eating ourselves silly," the housekeeper insisted.

"I don't know." Phyllis sliced into a bite of potato. "I think it makes the season all the more exciting."

Mrs. Jeffries ducked her head to hide a smile. When Phyllis first arrived at the household, she was so terrified of losing her position that she refused to help. Now Phyllis was a confident and useful member of their band of sleuths. The young woman was excellent at getting local merchants and shop clerks to divulge details and information about both murder victims and their suspects.

"Let's not worry about whether we've a case or not," the cook declared as she tucked into her own dinner. "I, for one, am more concerned that our poor inspector has to eat overly boiled cabbage with those nasty sausages for his supper."

"Constable Barnes says the food at the café isn't that bad," Wiggins said.

"We can always leave him a plate in the warming oven," Mrs. Jeffries pointed out.

"But he's not due home until late and no one should be eating at that time of night . . ." She broke off as they heard a knock on the back door. "Who can that be?"

Fred, the household's black-and-brown mongrel dog, looked up from where he'd been sleeping on his rug by the cooker. Mrs. Jeffries started to get up, but Wiggins got to his feet first. "Let me go, Mrs. Jeffries. It's already dark." Without waiting for her reply, he raced off to the back door. Fred got up as well and started after the footman.

A few moments later, they heard the door open.

"It's Constable Farley, isn't it? What are you doin' 'ere?" Wiggins said, making sure to be loud enough for the others to hear him.

"I'm just on my way home," Farley replied. "Inspector Witherspoon asked me to stop by and let you know he might be very late tonight."

"Did something 'appen?"

"We got a report that a woman had been murdered. The inspector wanted you to know so you'd not worry."

"Where was this?" Wiggins pressed.

"At a posh address, Number One Princess Gate Gardens," Farley said. "If there's nothin' else, I'll be off."

"Ta, thanks for lettin' us know." Wiggins closed the door and threw the bolt lock at the top. He reached down and patted Fred on his head. "Come on, boy, let's get crackin'." Grinning broadly, he and the dog charged into the kitchen. "Sounds like we've got us a murder."

* * *

Inspector Witherspoon and Constable Griffiths waited by the door leading into the house while Dr. Procash examined the body and prepared it to be moved to the hospital morgue.

Witherspoon glanced at Constable Griffiths. The tall, red-haired young man was a good lad—smart, capable, and more than competent—but when it came to murder, the inspector dearly wished Constable Barnes were there. Nonetheless, one needed to use the resources one had at hand, and he'd bring Barnes on board tomorrow. "Constable, please take charge of taking statements from the servants."

He broke off as Dr. Procash waved at him, indicating he was finished and they'd now be moving the corpse. Witherspoon nodded back and then continued speaking to Griffiths. "A house this big generally has a lot of servants, and we need to make sure we get statements from all of them."

"Yes, sir."

"I'll be in the drawing room taking statements from the family." Witherspoon stepped through the door and walked down the hallway. He stopped at a set of double oak doors and knocked softly before going inside.

He stopped just inside the door, blinking as his eyes adjusted from the dimness of the hallway to the brightness caused by the blazing lights in the overhead crystal chandelier. The room had been done up for Christmas.

Wreaths of holly were hung along the pale-yellow-painted walls interspersed among portraits of stern-looking men in old-fashioned high collars and women in elegant gowns. A thick blue, red, and cream oriental carpet covered the oak floor. Directly opposite the door was a huge fireplace with a mantle topped with ivy and evergreens intertwined with gold and red ribbons, above which hung a large mirror in a gilded silver-and-gold frame. Gold and green tiles surrounded the fireplace proper in front of which was a glass fire screen filled with brilliantly colored stuffed birds posed on branches.

A Christmas tree loaded with unlighted candles, painted ornaments, and bright paper chains stood on one side. Two Louis the Fifteenth–style settees upholstered in blue-and-yellow linen and four matching chairs were arranged artistically in front of the fireplace. A man who looked about sixty sat on one of them. He was thin, with gray hair balding in spots and bushy eyebrows.

He stared at the carpet, his expression one of stunned surprise. Next to him was a slender, very attractive blonde woman, who appeared to be in her early forties. She was staring into the unlighted fireplace. A younger man, who very much resembled the older man except that he had a weak chin, sat in one of the chairs, and next to him was a brown-haired woman with a long face. She looked to Witherspoon to be in her mid-thirties. But it was the slender, dark-haired man in the farthest chair who noticed the inspector and rose to his feet. "I presume you're here to speak with the family," he said.

"I am. I'm Inspector Gerald Witherspoon of the Metropolitan Police Department," Witherspoon introduced himself.

His voice seemed to shake the others into awareness. The older man got up and turned to Inspector Witherspoon. "I'm Jacob Andover. This is my daughter"—he pointed to the brown-haired woman—"Mrs. Ellen Swineburn, and this is my son, Percival Andover." He waved at the younger version of himself. "These are our houseguests, Mrs. Blakstone and the Reverend Daniel Wheeler."

The blonde acknowledged the introduction with a barely perceptible nod of her head.

"I'm pleased to meet you, Inspector." Daniel Wheeler wasn't wearing a clerical collar and had a faint American accent.

"Thank you, sir," Witherspoon replied. He turned his attention to Jacob Andover. "Mr. Andover, I'm sorry to intrude on your grief, but as I'm sure you're aware, I need to take statements from each of you."

"Tonight?" Andover looked surprised. "Can't it wait until tomorrow? We've had a dreadful shock, Inspector."

"I'm aware of that, sir. But one thing we've learned is that in cases like this, time is of the essence," Witherspoon explained.

"But, but that's barbaric," Andover protested. "No one's going anywhere. We'll all be here tomorrow."

"Nonetheless, it's best if we start the investigation immediately. Is there somewhere we can speak privately?"

"Father, the inspector is right. It's best to get this sort of thing over and done with." Ellen Swineburn smiled sadly and got up. "We'll go into the small drawing room. I don't know about the rest of you"—she glanced at the others—"but I could use a drink, and that's where Father keeps his whisky." With that, she turned and headed for the door. The others, except for Jacob Andover, got up and trailed after her. Witherspoon stepped aside as they all trooped into the hallway.

Witherspoon moved closer to Jacob Andover, who looked up as the inspector approached, and pointed to one of the chairs. "Sit down, please, Inspector. I understand you must do your job, but you should realize I've no idea what you want to ask me. I've no idea what happened or who would do such a thing to Harriet. Truthfully, I've no idea about anything anymore."

"I'm sorry for your loss, sir." The inspector took a seat. Reaching into his pocket, he pulled out a pencil and a small notebook. "When did you last see Mrs. Andover?"

"Last see her?" His bushy eyebrows came together in a puzzled frown. "I see her every day. She's my wife."

"I meant when did you last see her today?"

"Oh yes, of course. I'm sorry, that must have sounded very stupid." He shook his head. "Uh, let me see. We had luncheon together at one o'clock with the rest of the household."

"Everyone was there?"

"No, Daniel was at the British Museum. He's from America and doing research for a book," Andover explained. "And my son was at his office. So it was my daughter, Harriet, myself, and Mrs. Blakstone. After luncheon, I went for a long walk, and when I came home, I lay down and promptly fell asleep. When I woke up, I came downstairs . . ." He frowned. "Let me see, I went to my study, and yes, yes, that's when I last saw Harriet. She was in the library. The two rooms are next to one another and she had the door open. I asked her what she was doing, and she replied that she was getting ready to go over her investments. She goes over all her business matters every Monday afternoon. She has a number of enterprises she's put money into and she watches them quite carefully."

"What time was this?"

"I didn't look at the clock, but I'm sure it was close to four."

"And that was the last time you saw your wife?" Wither-spoon asked.

"I saw her a few minutes later as she went into the con-servatory. She always went in at four; she liked to work in there." He smiled. "She said the greenery was quite soothing."

"And you're certain it was at four o'clock?" Witherspoon was a great believer in "timelines." To his mind, finding out who was where at any given time was a great help in solving even the most difficult cases.

"Absolutely, Inspector. My wife is a creature—" He broke off and caught himself. "Was a creature of habit. I went back into my study to work on some correspondence of my own, and not long after that, I heard Mrs. Barnard and the maids bringing the tea trolley to the drawing room. Tea is always served at a quarter past four."

"Did Mrs. Andover take tea with you?"

"No, Harriet didn't take tea in the afternoon, only in the mornings. Afternoon tea gave her indigestion." His voice shook, his eyes filled with tears, and he clasped his hands together. "I don't understand this. How could anyone have done such a thing? Why would anyone want to kill her? There were some who thought her nothing but a no-nonsense businesswoman, but that's not the truth. Admittedly, she could be short-tempered and she didn't suffer fools gladly, but my gracious, the simplest thing could make her happy. She was so pleased when her nephew came from America, she said he reminded her of her older sister, Helen. The three sisters were very close, Inspector, and though she didn't show her emotions, Harriet was devastated by her younger sister's death last year. Daniel coming here meant the world to her. He brought her a broach from his mother." He broke off and swiped at his eyes. "Harriet said it reminded her of the game she played with her sisters years ago. They called it the Secret Silly Game." He gave a bark of laughter that sounded slightly hysterical. "And it was, Inspector, it was. Harriet always won. They had an old shed in their back garden, and the girls used it as a playhouse. But the rule was that whoever got to it first had to latch the door shut, and the other two could only come in if they brought the winner a secret, silly present. Not real presents, of course, things like four-leaf clovers, or flowers, or nicely shaped pinecones." He shook his head and looked away. "How could someone do this to her? How could someone do it to anyone?"

Witherspoon nodded sympathetically. It was obvious the poor man was babbling, saying anything to fill the moment with words so he could delay facing the awful truth that was death.

"We'll do our best to answer that question, Mr. Andover," Witherspoon replied quietly. He, too, had often wondered how anyone could deliberately take a human life. On the other hand, despite Jacob Andover's apparent distress over the loss of his wife, the inspector took it with a grain of salt. He hated to think he was becoming cynical, but he'd met many a murderer who could shed tears at the drop of a hat. "But I do need to ask you some basic information. Aside from you and Mrs. Andover, how many other people live in your household?" He opened his notebook to a blank page.

"My daughter, Mrs. Swineburn, lives with us, as does my son, Percival. He works for an insurance company in

Knightsbridge, so it's very convenient for him here. And as I've mentioned, we also have my wife's nephew, the Reverend Daniel Wheeler, staying with us."

"So Reverend Wheeler lives here as well?"

"Yes, he was staying at a small hotel near the British Museum, I believe it's called the Pennington, but when he came to pay his respects, Harriet insisted he move in with us until he completes his research. He's researching a book on the life of Saint Matthew."

"How many servants are in your household?" Witherspoon dearly missed Constable Barnes. It was very difficult to write fast enough to get everything down properly.

"I'm not certain, my wife took care of household matters, but I think we've seven servants. You'll need to check with Mrs. Barnard; she'll be able to give you a more precise answer. We also have a houseguest here, Mrs. Blakstone. She's a dear friend of Harriet's and she's staying with us because she's having work done on her home."

"How long has Mrs. Blakstone been here?" Witherspoon asked.

"She's been here since the fifteenth of December and had planned on staying until the end of January—that's when the work should be completed." His voice trailed off. "At least that was the original plan. But now I'm not sure what will happen."

"And the Reverend Wheeler, how long has he been staying here?"

"Since the first part of November."

"I see." Witherspoon nodded. There was still much to ask, but it was getting late and he didn't want his witnesses too exhausted to answer questions. "Can you tell me exactly what happened here?"

Andover stared at him, his expression puzzled. "Someone killed Harriet."

"My apologies, Mr. Andover, what I meant was can you tell me the sequence of events that started when your wife went into the conservatory this afternoon." He'd ask for further details about the last day of her life at a later time. Right now, he wanted to establish the sequence of events that had led to her being alone in the conservatory.

"Oh yes, I see." He sucked in a deep breath of air. "I was in my study and Harriet popped her head in and reminded me that I needed to go over the painting estimates for the upstairs bedrooms. Then she went on to the conservatory. At a quarter past four when I went into the drawing room for tea, Percy and Mrs. Blakstone were already there."

"Mr. Percival Andover, your son? Shouldn't he have been at his office?"

Andover shook his head. "He'd come home early. He'd not been feeling well over the weekend so he came home early today. Daniel was still at the British Museum. He didn't come home until later. But I'm not certain of when he arrived here. You'll have to ask him. My daughter was out as well. She was gone for most of the afternoon, shopping or some such thing."

"Was the Reverend Wheeler generally present at teatime?" Witherspoon put his pencil down and stretched his fingers.

"Sometimes he was here, but often he was so engrossed in his research, he didn't leave the museum until it closed for the day."

"What time was your daughter home today?"

"I don't know, Inspector. You'll need to ask her."

Witherspoon said, "Mr. Andover, can you describe what you did between finishing tea and the discovery of Mrs. Andover's body?"

"You're asking me to account for my whereabouts?" Andover gaped at him for a few moments. "But why? I loved my wife. I wouldn't harm her."

"It's a standard question, sir," Witherspoon assured him. "We'll be asking everyone, and I do mean everyone, in the household to account for theirs as well."

Andover pursed his lips. "I suppose you have to ask. After tea, I went to my club. I was there until almost seven o'clock, and then I came home."

"Which club?"

"Brettons on Saint James's Street," he replied. "When I got home, I remembered I'd told Harriet I'd look over the estimates for the painting. I was in my study until half past seven. Then I went upstairs to change for dinner."

"What time is dinner served?"

"Eight o'clock."

"Were you concerned at that point that you hadn't seen Mrs. Andover?" Witherspoon asked.

"Not at all. As I said, my wife had many investments. She was a very good businesswoman. She didn't put her capital in any one given enterprise; she was a very active investor and corresponded with a number of company directors and managers. I just assumed she was either in the conservatory or she'd gone upstairs to change for dinner. But she was generally never late coming downstairs. I was going to send one of the maids up to her room, but Mrs. Barnard commented that she was still in the conservatory, so I asked her to please tell Mrs. Andover that we were waiting for her. But when she came back, she said the door was locked, so she had to go downstairs to get the other key. It took a few moments and that's when we got inside and saw her lying there." He blinked hard and looked away. "At first I thought she'd had a stroke or a heart attack, so I was going to carry her upstairs, but Daniel stopped me. He saw the thing around her neck. Dear God, why would anyone wish to harm Harriet?"

Constable Griffiths adjusted his rather bony backside on the rickety chair for what seemed like the tenth time. He was conducting the interviews in the servants' dining hall and doing his best to make the housemaid relax. Kathleen Judson was an attractive young lady with brown hair tucked into a tight knot at the nape of her neck, a rosebud mouth, deep-set brown eyes, and an expression of terror on her pale face. "Miss Judson, please don't be frightened. I only want to ask you a few questions."

"Yes, sir. Mrs. Barnard said we was to answer anything you asked. But I don't know nuthin', sir. I've no idea who might have wanted to kill Mrs. Andover. I'm just one of the upstairs maids, sir."

"Yes, I understand that," Constable Griffiths replied. "When was the last time you saw Mrs. Andover?"

"Just before she went into the conservatory. She came up to her study to get her letter box. Her study is right next to her bedroom and I was outside. I'd just finished dusting the landing when she came out. She asked me if I'd seen Mr. Andover and I said he was downstairs in his study. She went on downstairs and I heard her stop at Mr. Andover's study and say something to him. I couldn't hear what she said."

"What happened then?"

"I finished dusting the upstairs and then I went downstairs to get the furniture polish. Mondays we always polish the side tables on all the landings."

"I see." Griffiths gave her what he hoped was a reassuring smile. "Was that the last time you saw or spoke to Mrs. Andover?"

She cocked her head to one side. "I think so, unless you count me hearin' her lock the conservatory door."

"You heard her lock the door?"

"I did. The servants' stairs are opposite the inside conservatory door, and just as I got down there, I heard her locking it."

Griffiths realized this might be a very important point. "Did she always lock the door when she was working in the conservatory?"

"Oh yes." Kathleen leaned closer. "Once I overheard Mr. Andover complaining about it, and she told him that if she didn't keep the door locked, she'd have him and both his children in there snooping into her financial affairs."

"Her financial affairs?"

Kathleen looked at the closed door of the dining hall before she spoke. "You'll not tell anyone what I tell you? I mean, you'll not say anything to Mr. Andover or any of the family or even to Mrs. Blakstone?"

"I certainly don't plan on it," Griffiths said. "Uh, we generally don't repeat information we hear from witnesses. However, if you tell me something that becomes pertinent to catching Mrs. Andover's killer, you might be called upon to testify in court."

"Testify in court? You mean in front of a judge? I don't want to do that," she protested. "I need my job here, and now that she's gone, we've no one to protect us. Who knows what the Andovers will do if they get wind of what I say," she declared. "They'll have me out on my ear without so much as a reference."

Griffiths had been a policeman long enough to know when it was important to find out everything the witness knew. He said nothing as he tried to think of a way to get her to talk freely. The trouble was, he understood her point of view. Good positions were hard to come by, but she'd said something that he might be able to use. "You said that now that Mrs. Andover is gone, you've no one to protect you," he began.

"That's right," she interrupted. "If we did our jobs properly, she looked out for us. She made sure the rest of them didn't pick on us for every little thing, made sure we had decent food to eat, didn't make us pay for our own tea or sugar out of our wages, and paid us on time each quarter."

"Then don't you think she'd want you to tell me everything you know? If she looked out for you and the other servants, don't you think her killer should be caught? Don't you owe her that much at least?"

She drew back and then she looked down at her hands for a moment before lifting her head and meeting his gaze. "She'd want me to survive. But you're right, she was good to me and I owe her."

"Rest assured, we'll not pass along anything you tell me unless it's absolutely necessary."

She took a deep breath. "Right then, I'll just say it. She was the one with the money, Constable. Mrs. Fell—she's our cook and she worked here before Mr. Andover married the mistress—Mrs. Fell said that this house was tumbling down around his ears before they wed. But Mrs. Andover was smart. Before she put any money in this place, she made him sign an agreement or some such thing saying she owned half of it. But that's not the important part. She didn't like either of Mr. Andover's children, not Mr. Percy and certainly not Mrs. Swineburn. She thought both of them were lazy and stupid. Once, I overheard her telling one of her friends that the trouble with this country was the upper classes produced half-wits like Mr. Andover's children. She said that one day, if they didn't get rid of the 'half-wits' running the country, England would be in big trouble."

"She shared her opinions freely?"

"Not really. I think she was a bit more careful about what she said in front of the Andover family."

"When did she make this comment, and do you know who she said it to?" Griffiths asked.

"It was December fifteenth," Kathleen said. "The day that Mrs. Blakstone arrived here. I remember because I overheard it when I was unpackin' Mrs. Blakstone's trunk. She and the mistress were in the little sittin' room attached to the guest bedroom when she said it."

"Did Mrs. Blakstone make any comment?"

Kathleen shrugged. "I don't know. I'd finished the unpacking and I was in a hurry to get downstairs for our supper. But when I went out into the hall, I saw Mrs. Swineburn scurrying off like a rat that had just heard the cat coming."

"Do you think she overheard her stepmother's comments?"

"I know she did." She snickered. "Mrs. Swineburn likes to eavesdrop. It wasn't the first time I'd seen her hurrying away from a closed door."

Griffiths scribbled down the information and then looked up. "Thank you for telling me. Now, let's get back to this afternoon. What did you do after hearing Mrs. Andover lock the door to the conservatory?"

"I got the polish and went upstairs to finish my work. After I did the landings, I still had Mrs. Andover's bathroom to clean. It's one of them modern ones, sir, and it's ever so nice. I guess that Mr. Andover will get it now that she's gone."

"Did Mr. and Mrs. Andover have separate rooms?" Griffiths knew that most upper-class couples had their own rooms.

"They did. They used to both have rooms with a connecting door, but she made him move up to the next floor so she could turn his room into her study."

"Mr. Andover's room is on the floor above hers?" Griffiths wanted to be sure he understood.

"That's right, sir."

"Where was the key to the conservatory kept?"

"In Mrs. Andover's pocket . . ." She broke off and laughed. "You mean the second one. That's kept on Mrs. Barnard's peg wall, sir. All the household keys are there."

"What about the key for the outside door?"

"It's the same one as for the inside one, sir. The one key locks both doors."

"Where exactly is Mrs. Barnard's pegboard?" Griffiths now wished he'd spoken with the housekeeper first. This could be very important.

"In her little alcove."

"And where's her little alcove?"

"In the kitchen, sir. Mrs. Barnard doesn't have a proper housekeeper's pantry or office. She does all the menus and ordering from an old closet. They just took the door off and put a little desk and chair there."

"Are the keys visible from the kitchen?"

"Oh yes, sir, and from what Mrs. Fell told Mrs. Barnard, they'd been there in full view of the kitchen servants right up until Mrs. Barnard came down to get the one for the conservatory."

CHAPTER 2

The ornate carriage clock on the table struck the half hour, and Witherspoon noted it was now half past ten. If he was going to finish taking their statements before the sun rose, he was going to need more help. He glanced at Jacob Andover, who was sitting hunched over and staring at the carpet. His skin was slightly greenish in color, his lips were pale, and his right hand trembled. Witherspoon decided that the more in-depth interview could wait until tomorrow. He didn't want the man keeling over from a stroke or a heart attack. "Mr. Andover, you don't look well. Please, go get some rest. We can finish your statement tomorrow."

"Thank you, Inspector." Andover straightened and got slowly to his feet. "I'm grateful. I'm suddenly so exhausted, I can barely move."

The inspector accompanied him to the hallway, watched him move slowly toward the staircase, and disappear up it.

Witherspoon then went to the door that hopefully led to what the household called the small drawing room. He looked inside and surveyed the solemn group. "Mrs. Swineburn," he said, "if you'd be so kind as to come with me, I'd like to take your statement."

"Is my father alright?" She put her whisky glass on the table and stood up.

"He's as well as can be expected. He's very tired, so I told him we'd continue taking his statement tomorrow." Witherspoon moved back into the hallway as she reached the door and came outside. The two of them stepped into the formal drawing room.

"How long is this going to take?" She took a seat in the middle of the settee. "It's very late and everyone is shocked as well as drained by what's happened."

"I'll be as quick as possible," Witherspoon assured her. He went back to the chair he'd been using, flipped open his notebook to a clean page, and picked up his pencil. "First of all, when was the last time today you saw your mother?"

"She's my stepmother," she replied. "And the last time I saw her today was at luncheon."

"You didn't see her this afternoon?"

"No, I had a very busy day and I left the house directly after luncheon."

"What time did you arrive home this afternoon?"

"I didn't notice the exact time." She rubbed her forehead. "My best guess is it was six forty-five or thereabouts."

He made a note of her answer and then looked up. "What did you do this afternoon?" he asked softly.

Clearly annoyed, she drew back. "Is that really the concern of the Metropolitan Police?"

"Mrs. Swineburn, I'm not asking these questions to be intrusive. But a murder has been committed, and finding out the movements of everyone in the household is important."

Shocked, she stared at him as she understood the implication of his words. "Do you consider me a suspect? That's absurd."

"Someone took your stepmother's life, Mrs. Swineburn." He held her gaze. "And it's my task to find out who might have done it, so please, as you pointed out, it's late and I'm sure you're tired. If you'll just answer my questions, we can conclude this unpleasant business quickly."

She closed her eyes briefly as she shook her head. "I'm sorry, Inspector. I know you're just doing your job. The truth is, I'm feeling a bit guilty. My stepmother and I weren't close, but I assure you, I'd never harm her nor would I wish her any ill. As to my whereabouts this afternoon, they were quite ordinary. After luncheon, I went to my dressmaker's shop for a fitting."

"What's the name of your dressmaker?" Witherspoon wiggled his fingers in an attempt to stop a cramp in his thumb. How on earth did Constable Barnes take notes so quickly and so efficiently?

"Lanier's on Morecomb Road in Belgravia," she replied. "I was there until half past two. After that, I went to visit a friend."

"What's the name of your friend?"

"Mrs. Arthur Jennings. She lives at Number Five Rothwell Crescent in Mayfair. Are you going to speak to her?"

"I'm afraid so, Mrs. Swineburn. It's proper police procedure to verify everyone in the household's movements for this afternoon."

"That's a bit embarrassing, Inspector. My friends aren't the sort of people who'll appreciate having the police on their doorstep." She pursed her lips. "But I suppose you have to do it."

"What time did you arrive at Mrs. Jennings' home?"

"Let me see," she murmured. "It must have been three o'clock or thereabouts. I walked from the dressmaker's shop. But I took my time and went around the edge of Hyde Park. Cecily has not been well and I knew she rested after luncheon. I didn't want to arrive while she was still napping."

"Do you remember what time you left?"

"Of course, it was a quarter to four." She smiled self-consciously. "I didn't want to stay for tea because I wanted to stop by Liberty's before they closed."

"You went to Liberty's upon leaving the Jennings home?" he clarified.

She nodded. "I did. I was there until closing time—"

He interrupted, "What time was that?'

"Six o'clock, and then I came home," she replied.

"How long have Mr. and Mrs. Andover been married?" Witherspoon had no idea why that question popped out of his mouth, but since it had, he decided the answer might provide useful information.

"About ten years." She shrugged. "I wasn't at their wedding, so I don't recall the exact date."

"I see," Witherspoon murmured. "How long have you lived here?"

Her face creased in annoyance. "I don't think my personal circumstances are any of your concern."

"Mrs. Swineburn, as I said before, your stepmother has been murdered. I'm assuming you do want me to find the person who took her life? You may think my questions are impertinent, but I assure you, answering them can help us greatly. Background information is always important."

She said nothing for a moment; she simply stared at him. "It's something you can easily find out by asking the servants. I moved here after my husband died. That was five years ago."

"I'm sorry for your loss," Witherspoon said. "Has your stepmother had any conflicts or disputes with anyone lately?"

"Conflicts or disputes? How should I know? It's certainly possible; she wasn't an easy person to get along with."

"You lived in the same house, Mrs. Swineburn. Surely if Mrs. Andover was having difficulties with someone, you'd have heard of it."

"As far as I know, she wasn't," Ellen replied. "But you're wrong in thinking I'd know about it, even if it had been true. She was a very self-contained woman who kept her own counsel and didn't share her problems with others."

"Not even her own family?" Witherspoon pressed. He stopped scribbling and looked at Mrs. Swineburn. Her eyes were narrowed and her expression belligerent as she spoke about the murdered woman.

She sat up straighter. "My stepmother was very strong-minded, Inspector. She didn't seek the family's approval or advice on any matter other than the color of paint for the upstairs bedrooms. I believe she was consulting with my father about that."

"Are you saying she was domineering?"

Ellen shrugged. "Not especially, Inspector, she simply assumed she was always right. She left you alone as long as you didn't try to interfere in her life or countermand any of her household decisions."

"Such as?"

"Such as when she and my father were buying new carpeting for the downstairs hall." Ellen pointed at the door. "My father wanted a deep royal blue, but Harriet insisted it wouldn't wear well, so we've got that awful brown-and-green-patterned monstrosity."

Witherspoon put his pencil down, stretched his aching fingers, and picked it up again. Ellen Swineburn had already admitted she and her stepmother weren't close, but he was beginning to think there was more animosity between the two women than Mrs. Swineburn had indicated. "Your father commented that Mrs. Andover took her business interests very seriously. Was that your impression as well?"

"Yes."

"As far as you know, had there been any problems with her investments? Had she complained about someone cheating her or anything of that nature?"

She gave a negative shake of her head. "Not as far as I know, but as I've said, she wasn't one to discuss business with our family, not even my father. The only person she may have confided in was her nephew."

"Reverend Wheeler?"

"That's right. He's a very kind person, and one of the few people whose company Harriet seemed to genuinely enjoy."

"I understand he's been here since the beginning of November?"

"Right again, Inspector. He came to pay his respects, but once Harriet met him, she insisted he come stay with us instead of that dreary little hotel near the British Museum. She said he was the spitting image of his mother, her oldest sister, Helen."

"Thank you, Mrs. Swineburn," Witherspoon said. "That'll be all for right now."

She stood up. "Well, let's hope this matter can be resolved as quickly as possible." She moved toward the door.

"Would you please send your brother in?" he asked.

Because of the lateness of the hour, Witherspoon took only the briefest of statements from the others in the household. Percy Andover confirmed he'd left his office early and had come home at half past three with a headache and the sniffles, though he seemed just fine to the inspector. Marcella Blakstone had spent the afternoon taking care of matters at her home, and the Reverend Daniel Wheeler said he was at the Reading Room of the British Museum until almost six o'clock.

None of them admitted to seeing, hearing, or knowing anything about the death of Harriet Andover. After making it clear that he'd be back the next day for more in-depth interviews, the inspector collected Constable Griffiths, who reported that he'd managed to speak to only two of the housemaids, and the two policemen left.

It was past midnight before Inspector Witherspoon let himself into the front door of his home. He took off his bowler and hung it on the coat tree, and was unbuttoning his heavy black overcoat when he heard footsteps. Turning, he saw Mrs. Jeffries hurrying toward him. "Gracious, Mrs. Jeffries, didn't you get my message? I certainly didn't expect anyone in the household to wait up for me."

"We got your message, sir. But I wasn't tired, and you know how I love hearing about your cases. I couldn't possibly go to sleep after learning you'd been called out on a murder. Are you hungry, sir? Mrs. Goodge made a lovely roast beef tonight, and I can easily make you a sandwich, or even a plate."

"Thank you, but no. Eating this late at night always gives me indigestion. However, I would love to have a sherry with you. I'll tell you all about what happened this evening." He headed down the corridor to his study with Mrs. Jeffries on his heels.

As he settled into his overstuffed leather chair, she went to the liquor cabinet, pulled out a bottle of Harveys Bristol Cream sherry, and poured both of them a drink. After handing him his glass, she took her own seat. "Now, sir, do tell."

"As you know, I was only on duty because Inspector Tarrant has the shingles. Nonetheless, I was there when the call came in that a woman named Harriet Andover had been murdered. It was quite close by." He took a quick sip. "The Andover home is on Princess Gate Gardens."

"That's a very expensive area, sir," she murmured.

"Indeed it is. You should see the house—even in the dark, there was enough light to see that there's a lovely cream facade on the outside and six full floors. But I digress. When we got there, it was obvious that Mrs. Andover had been strangled."

"Strangled? With what?"

"With a sash from a dressing gown." His brows drew together. "According to what Constable Griffiths overheard from one of the housemaids, the sash seems to have come from Mr. Jacob Andover's dressing gown. He's the victim's husband. The constable confirmed that the sash was from the dressing gown when one of the staff identified it."

"I take it you interviewed him? What did he say about it?"

"He was the first one I spoke with, but at the time I was taking Mr. Andover's statement, it was only something that

Constable Griffiths had overheard; he'd not verified it till much later. I didn't want to mention the sash until it was confirmed as belonging to Mr. Andover. So that's a question I'll need to ask him tomorrow."

She nodded. She could tell he was exhausted and she didn't want to keep him up longer than absolutely necessary, but the more information she had about the crime, the faster they could get out and about hunting for clues. "Is it just Mr. and Mrs. Andover who live in the household?"

He shook his head. "No, there are a number of people I'll need to speak to again." He took another drink and then continued his narrative. He spoke slowly, taking care to tell her every detail that he could recall. He wasn't just speaking to hear the sound of his own voice or to satisfy her curiosity; over the years he'd learned that talking about the case helped him see the facts.

Mrs. Jeffries listened carefully. She silently repeated the names he mentioned as she listened. Her memory wasn't what it used to be, but she knew that if she had names to give to the others tomorrow morning, they would have a starting point. They were at the ready, and everyone should be there for the morning meeting—she'd made sure of that.

Right after Wiggins announced they had a murder, she'd sent him to Knightsbridge to notify Luty Belle Crookshank and Hatchet. She'd also sent Phyllis to tell Betsy and Smythe, Inspector Witherspoon's coachman and his former housemaid, that they needed to be here as well. She herself had walked across the communal garden to leave a note with Lady Cannonberry's butler that she should be here, too.

Witherspoon continued speaking, telling her what Constable Griffiths had learned from speaking to the housemaids before circling back to the interviews he'd conducted. "I spoke at length to Jacob Andover and his daughter, Ellen Swineburn," he continued. "But even so, I'll need to speak to them again. Mrs. Swineburn didn't arrive home today until a quarter to seven, at which time she had a rest and changed for dinner. Mind you, as Mrs. Andover locked herself in the conservatory at four o'clock today, we'll need to confirm everyone's alibi from that time up until the body was discovered."

Mrs. Jeffries took a sip of her sherry. "Will that be difficult, sir?"

"Mrs. Swineburn was at her dressmaker's, Lanier's in Mayfair."

"Lanier's?" Mrs. Jeffries repeated.

Witherspoon looked at her over the rim of his spectacles. "You know the establishment?"

Indeed, she did, but she didn't want to remind him of it as yet. "No, no, sir, but I have heard of them. They're quite exclusive."

"Well, exclusive or not, I'm going to send a constable to verify that Mrs. Swineburn was actually there." He took another drink.

"I take it you'll be checking Mr. Andover's whereabouts for the afternoon as well," she murmured. "He was at his club?"

"That's right." Witherspoon sighed heavily. "This case is going to be difficult, Mrs. Jeffries. The victim was in a locked room, and both keys are accounted for—so how did the killer get in, and more importantly, how did he get out? The house was full of people—there are seven servants, two houseguests, and three family members—but no one heard or saw anything. Mind you, it would be helpful to know exactly when the woman was murdered, but despite so many scientific advances, all a postmortem can do is give us a reasonable estimate of the time of death, and I'm fairly sure Dr. Procash's report is only going to tell us what we already know; she was killed sometime between four o'clock and eight that evening."

"Now, now, sir, don't be discouraged. You've solved complex cases before. You'll solve this one."

"That's kind of you to say." He brightened. "You're right, I mustn't let myself get disheartened. I suppose I'm just very, very tired." He covered his mouth and yawned.

"You've had a long day, sir."

"But you've made me feel much better. Even though the interviews were hardly more than perfunctory, we learned quite a bit tonight. I mean, it was getting rather late. Everyone in the Andover household appeared to be shocked, but I still got the impression that, other than her husband, Mrs. Andover wasn't particularly well liked by her family." He drained his glass and sat it on the side table. "Mind you, that's merely an impression."

"But you're very perceptive, sir," she told him. "I'm sure your sense of the situation is correct."

He put his hand up to stifle another yawn as he got to his feet. "I hope so, Mrs. Jeffries. But over the years, I've learned that first impressions sometimes aren't to be trusted."

"Luckily, I got to the station early this morning and they told me the inspector had caught a murder." Constable Barnes nodded his thanks as Mrs. Goodge handed him a mug of tea. He was a tall man with wavy iron gray hair, a ruddy complexion, and a ramrod-straight spine. He and the inspector had worked on every homicide case together since Witherspoon had left the records room and been assigned to the Ladbroke Road Station. As was his habit when they were on a case, he made a quick stop in the kitchen before going upstairs.

When the constable first noticed the inspector was getting information and clues outside the scope of their investigations, it hadn't taken long before he realized it was Witherspoon's own household that was helping him. At first, he was alarmed by this turn of events—after all, they were amateurs who shouldn't have been mucking about with murder. But something had stopped him from pursuing the matter and exposing them. Instead, he'd kept a close watch on the situation. Then he'd seen that the household and their friends were careful, smart, and clever. Even better, they could get answers out of people who wouldn't give a policeman the time of day. What's more, several of them had access to places and information that were strictly off-limits for the Metropolitan Police Force.

"What do you know so far?" Barnes asked.

Mrs. Jeffries told him and Mrs. Goodge what she'd learned from Witherspoon last night. He drank his tea as he listened and mentally made up a list of questions that might need answering.

"Was the inspector sure both doors leading into the conservatory were locked?" he asked when she'd finished.

"He was and that alone made him think this one was going to be hard to solve." Mrs. Jeffries smiled at Barnes. "He'll be happy you're with him today."

"I'm sorry the inspector had to start this one on his own." The constable put his now empty tea mug on the table and rose to his feet. "But I'm sure Constable Griffiths did a good job in my stead."

"He was very competent." Mrs. Jeffries got up as well. "But the inspector missed you dreadfully. He told me this morning that it didn't feel right without you there."

"And he can't understand how you can take notes so fast," Mrs. Goodge added. "He said he got a terrible cramp in his fingers last night."

Barnes chuckled. "Good to hear that I'm still needed. I'll see you tomorrow morning, and hopefully, we'll have made progress on this one."

As soon as he'd disappeared up the back stairs, the two women set about getting the kitchen ready for their meeting. Ten minutes later, they heard the men leaving out the front door, just as the back door opened and footsteps pounded up the corridor.

"Amanda, stop running, you'll fall," Betsy ordered.

But the little girl only giggled and ran into the kitchen. She skidded to a halt as she spotted her godmother, Mrs. Goodge. The cook put a plate of brown bread on the table and then held out her arms. Amanda raced over and Mrs. Goodge scooped her up. "Let's go have us a cuddle before your other godmother gets here." Using her foot, she shoved her seat away from the table and sat down with the child.

Amanda immediately waved her chubby fingers at the plate of bread. "Want bread, Goma," she said, using the only name she could pronounce, as the word "godmother" was too difficult for her. Luty Belle Crookshank, her other god-mother, was called "Gama."

Betsy—a lovely, slender, blonde matron in her late twenties—swept into the kitchen. She was followed by her tall, muscular husband, Smythe. The coachman was a good fifteen years older than his wife. His dark brown hair was liberally threaded with gray, his features strong, and his face saved from being harsh by the smile on his lips and the twinkle in his brown eyes.

"I thought we'd have this Christmas all to ourselves, but it looks like we've got us another murder." Smythe pulled out a chair for his wife.

"I don't mind. They've always been solved before Christmas Eve or Day." Betsy sat down and frowned at her daughter. "You can't possibly be hungry. You just had breakfast."

"Jam and bwead. Goma's jam." Amanda pointed to a pot of strawberry preserves sitting by the bread plate.

Mrs. Goodge shifted Amanda on one side and pulled the jam pot closer. "Now, now, Betsy, as you just pointed out, it's Christmas. Surely the little one can have a bit of jam and bread."

"Alright, but just half a slice. She's developing a real sweet tooth."

They heard the back door open and, a moment later, Hatchet's strong voice. "Do slow down, madam." But the sound of heels clicking against the dark wood of the corridor just got faster, and a moment later, Luty Belle Crookshank burst into the room. The tiny white-haired American who loved bright clothes was dressed in a peacock blue cloak and matching hat decorated with streaming lace and feathers. "Where's my baby?" she called as she dashed across the kitchen.

"Gama, Gama." Amanda giggled as she saw her other godmother.

"You can have her in a minute." Mrs. Goodge cut a slice

of bread in half and pulled the jam pot close enough to reach. "Let me do her bread and jam first. Besides, I've only just put her on my lap." There was a good bit of friendly rivalry between the two godmothers.

A tall white-haired man dressed in a black frock coat and holding an old-fashioned black top hat stepped into the room. "Really, madam, you're going to hurt yourself if you keep racing off like a street lad."

Hatchet was supposedly Luty's butler, but their relationship was far more than employer and employee. They were devoted to each other. He put his hat down on the edge of the table and pulled Luty's chair out.

"Humph." Luty sat down and fixed the cook with a mock frown. "Now don't you go hoggin' that child. I want my turn, too."

"Stop your complaining." The cook snickered as she slathered jam on the bread. "You can have her as soon as she eats her treat."

Amanda's smile disappeared as she looked from Luty to Mrs. Goodge. "No, no, Goma, Gama, no fight . . ."

"We're just teasin', sweetie," Luty assured her.

"Don't fuss now, your Gama and I are good friends, we're just havin' a bit of fun." Mrs. Goodge handed the bread to Amanda.

"Luv Gama, luv Goma." Amanda grinned and then stuffed a bite into her mouth.

Mrs. Goodge looked at Luty. "She's at the age where she understands more than we think—we'll need to be careful. She doesn't realize we're just amusing ourselves."

"Understood," Luty agreed. "And she's a sensitive little one."

Phyllis put a fresh pot of tea on the table and took her seat just as they heard the back door open again, and a few moments later, Lady Cannonberry—or Ruth, as she was known—arrived.

"I do hope I haven't kept you waiting." She shrugged out of her coat as she crossed to the table. She was a woman of late middle age, slender as a girl, with blonde hair that tended to darken in the winter. She was the widow of a peer and the daughter of a country vicar who took Christ's admonition to love thy neighbor as thyself seriously. She was also dedicated to working for the rights of women.

"You're fine, Ruth," Mrs. Jeffries assured her. "We've only sat down and we're waiting for Wiggins."

"I'm 'ere." He stepped into the kitchen, wiping his hands on a clean rag. "It took longer to fix that latch than I thought it would." He pulled out his chair and sat down.

"Let's get started now," Mrs. Jeffries said when they were all settled. She told them most of what she'd learned from the inspector. She did keep one detail out of her narrative—she was saving that. When she was finished, she sat back and waited for their questions.

"Do we know for certain that both the doors to the conservatory were locked?" Hatchet asked.

"We do; both the inspector and Constable Griffiths confirmed it with the household. One of the keys was in the victim's pocket, and the other was hanging in full view of the kitchen servants until it was used."

"And the names you gave us, they're the only people we should be investigating?" Ruth clarified. "Oh dear, that didn't come out as I meant it. What I'm trying to ask is if we know who else might have disliked Mrs. Andover. From what you've just told us, she had a number of business interests and that could imply she also had some enemies in that quarter."

"We don't know who else might have had a reason to kill her. However, from the way the murder was described, it would have to be someone who had access to the conservatory." Mrs. Jeffries frowned as she said the words. "But that might not have been a problem for the killer. We know very little as yet. But you're right, Ruth, there is an outside door to the conservatory, and the inspector said it was Mrs. Andover's habit to work there every Monday afternoon."

"Which means there were lots of people that could have known she'd be there and that she'd be alone," Mrs. Goodge added.

Ruth nodded in agreement. "If it's all the same to everyone, I'll use my sources to find out if the victim was part of the women's suffrage movement. I know you think that might be a pointless exercise, but she was a businesswoman, so she might have had some connection to the organization. More importantly, some of our members might know about her. Many of them are very much in favor of women getting out in the world and making their own money."

"I'll have a gander at her financial situation," Luty volunteered. She had a number of sources she could tap in the banking community, as well as a network of wealthy friends. She had the knack of getting a person to open up to her, be they a beggar or a banker, and within a few minutes of meeting her, they'd be telling her their life story.

"I'll take the merchants on the local High Street," Phyllis offered. She shot a quick look at Betsy. "Unless you'd like to do that?" Before marrying Smythe and having a child, Betsy had been the one to tackle the shopkeepers and clerks in whatever neighborhood the murder had occurred. Since the change in her life, Betsy now took a less active role—but she did her fair share in other areas. Yet Phyllis knew Betsy could be sensitive about her contributions to their investigations, and the maid didn't want her friend thinking she was being pushed aside.

"No, I'm going to go to the British Museum." Betsy grinned. "I've always wanted to go into the Reading Room. Now I have an excuse."

"You're going to have a look at the Reverend Wheeler?" Mrs. Jeffries nodded in approval. "Good, we need to look at everyone in the household. But if you don't mind putting the British Museum off for a bit, I've another task for you. Remember Nanette Lanier?" she asked. This was the one detail she'd held back.

"I remember her. It was ages ago, but she was that French lady who we helped when her friend went missing," Luty put in.

"That's right, and she owes us a favor or two. Back then, she owned a hat shop. But now there's a dressmaker's shop in Mayfair with the same name, and I'm wondering—"

"It's her," Betsy interrupted. "I know the shop. I don't know why I never mentioned it, but when I happened to be passing by, I saw her inside and I went in to say 'hello.' We had a lovely chat." She glanced at her husband. He smiled faintly, and she knew he understood exactly what had happened and why she'd never mentioned it before. The truth was, she'd gone in to have a dress made and buy a new hat, but as most everyone sitting around this table thought she and Smythe merely a former housemaid and a coachman, they'd wonder how she could afford a dressmaker in Mayfair. "What do you want me to ask her?"

Mrs. Jeffries, who'd seen the quick look between husband and wife and was one of the few who knew the truth about their financial situation, went right to the heart of the matter. She knew this was a sensitive issue for both of them and wanted to focus the conversation elsewhere. "I'd like you to confirm that Ellen Swineburn was at the shop yesterday and that she was there until half past two getting a dress fitted."

"That shouldn't be a worry," Betsy said. "As you've said, Nanette Lanier owes us a favor or two."

"If it's all the same to everyone, I'll see what I can find out about Jacob Andover and Marcella Blakstone?" Mrs. Goodge shifted Amanda to a more comfortable angle. "The laundry boy will be here this morning, and as the Andover house is so close, he might do them as well. In which case, he might know something."

"I'll see if I can make contact with one of the Andover servants." Wiggins put his mug down.

"And I'll start with the local hansom drivers." Smythe looked at the housekeeper. "We don't know exactly when the lady was murdered, do we?"

"No, only that it had to be sometime between four o'clock and eight fifteen or thereabouts when the body was discovered. The inspector didn't have time for more than a passing word with Dr. Procash, so he wasn't able to get his opinion on the time of death."

"That's more than four hours," Hatchet mused. "That's a fairly large window of time. Oh well, we've got to start somewhere. I shall have a word with my friends the Manleys. They might know something worth learning."

"Good, then let's get to it. We need to get this solved before Christmas!" Mrs. Jeffries exclaimed.

Chairs scraped, elbows bumped, and dishes rattled as everyone rose to their feet and readied themselves for the hunt.

Constable Barnes flipped his notebook open and put it on the rickety table next to his pencil. He sat back and glanced around the small, cluttered room. On the far wall, there was a row of glass-fronted cabinets filled with mismatched dishes, crockery, and cooking utensils. The walls were painted a pale, ugly green; the green-and-black linoleum floor was cracked and scuffed with boot marks. The tabletop was scratched, and most of the straight-backed chairs didn't match. A pale winter light filtered in from the one window, which was draped with a limp, wheat-colored curtain. In short, it was very much like every other servants' dining hall he'd seen.

He shifted on the uncomfortable chair as he waited for Mrs. Barnard, the housekeeper. He and the inspector had stopped in at the Ladbroke Road Station, and he'd had a chance to go over the two statements taken by Constable Griffiths. Inspector Witherspoon was upstairs speaking to the family and the houseguests.

The door opened, and a middle-aged woman dressed in a black bombazine dress stepped inside. "I'm so sorry to keep you waiting, Constable, but there were matters I absolutely had to tend to." She closed the door softly before crossing to the chair opposite him and sat down.

"I'm Constable Barnes," he introduced himself. She was tall, with brown-gray hair neatly fashioned into a chignon, thin lips, and hazel eyes. "Please don't apologize, Mrs. Barnard. I realize the household is probably a bit overwhelmed at the moment."

"It's far worse than overwhelmed," she murmured. "But you're not here to listen to complaints about our domestic affairs. Mr. Andover has instructed me and the other servants to answer any and all of your questions."

Barnes picked up his pencil. "When was the last time you saw Mrs. Andover?"

"Just before four o'clock yesterday afternoon. I saw her as she went into the conservatory."

"According to what we've been told, Mrs. Andover always worked in there on Monday afternoons and she always kept the door locked. Is that correct?" He looked up from his notebook.

"That's correct. Though I didn't hear her lock the door when I was in the hallway. She'd just gone in and her arms were filled with her letter box and her correspondence."

"One of the housemaids has confirmed that she locked the door," he said. "Did you see anyone hanging around the area, specifically anyone showing undue interest in your garden?"

"As far as I know, the only person who was in the garden yesterday was Mr. Debman—he's the gardener."

Barnes looked up sharply. "He was in the garden?"

She shook her head. "Only until one o'clock or thereabouts. He only does a half day on Mondays."

"I understand that Mrs. Andover's body was discovered after you sent a housemaid down to get the spare key? Is that right?" After reading Griffiths' report, he'd made sure to take a good look at the housekeeper's alcove as he went past.

The maid was right. The key would have been in plain sight of all the kitchen staff yesterday afternoon.

"That's correct. When Mrs. Andover didn't answer us, I sent Marlene down for the spare key. Mrs. Andover had her own key."

"Yes, a key was in the evidence list; it was found in her pocket," he said. "What time was this?"

She frowned. "I didn't look at the clock, but it was probably eight fifteen or so. Dinner is served at eight, and the family waited a good ten or fifteen minutes for Mrs. Andover. It was actually quite alarming. Mrs. Andover likes her food. She doesn't take afternoon tea and she's never late for dinner."

"Was Mr. Andover alarmed by his wife's tardiness?"

"I don't know, you'll need to ask him." She glanced at the closed door and then leaned closer. "The truth is, they were all more annoyed than worried. I was in the butler's pantry right off the dining room waiting to bring out the first course. Mrs. Swineburn and Mr. Percy Andover both complained about having to wait for their dinner. I can't serve until both Mr. and Mrs. Andover are at the table. That's the house rule."

"Did Mr. and Mrs. Andover get along well with one another?" Barnes thought of the sash used to strangle the poor woman.

"As far as I know, they got along as well as most married couples." She looked down at the scratched tabletop.

"Did Mrs. Andover get along well with her stepchildren?"

Mrs. Barnard shifted uneasily and then looked up. "Not really. In my opinion, she didn't like them, and they certainly didn't like her."

"Can you be more specific, Mrs. Barnard?" he pressed. "I'm not asking you to tell tales out of turn, but it's been our experience that household staff often see and hear things that can have a bearing on the case."

She said nothing for a moment, then she sat up straighter and looked him directly in the eye. "Mr. Percy and Mrs. Swineburn considered Mrs. Andover a low person."

"A low person," he repeated. "I'm not certain I understand."

"The Andovers consider themselves landed gentry, one tiny rung lower than the aristocrats. When Mr. Andover married the late mistress, they thought he'd taken a step down in status. They are dreadful snobs, Constable, but like so many of that class, they've no money."

"I thought Mr. Andover owned this house." Barnes knew that to be true, but he wanted to keep her talking.

"He does, but it's her money that keeps it up. I once overheard Mrs. Swineburn describe Mrs. Andover as 'common as mud,' and Mr. Percy had a dreadful argument with both her and his father when she insisted he find employment. He kept claiming that 'a gentleman' shouldn't work. Mrs. Andover reminded him that he could only call himself 'a gentleman' if he had independent means to support himself. Which, of course, neither Mr. Percy nor Mrs. Swineburn had. Mind you, both Mrs. Swineburn and Mr. Percy kept a civil tongue in their heads. Mrs. Andover controls the purse strings." She broke off. "Well, she did control them. But now that she's gone, it looks like none of them have to dance to her tune anymore."

Upstairs, Inspector Witherspoon watched a sweat break out on Percival Andover's forehead. He thought it odd—the room was quite cold and he'd only asked the most mundane of questions. "Excuse me, Mr. Andover, but you haven't answered me."

Percy blinked. "Oh dear, sorry, this has been most upsetting, Inspector. My mind keeps wandering. What was it you asked?"

"What time did you leave your office yesterday?" It was a simple enough inquiry.

"I'm not certain." He swallowed. "Midafternoon, I think it was close to three."

"You left because you felt ill?"

"Yes, I wasn't feeling well over the weekend but I went in to work on Monday morning. I should have stayed home."

"When was the last time you saw your stepmother?"

"At breakfast yesterday morning."

"You didn't see her when you came home yesterday?"

"No, I went straight up to my room and took a rest. I didn't get up until teatime."

"Do you know of anyone who has had a conflict with Mrs. Andover?"

"My stepmother was a very opinionated woman. She had conflicts with a number of people. She's quarreled with Mr. Cragan. He's one of our neighbors. She wanted him to pay his share of fixing the wall between our adjoining properties. Oh, and she's also threatened to sue one of her stockbrokers; his name is Peter Rolland."

"I see." Witherspoon nodded and made a mental note to ask Mr. Andover about these two items. "Had either of these two people threatened your stepmother?"

"Not as far as I know."

"You say your stepmother threatened to sue this Mr. Rolland. Had she actually done so?"

"No, but she did speak with her solicitor about the matter."

"When was this?"

"About two months ago," he said.

"What exactly do you do, Mr. Andover, and what's the name of your place of employment?" Witherspoon asked.

"Why do you need to know that?"

"You said you were at your office for most of the day yesterday. We'll need to confirm that with your employer."

"But my stepmother was killed last night, not while I was at my office," he protested. "I don't see why you need to speak to them. Frankly, my employers will not look kindly at the police arriving on their doorstep."

His chin quivered slightly, and for a moment, Witherspoon was reminded of a rabbit. "We don't know precisely when Mrs. Andover was murdered. So please, answer my question."

He clasped his hands together and brought them to his chest. "Alright, if you insist. I'm a manager for the Banker's Insurance Trust. Their main offices are in the City, of course, but as there are so many of their clients in this part of London, they opened a small branch in Knightsbridge." A bead of sweat rolled down the center of his forehead and picked up speed until it dangled at the end of his nose.

Unable to tear his gaze away, Witherspoon stared at it until finally it fell off. He realized that Percy Andover had asked him a question. "Excuse me, could you repeat that?"

"I asked if you could possibly see your way clear to not speaking to my employer. My position there isn't very good right now. I'm afraid if the police show up, it will get even worse." Percy swallowed so heavily, his Adam's apple bobbled.

"I'm sorry, Mr. Andover, but I've just explained that we've no idea exactly when Mrs. Andover was killed. Confirming everyone in the household's movements yesterday is important."

Percy's face paled. "Actually, Inspector, this is quite embarrassing. But I'd prefer it if you could see your way clear to . . . oh dear, oh dear . . . I don't know what to say."

"Why don't you just tell me the truth?" Witherspoon asked. "That's really all an innocent person ever has to do."

"I am innocent," he protested. "My stepmother and I weren't close, but I had nothing to do with her death. Oh my goodness, you must believe me."

"Then why are you so upset, Mr. Andover?" Witherspoon asked.

"But I'm not."

"You are, sir. You look as if you've run for miles, your face is noticeably paler than ten minutes ago, and you apparently can't think of what to say."

"You don't understand, Inspector. Going to them could cause me a great deal of trouble and embarrassment."

"Come now, Mr. Andover, your own actions are making you look guilty. Surely you'll not lose your position simply because we ask them to verify your statement."

"I've already lost it," he blurted out. He glanced quickly at the closed door of the drawing room. "I was sacked months ago, but I couldn't let my family find out."

CHAPTER 3

"Sacked?" Witherspoon repeated. "And your family has no idea you no longer have a job?"

Percy nodded. "That's correct. I wouldn't have said anything about the matter except you're going to speak to my former employer. I know this makes me look very bad, but I assure you, I've nothing to do with my stepmother's murder. I simply don't like working. Well, that wasn't the exact situation. It was more a case that my employer didn't appreciate the hours I wanted to keep. Apparently, they expect you to be there from early in the morning until half past five or even six o'clock in the evening."

Surprised, Witherspoon simply stared at the man. It took him a good thirty seconds to recover and ask another question. "When were you sacked?"

"At the end of September."

"You've been pretending to have a job since the end of

September?" Witherspoon pressed. He wanted to understand, to ask how on earth anyone could possibly keep up such a tiring charade? But other than satisfying his own curiosity, the man's employment situation probably had very little to do with Mrs. Andover's murder. On the other hand, from what he'd learned of the dead woman, she might have been the driving force behind Percy hiding his employment situation. He could well have kept up the pretense because he was worried she'd ban him from the house.

"I think my sister is starting to suspect." He frowned, then brightened. "But the others are completely in the dark, and if you don't mind my asking, I'd like to keep it that way. At least until after the funeral. Father doesn't need any additional unpleasant surprises."

"If you weren't at work yesterday, where were you?"

Percy steepled his hands together under his chin in a thoughtful pose. "Let me see, to begin with, I generally go to the park—"

The inspector interrupted, "Which park?"

"Hyde Park, of course. I love watching the horses and the riders trotting down Rotten Row. Though lately there haven't been so many of them because the weather has been so dreadfully miserable."

"What time did you leave the park, and where did you go after that?" Witherspoon asked.

"It was very cold yesterday morning, so I didn't stay very long." He drew in a deep breath and expelled it slowly. "I went to Paddington Station—it's a nice walk and gets me a bit of exercise, which I understand is quite good for one. Once there, I bought a copy of *The Standard* and then had a cup of tea in the café. Train stations are very useful, especially this time of year." He paused and shoved his spectacles back up his nose. "They're warm, and if someone happens to see you there, they'll simply assume you either stopped in for a quick cup of tea or are going on a business trip. In other words, Inspector, if someone spotted me at Paddington or one of the other train stations at that time of day, they'd think nothing of it. No one would assume I was there because I was unemployed."

"How long were you at the station?"

"I always stay until it's close to morning opening time for the pubs, then I find a nice place and settle in."

"A pub near the station? Then someone should remember you being there," Witherspoon began, only to be interrupted.

"Oh no, no, the pubs around that area are far too close to here," Percy explained. "I always go to one further afield, if you get my meaning. Yesterday I went to the White Horse in Islington. I was there from right after morning opening until just after lunchtime, so I'm certain the barman or the barmaid will remember me."

"You didn't meet anyone at the pub?"

He shook his head. "No, the point of going there was simply to have a warm place to sit while I waited for the hours to pass. After that, I went for a long walk." He laughed self-consciously. "Usually I limit how much I drink, but I had a bit more than I should yesterday so I walked until midafternoon, by which time I judged I was sober enough to come home."

Witherspoon couldn't help himself—he had to ask. "Mr. Andover, is going to a pub a daily habit?"

"Oh no, Inspector," he replied. "I don't always go to a

pub. Sometimes I go shopping on Bond Street or I go to a museum—not the British Museum, of course. Running into Daniel wouldn't be helpful to me, would it? I rather like to read, so sometimes I'll go and explore the wonderful book shops on Charing Cross Road."

The inspector nodded as if he understood, but he didn't. He couldn't fathom how someone could keep up such a strange pretense. "Did you see anyone you know when you were walking yesterday?" Percy Andover's whereabouts for the afternoon were almost impossible to verify. Witherspoon wondered if they should even bother trying. Mrs. Andover was definitely alive when Percy arrived home yesterday.

"Of course not, Inspector." Percy looked at him as if he were a half-wit. "Haven't you understood what I've been telling you? The only place where it would be safe to be seen is the train station. But once I'm away from there, the whole point of the exercise is to avoid being spotted by someone who knows me. I take great pains to avoid streets and neighborhoods where I might be seen by a friend or an acquaintance. I must say, it's getting a bit tiresome. Once Father gets over Harriet's death, I'll tell him the truth."

"Are you suggesting it was your stepmother more than your father who would have been the most upset by your losing your position?" Witherspoon watched him carefully as he asked the question. Surely Andover realized this could well be a motive for murder.

"Of course it was her doing. Do you think my father would have insisted his only son work in some nasty little office? My father is a gentleman. She's the one who forced the issue," he complained. "Her middle-class sensibilities were ridiculous. She had no idea about how a true gentleman should live. It was her idea that I should spend my days grubbing around with accounting lists in that silly office."

"If she'd found out you were sacked, would she have asked you to leave this house?"

"She might have tried such a thing. But that would have been one battle she wouldn't have won. My father owns this house, and he'd not let his own flesh and blood be tossed into the street. Once this situation has been sorted out, it'll be a relief to start living like a gentleman again." He smiled as he spoke, but his good mood quickly disappeared. He leaned closer to Witherspoon. "Since I got the sack, Inspector, I've had to dip into what little savings I have just to pay my club fees and other bills. She was a most unreasonable person. Before she insisted I work, she gave me a quarterly allowance. But once I had the job, she cut it off completely!"

Wiggins kept a sharp lookout for constables as he made his way past Number One Princess Gate Gardens. He didn't want to have to explain what he was doing here to Constable Griffiths or any of the other constables who knew him by sight. But if it did happen, this neighborhood was close enough to the inspector's home that he could come up with something.

He slowed his steps as he surveyed the Andover home. Wiggins knew today was probably his best chance of making contact with a housemaid or a footman. There was a death in the family, so the normal routine of the household would be disrupted. There would be extra telegrams to send, additional mouths to feed due to family and friends making condolence calls.

He dropped to one knee and pretended to tie his shoe as

his gaze swept the entire property. It was the end house on a row of identical attached Georgian homes. The cream-colored facade looked recently redone, and the black door gleamed as if freshly painted. There was a narrow walkway on one side that extended down the length of the building to the back. The servants' entrance was probably along there somewhere, he thought.

Wiggins looked up and down the block as he stood up, searching for a darkened alcove or clump of bushes where he could stay out of sight while watching the place. But the elegant town homes across the street had tiny front gardens with nary a bush or tree in sight, and there was no place to hide on this side of the road, either. "Cor blimey," he muttered, "you'd think there'd at least be a post box I could duck behind."

He circled the block twice, but decided against a third time when he saw the curtain of the house across the street twitch. Blast a Spaniard, he thought, he'd been spotted. Stopping, he reached into his pocket and pulled out a blank piece of paper. He held it up and pretended to read it. Hopefully, whoever was watching him would think he was lost and trying to find an address.

Just then, he heard a door slam, and to his delight, it came from the Andover home. From the corner of his eye, he watched a young woman hurrying up the walkway. She had a shopping basket tucked over one arm. Wiggins pretended to read the paper as she approached, frowning as if confused. He'd dressed carefully in his best coat and matching flat cap, his polished shoes, and a proper shirt and tie. In a neighborhood this posh, being dressed like the locals could be helpful.

He scrutinized her as she came closer. She was a tall young woman with flaming red hair under her neat house-maid's cap. He stepped back almost off the pavement to give her room to pass. She gave him a swift, assessing glance, her gaze lingering a split second longer on his nice clothes and expensive shoes.

"Excuse me, miss," he said politely as he whipped off his cap. "I'm hoping you can help me. I think I'm lost." He took care with the way he spoke. He wasn't acting like a footman here.

She stopped. "Where are ya goin'?"

"I'm looking for Malcolm and Sons, the haberdashers. I thought the High Street was along here somewhere." He continued to fake confusion. "But I've taken a wrong turn. If you could just point me in the right direction, I'd be ever so grateful."

She studied him for a moment and then cast a quick look over her shoulder. Wiggins knew he had her then; she was making certain no one from the house had seen her talking to a young man.

"I know where Malcolm's is," she said. "I'm goin' that way myself. You can walk with me if you've a mind to."

"Thank you, miss." He gave her his best smile. "That's very, very kind of you. My name is Arthur Harley-Jones."

"I'm Angela Evans. It's this way." She pointed straight ahead and started walking. He fell into step beside her.

"I'm so sorry to trouble you," he apologized. "I hope this won't take you out of your way."

"As I said, I was going that way." She tossed another quick look over her shoulder as they walked away from the Andover house. "And I'm in no hurry to get back to work."

"That's kind of you, miss." He gave her another smile. "But I'd not like you to get into trouble with your household because you were kind enough to help me."

She laughed. "Don't worry about that. They're all in such a blather, they'll not notice whether I'm there or not, not with what's happened."

"Forgive me, miss, but you've aroused my curiosity. What happened?" They turned the corner and came to the High Street. Wiggins realized that he might be running out of time. He came to a complete stop and turned to face her. She was so surprised, she halted as well.

"The mistress has been murdered, and it's upset everything," she blurted out. She sucked in a deep breath and continued speaking. "Mrs. Barnard, she's the housekeeper, has already been questioned by the police, as have two of the upstairs maids—Mrs. Fell, she's the cook, says we're all going to be questioned and we must all tell the truth, otherwise we'll go to hell. But it's not like any of us would deliberately lie to the police. Why should we? The mistress wasn't perfect, but she was always decent and fair, and that's more than I can say for the Andover family."

"Oh dear, a murder?" He tried his best to look shocked and hoped he wasn't overdoing it. "That must have been awful for you. I hope you're alright."

She smiled shyly. "I'm alright. I'm the scullery maid, so I've been downstairs most of the time. But it's been terrible for everyone else. Everyone's walking about tight-lipped and miserable. Thank goodness we've Reverend Wheeler, he's Mrs. Andover's nephew and he's a houseguest. The poor man has spent the whole day trying to give aid and comfort to the family as well as us." She started walking again.

"Now Colleen Murphy, she's one of the upstairs maids, has got her eye on Reverend Wheeler. You know, thinking that as he's an American, he'll not notice she's just a housemaid who hasn't ever been out of London."

Wiggins wasn't sure how to steer the conversation, but as Miss Evans didn't show any signs of slowing down, he stayed silent.

"What's more, just because he's from America doesn't mean he's goin' to take her seriously." They stopped as they reached a corner. "But she goes on and on about how he's always smilin' at her. I tried to tell her not to get her hopes up high, but she won't hear of it. She thinks that just because he's given her a bit of attention that he likes her special. But if you ask me, he's just one of them men that treat everyone nice—I mean, after all, he's a priest, even if he's an American." She snorted delicately. "As a matter of fact, I told her she better be careful. Just because he's been nice to her, he'll not like her snoopin' in his things, and I know for a fact she was havin' a look in his desk and it wasn't the first time, either."

"She admitted to going through his desk?" Wiggins hoped he sounded scandalized.

"Well, she didn't actually admit it, but how would she know what was in the telegram Reverend Wheeler got yesterday morning if she hadn't been snooping? Reverend Wheeler left the house just a few minutes after he took the telegram up to his room, so it isn't like he would have had time to confide in her." She snorted again, only this time it wasn't in the least bit delicate. "If you ask me, Colleen needs to be careful. But she's not one to hold her tongue, and she thinks that because she's pretty, all she has to do is bat her eyes at a man and she can get away with anything. It wasn't that interesting a telegram, either. All it said was some old uncle of his was going to Tombstone. Don't they have strange names in America? Tombstone, who would want to live in a town with a name like that?"

"Not me," he murmured.

"Now I ask you, how would Colleen have known those details if she'd not read that telegram?"

"It sounds as if she did."

"It's been a terrible day." Angela sighed. "I'm upset and I'm chattering like an angry magpie."

Wiggins shot her a sympathetic smile. "You've every right to be upset, miss. I imagine being in a house where there was a murder is right nasty."

"Thank you, you're very kind. I was glad when Mrs. Fell insisted we had to get in more provisions, in case they have relatives come for the funeral. She wasn't the only one havin' a bit of a fit, either. Mr. Debman, he's the gardener, he spent twenty minutes today complainin' that someone has been muckin' about with his coat and hat."

"Why would anyone do such a thing?" Wiggins slowed his pace.

"That's what we tried to tell him, but once Mr. Debman gets an idea in his head, he'll not let it go. He went on about it so long that Mrs. Barnard told him if he couldn't stop his complaining, he needed to leave the kitchen, because everyone was upset enough without him addin' to it over somethin' silly like someone puttin' his ruddy hat and coat on the wrong peg. He keeps them out in the shed and he said that, twice now, someone's moved them. But if you ask me, he's goin' a bit senile, you know, startin' to forget things."

*   *   *

"I understand you wish to speak to me." Reverend Wheeler stepped into the drawing room. He wore a dark suit, a white shirt, and a black tie.

"I've a few more questions," Witherspoon replied. "It won't take long, Reverend Wheeler."

"Thank you." He crossed the room and took a seat on the settee opposite the inspector. "Mr. Andover has asked me to help organize my aunt's funeral service and, well, as I'm sure you can imagine, the household is in shock. I'm doing what I can to help both the family and servants, but everyone is most upset. Please, ask your questions, Inspector. I'll do anything I can to help find my aunt's murderer."

"I understand you've been here since the beginning of November, is that correct?" Witherspoon said.

"Yes, I stopped in to pay my respects and to pass along a broach of my late mother's." He sighed and looked away. "I'd been at the Pennington Hotel for several weeks prior to that. Sorry, forgive me, even though I've only known my aunt Harriet for a short time, she's been so very wonderful to me that I'm quite upset myself. She insisted I move in here and has been nothing but kind and generous to me. We've grown quite close in the weeks that I've been here."

"Did she confide in you?"

His eyes narrowed thoughtfully. "Perhaps a bit. I was both a blood relative and a bit of an outsider, if you understand what I mean."

"Did she ever mention that she was concerned for her safety? Was there anyone in her life that she was worried might try to harm her?" Witherspoon would generally have led up to this sort of question slowly, after asking for more background information, but the opening here was too good to pass up.

Reverend Wheeler shook his head. "Not as such, Inspector, but she did tell me she was worried about someone here in the household."

"She was concerned someone would hurt her?" he pressed.

"No, no, Inspector, I wouldn't go that far." He smiled self-consciously. "She merely stated that she wished she could trust everyone in her household, that's all. When I pressed her on the matter, she got embarrassed and said she shouldn't have said anything. She appeared upset, and I was hoping to ease her mind, but my aunt was a very proud woman. She didn't like to admit to weakness or fear."

"I see." Witherspoon nodded. "When was the last time you saw your aunt?"

"At breakfast yesterday morning."

Witherspoon started to ask the standard questions, but then realized there was something else he wanted to know first. "I understand it was you who insisted the police be called, and it was you who realized she was dead."

He nodded. "That's true, Inspector. I've no real medical training, but I've assisted the medical men at the mission house in Sacramento enough to know death when I see it. When I saw the plaid sash around her neck, I realized that something dreadful must have happened."

"Do you know whose sash it is?" Witherspoon asked. He was fairly sure the sash belonged to Jacob Andover, but he wanted to know if Daniel Wheeler knew the answer.

His brows drew together. "I'm not certain, Inspector. I've a feeling I've seen that particular plaid before, but I don't recall where it might have been." He shrugged. "Still, it's probably a very common pattern, and that's why it looked familiar."

"I understand you spend most of the day at the British Museum?"

"I do, Inspector. I'm writing a book on Saint Matthew. There isn't much factual material on him, of course, so I'm researching general information on what that specific time period must have been like. You can learn so very much about how people behaved, why they did the things they did, why a tax collector making a good living would up and walk away to follow our Lord. It's fascinating."

Witherspoon watched his face as he spoke, noting that his enthusiasm for his subject made him look simultaneously intelligent and boyish. "Yes, I'm sure it is. Is there anyone who can confirm you were there yesterday afternoon?"

"I'm sure the librarians will remember me. I'm there most days. But if you'd like to speak to someone specific, there's a nice lady who is doing research on medicinal herbs that often sits at the same table as I do. Her name is Miss Nora Barlow."

"Thank you, that's very helpful, but I'm sure all we'll need to do is get verification from the librarian. What time did you say you left the museum yesterday?"

"It was close to six o'clock. I wanted to get back here in time to change for dinner."

"Did you have a parish or a church in America?"

"I was at Saint Peter's Episcopal Church in Carson City for ten months, then the diocese moved me to the Episcopal mission house in Sacramento."

Witherspoon picked up his pencil and notebook and

wrote down the information. "Your mother and Mrs. Andover were sisters, is that correct?"

"That's right, but I only met my aunt this past October. My parents left England right after I was born to live in North America. We spent some years in Vancouver—my father was a fisherman and had his own boat. When he passed away, my mother and I moved to San Francisco to be near family. Uncle Teddy, as she called him, was all the family we had left, save for each other." He looked away. "My dear mama died four years ago and I miss her dreadfully each and every day."

"She never thought of coming back to England?"

"Oh yes, she did. As a matter of fact, we'd made plans to come for a long visit, but she caught pneumonia and passed away." He closed his eyes briefly. "As much as my faith sustains me, Inspector, that was a hard blow, and I didn't have the heart to come without her."

"Thank you, Reverend, background information is always important. How long have you actually been in England?"

"I've been here since October fifteenth. I'd been in France doing some research in Paris."

"You speak French?"

"Not very well. My reading comprehension is better than my ability to speak the language."

"How long were you in Paris?"

"Two weeks," he replied. "Then I came here and moved into the Pennington Hotel so I could be close to the British Museum."

"Have you noticed anyone hanging around the neighborhood?"

Wheeler's boyish face looked confused for a moment. "You mean, someone who I'd not seen here before? I'm a stranger here myself, Inspector. I wouldn't really know who does or doesn't belong here."

"I'm sorry, Reverend, I wasn't clear. What I meant to ask was have you seen anyone recently who showed undue interest in this house? Someone who struck you as suspicious?"

He steepled his fingers under his chin, his expression now thoughtful. "Not really, no—no, I tell a lie. For the last few days, I have noticed an older gentleman who I'd never seen before. The reason I remember him was because he was standing across the street staring at the house. I thought nothing of it at the time. Elderly people occasionally get a bit confused when they're on their own. The truth is, I thought he might be lost. I started to cross the road and ask him if I could be of service, but when he saw me looking his way, he hurried off."

"What did he look like?"

"Let me see, he had on an old-fashioned black top hat and a black greatcoat. I didn't get a close look at his face, but he had a beard and mustache. Oh, and his hair was gray."

"When was the last time you saw him?" Witherspoon put his pencil down and stretched his fingers.

Wheeler's eyes widened. "Oh, gracious, Inspector, it was yesterday morning. How stupid of me, I should have told you this right away."

"How long is this goin' to take? I've bread rising and I can't trust that silly girl to punch it down properly." Mrs. Fell, the cook, crossed her arms over her ample bosom and gave Barnes a flat-eyed stare. Beneath her floppy cook's cap, her hair was gray, her cheeks rosy, and her blue-and-white-striped apron dusted with flour.

"Not long, Mrs. Fell. When was the last time you saw Mrs. Andover?" Barnes picked up his pencil and flipped open his notebook to a clean page.

"Yesterday afternoon. She came down to the kitchen to have a word with Mrs. Barnard."

Barnes looked up. In a household like this, he'd have expected the mistress of the house to call the housekeeper upstairs. "Was that her habit? Coming down here instead of calling the housekeeper up to her study or morning room?"

"Mrs. Andover didn't believe in such nonsensical airs." Mrs. Fell uncrossed her arms. "She wasn't an easy mistress, but she was decent and fair to the staff. She used to call her up to her study, but after she found out Mrs. Barnard's arthritis was so bad, she took to coming down here."

"So the servants liked Mrs. Andover?" Barnes pressed.

"Yes, once the master married her, things got easier for all of us, but especially for those of us who've been here a long while. She took over the household, and she was easier to deal with than the others."

"By the 'others,' you're referring to Mr. Jacob Andover and his children?"

Mrs. Fell glanced at the closed door before answering.

Barnes noticed that all the servants he'd interviewed did the same thing—they made certain they wouldn't be overheard before they answered the questions.

"That's exactly what I'm saying," the cook continued. "Before Mrs. Andover was here, this place was tumbling down around our ears. She put a fair amount of money into it, with a new heating system and fixing the windows in the attic rooms so the housemaids didn't freeze to death. What's more, she made sure that us servants had decent food to eat and enough of it so we weren't half-hungry all the time."

"I see," Barnes said. "Did the rest of the Andover family like Mrs. Andover?" The answer to that question was obvious, but he wanted to hear what she had to say.

She snorted. "They'll pretend they did, but they didn't like her at all." Once again, she glanced over her shoulder at the closed door. "Mr. Percy Andover, he and his sister were always making nasty comments about her when her back was turned. Mind you, I don't even think it was anything personal with them two, I think they just got their noses out of joint because they considered her common and themselves better than gentry. But the truth is, she was the one with the money, and if you don't mind my sayin' so, she didn't let them forget it, either."

"I understand that, last night, the housemaid came down to get the spare key to the conservatory door."

"That's right, we wondered what was going on." She leaned closer. "Mrs. Barnard and Marlene had taken the first course up, but then it seemed like ages passed and she'd not come down to get the main course. Then all of a sudden, Marlene come flying down the stairs like the hounds of 'ell were after her, grabbed the key, and raced back upstairs. Well, of course, Angela—she's the scullery maid—had to know what was going on, so she dashed up after her. A few minutes later, she come back and told us they'd found Mrs. Andover murdered."

Barnes looked up sharply. "She said 'murdered,' not 'dead'?"

"That's right, she overheard the Reverend tell Mr. Andover to send for the police and that Mrs. Andover had been strangled." She shook her head, her expression one of disbelief. "It was shocking, terribly shocking. In all my years in service, I've never worked in a house where there was a murder, and frankly, I don't much like it."

"Lady Cannonberry has come to call," Winslow—Octavia Wells' butler—announced from the open double doors of her study.

Octavia looked up from the open ledger on her desk. "Oh, do send her in, and ask Mary to bring up some tea. I've not seen Ruth in forever."

"Yes, ma'am." Winslow retreated, only to return a moment later with Ruth. "I'll see to the tea, ma'am," he said as he withdrew, closing the door behind him.

Octavia leapt up and came around from behind her desk. "This is a delightful but not unexpected surprise."

Ruth laughed. "You've read the papers?" She smiled at her friend. Octavia Wells had bright red hair, a very ample figure, and an excellent dressmaker. Today she wore a serviceable white blouse with fashionable puffy sleeves, a gray serge skirt with a wide emerald green sash, gold earrings, and an emerald-and-gold broach the size of a goose egg.

If one didn't look carefully, one would think her a typical, upper-class society matron obsessed with clothes, the London social scene, dinner parties, and elegant balls. In reality she was smart, savvy, and the treasurer of the London Society for Women's Suffrage. She knew everyone who had money, everyone who had influence, and everyone who could possibly lend support to the cause she believed in with her whole heart.

"Indeed I have." Octavia gestured toward the forest green love seat opposite her desk. "Come, let's sit down and have tea. Mary will bring it up in a minute."

Octavia sat on one end, and Ruth took the other and then pulled off her gloves. She glanced around the study and smiled in delight. "You've even decorated in here."

Paper Christmas streamers in white, red, and gold were intertwined overhead and attached at each corner. Over the small fireplace next to Octavia's desk was a huge Christmas wreath bedecked with miniature colored birds, ribbons, and holly berries. A lovely little tree, decorated with brightly painted wooden ornaments, more ribbons, strings of red berries, and even a few unlighted candles stood next to the fireplace.

"But of course. I spend most of my time in here," Octavia explained. "And I love to enjoy the season. Now, please tell me you've come to ask me about Harriet Andover. I know your inspector is on the case, and I was so upset to see she'd been murdered."

Ruth nodded. There was no point in being coy—Octavia was well aware of her activities and was happy to provide any information she could. Despite her reputation as a dreadful gossip, she was, in fact, discreet, taking care only to repeat things that were already common knowledge in their social circle. "I'm so sorry, Octavia, I didn't realize she was a friend of yours."

"She wasn't, but I did know the woman and I quite liked her. Luckily, I have no doubt her killer will be caught, as your inspector is in charge of the case."

"He is." She smiled, proud that Gerald was being acknowledged and equally proud that she and the others did their part to see that justice was served. "It seems we always have a case at Christmas."

"Not to worry." She patted Ruth's hand. "Your inspector will get it solved."

The door opened and a housemaid carrying a silver tray entered.

"Put it on the desk, Mary," Octavia instructed. "I'll pour."

"Yes, ma'am." She put the tray down and withdrew.

Octavia got up, moved the short distance to her desk, and prepared their tea. "I liked Harriet Andover, but I will admit I don't know all that much about her," she said as she handed Ruth her cup. "We've been trying to interest her in our cause for some time now."

"She wasn't interested?" Ruth took a sip.

"I wouldn't say she wasn't interested." Octavia picked up her cup. "She kept telling us she'd think about it, but I had the feeling she was saying it more out of politeness than any conviction that women should have equal legal rights."

"What do you mean?"

"She was a very astute businesswoman, and more importantly, she controlled her own money. That's a rarity in this country, though I will concede that the passage of the second Married Women's Property Act helped enormously. But in our society's view, it certainly didn't go nearly far enough. Still, because of it, Harriet Tichner was able to hang on to her own money when she married Jacob Andover." Octavia took her seat again. "The last time I saw her, she made it very clear that she believed in some aspects of our cause. She supported the idea of women having the right to vote and control their own property. But she was too busy with her own business interests to be of much help to our group. She also said that she spent half her time making certain that she wasn't being swindled by 'stupid men,' all of whom assumed she was an idiot because of her gender." She chuckled. "And those were her exact words."

"She sounds quite fierce." Ruth was disappointed and struggled to hide it.

"She was. I first met her several years ago at the home of her sister, Henrietta Royle. The two women were as different as chalk and cheese. I approached her thinking she'd be sympathetic because Mrs. Royle was a great supporter of our cause."

"I don't recall hearing that name," Ruth said. Nor did she recall Mrs. Jeffries telling them that the victim had a sister.

"She wasn't a member—like so many of our supporters, her husband was an old hidebound reactionary that wouldn't hear of her actually joining us. But Henrietta had a bit of money of her own and was quite generous to the society. Unfortunately, she must have loved the old reactionary, because she committed suicide last year when he died."

"Suicide?"

"It was never officially ruled suicide, but that was the gossip," Octavia said, her expression solemn. "It was quite awful. She shot herself on the train back to London. She'd taken her husband's body to the Brookwood Cemetery in Surrey for burial. She was on the train coming home, and just as it pulled into Waterloo Station, she shot herself."

"I don't recall reading anything about it. When did it happen?"

Octavia tapped her finger against her chin. "About this time last year, and there is a good reason you didn't read about it. As I said, it was never ruled a suicide. Her husband's family managed to keep the details out of the papers. Not only that, but she was given a Christian burial right next to him at Brookwood." Octavia pursed her lips. "It's sickening when you think of it. Some poor girl throws herself in the Thames, and because she's a suicide, the local parish won't give her a decent service, but the rules for the rich are different." She shook her head in disgust.

"That's true, and it's wrong," Ruth declared. "That's one of the reasons we're working so hard to make the world a more equitable place. Once women have the vote, many of these outdated, autocratic ideas and unfair practices will end. Women can change the world."

"I hope you're right, but nonetheless, it's still very sad. Despite being wealthy, that poor woman must have been devastated to take such a drastic step."

"It happened on a train?" Ruth exclaimed. "And the authorities deemed it an accident?"

"They went to great lengths to avoid embarrassing the family." Octavia took another sip from her cup. "And this certainly isn't the first time something like this has been done, you know, making sure the rich aren't embarrassed by something as awful as a suicide. But the evidence supports the suicide theory. She was in a first-class compartment and the gun, a small derringer of some sort, was found on the floor by her hand. She was alone in the compartment. Mind you, she wasn't on the cemetery train. She'd taken an express train from Woking."

"Cemetery train, oh, you mean the Necropolis Railway," Ruth said. "I've been on that one a time or two myself. That's one of the reasons I was so surprised, it's always so crowded."

"True. But Henrietta didn't take it home that day—she'd stayed at the cemetery for several hours. She wanted to see her husband buried," Octavia said. "What's more, there was gossip at the time that Mrs. Royle had been diagnosed with stomach cancer only days before her husband's heart attack. All in all, it's simply one of those tragic stories one hears every day." She closed her eyes. "Sorry, I liked Henrietta Royle, and when we lose women like her, I despair we'll ever achieve our goals. It's just that we've worked so hard and we've barely made any progress. I had hoped to see women get the right to vote before I die, but Henrietta and I were close to the same age, and now she's gone, so I doubt that's going to happen."

This time, it was Ruth who reached across and patted her friend's arm. "We've made tremendous progress, and I, for one, am sure we'll win this particular battle."

"Don't mind me." She smiled. "Sometimes I get a bit maudlin, especially at this time of the year."

"As do I, Octavia," Ruth admitted. She made a mental note to ask Mrs. Jeffries to check with Constable Barnes. It would be interesting to see what the official coroner's or police report might have said about the death of Mrs. Andover's sister. "But be of good cheer, we have right on our side."

"You wish to speak with me, Inspector?" Marcella Blakstone stood in the open doorway of the drawing room. Like everyone else in the household, she was dressed in mourning. She wore a high-necked dark gray blouse with a black skirt topped with a wide black velvet cummerbund.

"I do, Mrs. Blakstone, please come in." He gestured toward the chair opposite him.

"I don't understand." She moved into the room and sat down. "I told you everything I know last night."

"As it was so late, I took very perfunctory statements last night. If you'll recall, I did make it clear I'd be back today," he reminded her. Up close he could see she was a lovely woman, but not as young as he'd first thought. There were rather deep lines around her eyes, and the veins on her hands were prominent and blue. "You said that yesterday you left the house right after luncheon, correct?"

"That's right, I had a busy afternoon. I went to Regent Street to look at fabric for the drawing room drapes."

He interrupted, "Where specifically did you go? Which shops?"

Her blue eyes widened in surprise. "If you must know, I called in at several shops. The first one was Manard's—they're right next to the Hanover Bank—and the second place was Harrington's."

"How long were you at these establishments?"

"Just a few minutes. Both of the shops were ridiculously crowded, and when I realized it would take ages to get served, I simply had a look at the fabrics and then left."

"You spoke to no one who can verify your account?" Witherspoon asked.

Again, she stared at him, her expression clearly surprised. "What on earth do you mean, Inspector? Surely you don't think I had anything to do with Harriet's death. She was my best friend."

"I'm not accusing you of anything, Mrs. Blakstone," he explained. "I'm simply trying to get a sense of where everyone was and what they were doing in the hours prior to Mrs. Andover's death."

"But that's absurd. Surely you don't think one of us murdered Harriet." Her eyes flashed angrily. "That's ridiculous. People like us don't commit crimes. We leave that to the lower classes. I'm sure you're going to find that poor Harriet was killed by some maniac who managed to get into the conservatory. It's probably that dreadful Ripper killer that you police never arrested."

Witherspoon took a deep breath. "Mrs. Blakstone, as I'm sure you're aware by now, Mrs. Andover was murdered in a locked room. Both the doors going into the conservatory were locked, and Mrs. Andover had the key in her pocket, so the chances of a maniac getting inside, killing the poor woman, and then miraculously finding a way to lock the outside door is rather small."

Betsy stopped outside Lanier's and stared at the display in the front window. Three hat stands, each topped with an elegant and fashionable bonnet, stood along the far side of the window. A swath of silky pink fabric covered the inside window floor, on top of which lay a black beaded evening bag, a pair of formal white evening gloves, and an open catalogue of dressmaker illustrations.

Stepping inside, Betsy paused by the door and surveyed the room. Directly opposite the front door, there were various-sized drawers from halfway down the wall to the floor. Two tall tables displayed more hats, evening bags, formal evening gloves ranging from pink to cream to white, as well as colorful feather boas and fur muffs. On a third table—this one closest to a door on the left side of the room—there was a stack of dressmaker's pattern books and several bolts of fabric.

Three well-dressed customers were in the shop, all of them being served by shop assistants wearing gray skirts and either pink or white blouses.

"Betsy, how lovely to see you. It'z been so long since you've come to my shop," a heavily accented voice said from behind her. Betsy turned and saw the lovely Frenchwoman, Nanette Lanier. The years had been very kind to Nanette. Her lovely blonde hair, done up in the latest fashion, was still devoid of gray, her blue eyes still sparkled mischievously, and her ivory complexion was as unlined as a baby's bottom.

"Nanette, I'm so glad to see you're doing so well." She nodded toward the staff. "You've got three assistants now. The last time I was here, you only had two."

"I've expanded to include zee dressmaking. Business has been good—everyone wants a French dressmaker." She broke off as a frown crossed her face. "I'm happy to see you, but if you've come because you think I betrayed your secret, you are wrong."

Betsy laughed. "That's not why I'm here, Nanette. I trust you completely." When she'd told the others she'd seen Nanette's shop, she hadn't mentioned that not only had she stopped in to speak to their old friend, but she'd bought three hats, a pair of gloves, and a muff while here. Naturally, she'd asked Nanette to keep the details of her visit confidential. It wasn't that Betsy enjoyed keeping secrets from the people she now considered family; it was because the whole situation with her husband's wealth was now so awkward.

Years earlier, Smythe had returned from Australia a very wealthy man. He'd struck it rich in mining opals, and as soon as he'd returned to England, he stopped in to pay his respects to his former employer, Euphemia Witherspoon, the inspector's aunt. He found her in dire straits, ill and being taken care of by a very young Wiggins. Her servants were stealing from her and, even worse, trying to keep Wiggins from bringing in a decent doctor to tend her. Smythe had put the situation right immediately, tossing the thieves into the streets and sending Wiggins for a competent doctor. But Euphemia Witherspoon knew her days were numbered, and she'd made Smythe promise that he'd stay on at the house when she passed away. She was leaving her home and a substantial fortune to her only living relative, Gerald Witherspoon, and she didn't want him taken advantage of by scheming servants or flimflam confidence tricksters. Even though her dear nephew was a police inspector, he was somewhat innocent about the ways of the world.

Smythe had promised he'd stay. By the time he thought the household was safely established with Mrs. Jeffries, Mrs. Goodge, Wiggins, and herself, it was too late.

By then, Mrs. Jeffries had them out investigating those Horrible Kensington High Street Murders, and even more important, Smythe had started to fall in love with Betsy. But even in those early years, he'd kept his wealth a secret from her and the others for a very simple reason: He didn't want them to see him or treat him differently. As time passed, the fact that he hadn't told them began to have more and more significance . . . not because he didn't love or care for them, but because he was now scared that they would think he'd deliberately hidden the truth from them.

Nanette took her arm. "Good, let's go to my leetle office and have a chat. I see that your inspector has another case." She led the way to one of the two doors on the far side of the room. Pointing to one, she said, "That's my fitting room. We took space from zee shop next door when Madame Dorleac—she's my dressmaker—came to work for me. But this one is my leetle office." She opened the other door and led Betsy into a small, windowless room.

An open rolltop desk was shoved against the wall. Receipts, order books, fabric swatches, and half a dozen pattern books cluttered every inch of the surface. Two chairs sat facing the desk, one of which held a stack of *La Mode Illustrée*s, a French fashion magazine, while a roll of diaphanous white material was on the other. Nanette scooped up the magazines in one arm and the fabric in the other. "Pleaze, you must sit and we can talk."

"I don't want to take you away from your business." Betsy sat down on the chair nearest the door as Nanette dumped the magazines and the roll of fabric on a side table.

"Don't worry about zhat. I've been on my feet for hours and I need to take a leetle rest." She sat down and grinned at Betsy. "Now, are you here because you need somezing new?"

"No, I came for another reason," Betsy replied. "As you've said, our inspector has a case."

"Oui, Mrs. Jacob Andover was murdered. I read about it in zee newspapers. It sounds terrible, zat poor woman."

"That's why I've come, you see. One of the suspects in the case, Mrs. Swineburn—she's Harriet Andover's stepdaughter—said that she was here at your shop getting a dress fitting on Monday afternoon. She said she was here until half past two."

Nanette tilted her head slightly, her expression thoughtful. "She told zee inspector she was here for a fitting?"

"That's what she said."

"Mais non, that's not true."

"She was lying about being here?"

"She was here, but it was not for a fitting. She came for a different reason. She owes me a great deal of money. Last week, I sent her a note telling her I could no longer extend zee credit. I told her she must pay what she owes. She came and begged me for more time. She said she was coming into money soon and that she'd pay me then."

"She said she was coming into money?" Betsy wanted to make sure she understood this correctly.

"That is what she said, but I did not believe her. But I have no choice . . . So many of her friends and acquaintances are my customers, I must give her more time." She shrugged. "If she does not pay, I will take a loss, but I could not risk giving offense, you understand."

CHAPTER 4

"You needn't be so condescending, Inspector," Marcella Blakstone snapped. "I am perfectly aware that a beloved friend was murdered. However, my point was simply that none of us in the household could possibly have done such a monstrous thing."

"I'm sorry if you felt I was condescending. That wasn't my intention," Witherspoon explained. "But it's important that you answer my questions."

She sighed and closed her eyes for a brief moment. "Of course, Inspector. Please, go ahead."

"What did you do after you left the shops?"

"As I mentioned last night, I went to my home to see how the repairs were progressing."

"How long did you stay at the shops?" Witherspoon suddenly realized that, with so many odd alibis, it was imperative to construct a proper timeline of everyone in the household's movements. Thus far, there were only two people who had alibis that could be verified, and that was Reverend Wheeler, who was at the British Museum, and Jacob Andover, who was at his club. Everyone else in the household seemed to be either shopping or, in the case of Percy Andover, going for a long walk to sober up.

She shrugged. "I've already told you I was only there for ten, perhaps fifteen minutes at each place. Both shops were so crowded, it was difficult to see the fabric selection properly, and the level of service was appalling, especially since the finest fabrics are kept on the shelves behind the counters. But they had far too few shop assistants. I even tried waving at one of them, but she pretended not to see me."

Witherspoon nodded as if he agreed, but what she'd just said was laying the foundation for no one at either shop remembering her. "So you left here right after luncheon yesterday and went shopping. Then you say you went to your home to check with the builders. What time did you arrive?"

She tapped her finger against her chin. "It was close to three o'clock."

"What's the name of your builder?" Witherspoon asked.

"Brownsley and Sons," she replied. "But the only person I saw was a day laborer who was outside tidying up."

Witherspoon gave her a puzzled look. "Really? Why is that? Didn't you go there for the express purpose of checking on the progress?"

"Of course, Inspector, but apparently, yesterday they'd wallpapered the entire downstairs and they couldn't do anything else until the paste had dried. It was annoying, but there is little I can do about such matters."

"Did you come directly back to the house?"

"No, I spent the next half hour having a good look around." She patted her dress pocket. "I have the keys so I let myself inside."

"Were you afraid they weren't doing it properly?" Witherspoon knew his question had nothing to do with the current inquiry, but he hoped her answer could give him a clue as to her character.

"One must always keep a sharp eye on tradespeople and workmen, Inspector. In all fairness, the quality of the work is fine, but it is progressing much slower than I'd hoped."

"Mr. Andover said you were here for tea yesterday, is that correct?" the inspector asked.

"Yes, my home is quite close and I was able to get here by four fifteen."

"What did you do after that?"

"As I said when you interviewed me last night, I went for a walk."

"I thought you'd be comin' today." Blimpey Groggins put his newspaper to one side and nodded toward the stool on the other side of the small table. "Do ya want anything?"

"I'm alright." Smythe sat down, whipped off his flat cap, and unbuttoned his coat.

The round-faced, ginger-haired man sitting across from him wasn't just the owner of the pub, he was also a buyer and seller of information, and Smythe was one of his best customers. Blimpey had paid sources among all the criminal gangs, the Old Bailey, every major London hospital, the newspapers, the docks, the shipping companies, the banks, insurance companies, and it was even rumored he had someone at Buckingham Palace. Smythe wasn't sure he believed that one, but he did suspect that Blimpey had a couple of old men from the House of Lords and the Commons in his employ.

"You've read the papers then?" Smythe said.

Blimpey's eyes narrowed. "Don't be daft. My sources tipped me off before your inspector saw the poor woman's body. I take it you want as much information as possible on Harriet Andover and the others in the household?"

"That's right. It's a strange one, though. From what little we've 'eard so far, Mrs. Andover was in the conservatory when she was killed, and it was locked good and tight. There's only two keys, both of which 'ave been accounted for, and the outside door was locked from the inside, so no one can say 'ow the killer could 'ave gotten out."

"Not all criminals are stupid, Smythe." Blimpey grinned. "If you'll recall my earlier profession, I've gotten in and out of locked rooms more than once."

He was referring to the fact that he had once been a burglar. But after a rather nasty fall from a second-story window and a run-in with an enraged mastiff on the very same occasion, he decided to use his prodigious memory rather than risking life, limb, and liberty. He might have once been a thief, but Blimpey had standards. No matter how much he was offered, he wouldn't pass along any information if it meant a woman or a child would be harmed.

Smythe laughed. "Maybe you should tell our inspector 'ow you did it."

"Mornin', Smythe," Eldon, Blimpey's man-of-all-work, called out as he put a small keg of beer behind the bar. "You want somethin'?"

"I'm alright," he replied. He turned his attention to Blimpey. "Did your sources give you the names of the others in the Andover house?"

"Not all of 'em. I know that Percy Andover and his widowed sister live there. Who else was in the 'ouse?"

"Two houseguests, Marcella Blakstone and the victim's nephew from America named Daniel Wheeler. 'E's an Episcopal priest and 'e's doing research at the British Museum. 'Ave you ever 'eard of either of them?"

Blimpey drummed his fingers lightly against the tabletop. "Blakstone, Blakstone," he murmured, "that name sounds familiar. But it wasn't a Marcella . . . Oh, I recall it now, Henry Blakstone, he owned the majority of shares in that bank that went under last year. He died shortly afterwards."

"'Ow'd 'e go?"

"Heart attack." Blimpey shrugged. "Guess owin' all that money was a bit worryin' for 'im. Never 'eard of the priest fellow."

"Why would ya? 'E's only arrived from America in the last few months."

"Right then, I'll get me sources workin'," Blimpey said. He crossed his arms over his chest and sighed. "I know you're wantin' to ask about that other matter, but you'll not like what I've found out."

Smythe went still. He knew that Blimpey was doing his best to let him down gently, that the task he'd given the man might be impossible. "You've found out somethin' more?"

"Yup, and none of it good." Blimpey stared at him sympathetically. "I know you love your Betsy as much as I love my Nell. Men like us, who find love later in life, we know how to cherish it, and we'd do anything to protect our ladies and make 'em happy. This isn't going to be easy to tell." He broke off and took a deep breath. "Betsy's mum and her baby sister are buried in a mass grave."

"A mass grave, are ya certain? No offense meant, Blimpey, but it's taken you months to find out anythin' at all, so is there a chance ya might be wrong?"

He'd come to Blimpey right after their last case. Betsy had done her bit in that investigation by going to her old neighborhood in the East End and learning what she could about their suspects and victim. But while there, she'd gone to the cemetery to pay her respects to her mum and baby sister. She'd realized that their pauper's grave wasn't marked, and she had no idea where they were buried. Smythe had promised her he'd find out where they'd been laid to rest and he'd use their wealth to have them properly reburied with headstones.

Blimpey shook his head. "I wish there was, Smythe, but one of the reasons it's taken so long to find out where they were buried is because the cemetery mucked up their record-keeping, and I 'ad to find someone who could get the local parish church into 'elpin'. Church parishes keep decent records."

"But Betsy's family was in Saint Matthew's parish and those records were burnt up in a fire."

"I know that. It's why it's taken so long to find out anythin' useful. My people 'ad to track down the old fellow who was verger at Saint Matthew's twenty years ago. But we found 'im. 'E's livin' in Liverpool with 'is daughter. My man says there was nuthin' wrong with the old fellow's memory or 'is mind, so we can trust what 'e said."

"And 'e was sure about Betsy's mum and sister?"

"'E was sure."

"Blast a Spaniard," Smythe muttered. "A mass grave . . . that'll break 'er heart and I'll not 'ave that."

"'Tis a pity, Smythe, but Betsy's family lived in one of the poorest parishes in all of England. Saint Matthew's had to pay for the buryin', and that cemetery was the cheapest because they was still doin' mass graves. The question now is, do you want me to move forward on this?" He looked Smythe directly in the eye, his expression somber. "Gettin' permission to open a mass grave is goin' to cost the earth. We'll 'ave to bribe an official or two as well as pay for the cost of the diggin' and the reburyin' of the others."

Smythe's eyebrows drew together in a thoughtful frown. "Let me think on that for a day or two. It's not the expense that's worryin', it's upsettin' Betsy. I'll speak to her before we do anythin' else."

"Sorry it took me so long to get down 'ere, but with the rain comin', I wanted to get them seed beds tucked in right and proper." Martin Debman yanked the chair out and slowly eased his lanky frame onto the seat. His grizzled face was square shaped, and he had close-clipped gray hair and watery blue eyes.

Constable Barnes nodded. "Mr. Debman, how long have you worked here?"

"It'll be ten years this February. Mrs. Andover hired me right after they got married," he replied. "Before that, I was only here once a fortnight, but the missus, when she come, she insisted I work 'ere permanently. She was right, the gardens were a right old mess." He pulled a crumpled handkerchief out of his trouser pocket and swiped at his eyes.

"Sorry," he apologized, "but she was decent to me. I'm goin' to miss her."

"She was a good mistress?"

"She was," he said. "Not soft, but fair and decent."

"When was the last time you saw Mrs. Andover?" Barnes asked.

"Yesterday, she waved at me from the upstairs window as I was leavin'."

"And what time would that be?"

"Half past twelve. I only work a half day on Mondays. Mrs. Andover let me have Monday afternoons off so I can visit me mum in Colchester. There's a cheap return fare on the railway then," he explained. "I don't know what they'll be doin' about the garden now she's gone, probably want to go back to the way it used to be. But then again, Mr. Andover can do what he pleases. I'm old enough now to retire, and if they make any changes I don't like, I can leave."

"Yes, well, perhaps the Andovers will keep things as they are for the time being," Barnes murmured.

"Not bloomin' likely," Debman muttered. "It was Mrs. Andover that appreciated the garden. The others could care less."

"Have you noticed anyone hanging around the neighborhood, someone who you didn't recognize?" Barnes broke off as a puzzled expression crossed the gardener's face. "You know what I mean, it's not as if you know everyone 'round here, but you know it when you see someone who isn't from 'round here. See what I mean?"

Mr. Debman nodded. "Yeah. I do, but I've not noticed anyone like that."

"I see. Do you know of anyone who might have wanted to harm Mrs. Andover? Had she had any quarrels with her neighbors, anything of that sort?"

"No, she didn't bother them and they didn't bother her. No, no, wait a minute, she did 'ave a bit of an argument with Mr. Cragan a few months back. He owns the property next door, and they had a bit of a spat over sharin' the cost of payin' for the repairs on the wall between their gardens, but they sorted it out and Mr. Cragan paid his fair share."

Barnes struggled to think of another question. "Have you noticed anything unusual going on lately? Anything that struck you as odd or out of place?"

Mr. Debman's brows drew together in a frown. "Well, not so's the police should notice, but someone's been movin' my coat and hat to the wrong pegs."

"What?" The constable was genuinely confused.

"It's happened twice now. I put my overcoat and hat on the same peg every day, but twice recently, they were put on a different peg."

"You're right, Mr. Debman, that's not the sort of information the police would notice. Can you ask Miss Evans to come in, please?"

"That it, sir?" Debman lumbered to his feet.

"Yes, thank you." Barnes forced a polite smile. "You've been very helpful."

Jacob Andover stepped into the drawing room, and Witherspoon politely rose to his feet. He stared at the inspector for a moment before crossing to the chair opposite and sitting down. "How much longer do you expect to be here, Inspector?"

Witherspoon was taken aback. Thus far, Jacob Andover had been very cooperative, and he didn't understand the man's apparent change of heart. He'd interviewed the others first to allow Andover to get a decent night's rest. Yet here he was, eager for them to be gone. Not quite the sorrowing widower he'd appeared to be last night.

"We're doing our best to take statements as quickly as possible," the inspector assured him. "But if we're going to get to the truth of this matter, we must be allowed to investigate properly."

Andover stared at him and then sighed heavily. "I'm sorry, Inspector. It's just been such a dreadful time and I'm at my wit's end. But that's no excuse for my rudeness."

The inspector gave him a brief, sympathetic smile. "I understand, Mr. Andover. We've been told that the object used to, uh . . ." He struggled to find the right word. "Take your wife's life, is the sash from your dressing gown. Can you confirm that?"

Jacob gave an affirmative nod. "Yes, it's mine. But I assure you, Inspector, I have no idea how or why it was used to murder my wife."

"You're not being accused, sir," Witherspoon said. "When was the last time you wore your dressing gown?"

"Last week. It was taken to be laundered on Saturday afternoon, and it wasn't returned until yesterday morning."

"Is that the usual course of events?" the inspector asked. He needed to know if everyone in the household was familiar with the laundry schedule.

"Yes, everyone knows the laundry is picked up on Saturday mornings and returned on the following Monday." He smiled bitterly. "I'm very aware of what this means,

Inspector—someone in my household murdered my spouse and deliberately used an article that was easily identifiable as belonging to me. It's a very depressing thought."

"It does look that way, sir," Witherspoon said. "But appearances can be deceptive, and even though it would appear to indicate that Mrs. Andover was killed by someone in the household, we're not eliminating the possibility someone from outside was able to get into the house. When the laundry is returned on Mondays, is it immediately taken out of the baskets and put in the proper rooms?"

Jacob looked puzzled again. "I'm not sure I understand what you mean."

His answer didn't surprise the inspector. Very few men of his class had any real understanding of the workings of their homes. The only thing Jacob Andover knew was that the house was scrubbed clean, his clothes were properly hung in his wardrobe, and his food arrived on the table promptly. He had no more understanding of the intricacies of running a huge house than he did of flying to the moon.

"Never mind, Mr. Andover, I'll have a word with the housekeeper about how the laundry is handled when it is returned to the household."

"Indeed, she'd be the person to ask about such matters." His mouth flattened into a grim line. "Thinking that someone here could have done such a monstrous thing to Harriet has been unbearable. I'm praying it was someone from outside, some maniac who saw her sitting in the conservatory on her own and was overcome by the urge to kill."

Witherspoon kept his face carefully neutral, but the real truth was that the odds of the murder being committed by an outsider were small. "Did Mrs. Andover have a will?"

"Yes. We both had new wills drawn up when we married," he explained. "Harriet has, or had, a great deal of money. As I've told you, she was a very successful businesswoman, and of course, I had my own assets to protect."

"Who is her solicitor?"

"Hamish McGraw. He's got an office on the High Street. He handled all of Harriet's legal work." He shifted in his seat. "He'll have a copy of her will."

"Is he your solicitor as well?"

"No, my family has always used Carstairs and Perry. They've offices on Regent Street."

"You kept your property and assets separate?" Witherspoon asked. It was only recently, since the passage of the second Married Women's Property Act, that wives had the option of controlling their own money and property.

"Yes, we married late in life and both of us wanted control over our estates."

"Do you know who is the main beneficiary of Mrs. Andover's estate?" Witherspoon asked.

Jacob looked down at the floor for a long moment and then lifted his chin and stared at the inspector. "I am." He shook his head. "When we married, Harriet left most of her estate to her sister, Henrietta Royle. Not that Henrietta needed her money; she most certainly didn't. Her husband was very wealthy. But last year Henrietta passed away, so Harriet changed the main beneficiary to me. She left some substantial bequests to several charities, as well as to the servants, but I doubt that any of the servants knew she'd included them in her will."

"She left nothing to her stepchildren?" Witherspoon fully intended to speak to Hamish McGraw. He watched Andover carefully, looking for a glimpse of his real feelings as he spoke of his late wife's estate.

"To be honest, Inspector, I don't know. My late wife and my children were never close, but when she made me her beneficiary, she did make some comments about including them as well. But I've no idea if she actually did it."

"Why didn't you ask her?"

"That simply isn't done, Inspector"—Andover looked away—"especially as I made such a fuss about keeping my assets separate for my children. I'm ashamed now; she had so much more to protect."

"You own this house, correct?"

"I did, but half of it now belongs to Harriet's estate. She bought in a half value of the property when we married. She didn't buy it outright, but we agreed that she'd use her money to pay for some badly needed major repairs up to half the assessed value of the property." He smiled self-consciously. "That sounds rather cold, but the arrangement worked for us."

"Did she make any changes to her will once she met her nephew?" Witherspoon asked.

He thought for a moment. "She was planning to do so, but I don't think she had done it as yet. As far as I know, the last time she spoke to Hamish McGraw was more than two months ago—I believe it was at the end of October—and she didn't meet Daniel until the beginning of November."

"And why did she meet with him two months ago?"

"She was considering suing one of her financial advisors, a stockbroker named Peter Rolland. She thought he'd deliberately misled her about the financial health of a company he'd suggested she invest in. But nothing came of it—when she took into consideration court costs and that she had no guarantee of winning, she decided against it."

"I take it she no longer used Mr. Rolland's services."

"Absolutely not," he confirmed. "Are you going to speak to him? I've got his address somewhere if you need it."

"We'll be interviewing him," Witherspoon confirmed. "I know I've asked you this before, but was there anyone else who might have had a grudge against Mrs. Andover?"

He shook his head, his expression weary. "I've done nothing but think on the matter, Inspector, and I can't think of anyone who would wish to harm her."

Constable Barnes read through the notes in his little brown notebook while he waited for Angela Evans. From the servants' statements, it was obvious that Mrs. Andover, while not warmly loved, had been liked and respected by her staff. On the other hand, Jacob Andover and his children weren't held in such high regard. He heard the butler's pantry door open, flipped to a clean page, and picked up his pencil.

But when he glanced up, instead of the housemaid he'd been expecting, Constable Griffiths stood on the other side of the table.

"Have you finished questioning the neighbors?" Barnes asked.

"Not yet, sir. We've finished with some of the houses, but we're still working on the others. But I've got news, sir. Constable Stuart popped in to drop off the postmortem report from Dr. Procash and you'll not believe what he told me."

It wasn't like Griffiths to gossip or spread silly rumors, so Barnes put his pencil down and gave him his full attention. "What is it?"

"It's Inspector Nivens, sir."

"Inspector Nivens," Barnes repeated. "What about him? Is he dead?"

"No, sir, he's alive, but the rumor is he's on his way to Bethnal Green Station. Mind you, it's just talk at this point. No one knows for sure where he'll end up."

"What are you on about? I thought we were rid of him once and for all. He's not been on the force since last March."

"But I've heard he's coming back now, sir."

"That's not possible." Barnes couldn't believe it. "Chief Superintendent Barrows would never have him back on the force, not after what he did."

"But his family has lots of influence, and the commissioner overruled the chief superintendent, and now he's back."

Barnes couldn't believe his ears. "That's ridiculous. Nivens has no respect for the law nor for his fellow officers. I can't believe they'd let him back on the force. Ye gods, the fellow resigned."

"But that's just it, sir—according to what Constable Stuart heard, Inspector Nivens didn't resign. He never sent in his letter, and apparently, the higher-ups at the Yard just assumed he was gone for good, but he's back."

"That's not good news; men like Nivens give us all a black eye." He sighed. "Good Lord, this is a nasty surprise."

"Maybe we'll get lucky and it'll be a rumor that turns out not to be true. Or if it is true, maybe he'll mind his manners." Griffiths turned as the door opened and a young maid with auburn hair and bright flushed cheeks stepped inside. She stood in the doorway, her expression wary as she stared at the two policemen.

"I'll get back to work, sir. Uh, I take it you'll mention this development to Inspector Witherspoon."

"I'll take care of it."

Griffiths nodded politely to the maid as he stepped past her and into the corridor.

"Please come in, miss." Barnes gestured toward the chair.

"Thank you, sir." She sat down. "I'm Angela Evans. I was told you wanted to speak to me."

"That's correct. Now, tell me a bit about yourself. How long have you worked here?"

"It will be three years in February, sir. I'm the scullery maid, but Mrs. Fell—she's the cook—is helping me learn to cook. That's what I eventually want to do, sir. Be a cook."

"You were here yesterday when Mrs. Andover was killed, is that correct?"

"Yes, sir. I was here in the kitchen when Marlene come flyin' down to get the key to the conservatory. I got a bit curious, so I followed her upstairs and heard that the mistress had been strangled with the sash from the master's dressing gown." She shivered. "I can't believe it. I was here in the kitchen when the laundry came back, and I saw the dressing gown when Colleen and Kathleen—they're the upstairs maids—took the clothes upstairs."

"Do you recall if the sash was with the dressing gown?" Barnes asked.

"I think so, sir, but I couldn't swear to it. You'll need to ask Mrs. Barnard, as she oversees the laundry. Or you might have a word with Colleen—she takes the master's clothing up to his room."

Barnes knew that Constable Griffiths had spoken with that housemaid, but perhaps hadn't asked that specific question. He'd have another word with the girl. "Were you in the kitchen all afternoon yesterday?"

"I was. Mrs. Fell was showing me how to stuff a leg of lamb. She let me do the whole thing."

"Did you go outside at any time yesterday afternoon?"

"No."

"Have you noticed anyone hanging around the area, anyone that struck you as odd or suspicious? Anyone who seemed to be taking too much interest in the house?" Barnes asked. He was fairly sure she, like the others, had neither seen nor heard anything.

"Not so that I recall, sir. The only odd thing I've seen lately was back in October when I saw an old man staring at the house. But I think he was just lost. I've not seen him since."

"Has anything else happened lately, anything untoward or out of the ordinary?"

"I don't think so, sir, not unless you're countin' the times the morning paper disappeared. Honestly"—she glanced at the closed pantry door—"I've never seen such a fuss over a few newspapers going missing. Mr. Andover had a fit and insisted the newsboys hadn't delivered them, so he sent me to the newsagent's for replacements. This happened three times in one week, and when I went in the third time, the newsagent made me pay for the paper. He claimed someone in the house must be taking it, because he was certain the boy had brought it that morning. Anyway, Mr. Andover wasn't going to reimburse me, but Mrs. Andover told him not to be so stingy. Why are the rich so tightfisted? They're the ones with the money."

Mrs. Jeffries was the last one to take her seat. Along with the tea, Mrs. Goodge had put out a plate of brown bread, jam and butter, as well as a loaf of seed cake. She glanced around the table and noted that everyone was present. "I'm so glad everyone is here. Let's get started, shall we? Who would like to go first?"

"Mine won't take long, so I'll 'ave a go," Smythe volunteered. At the housekeeper's nod, he told them what he'd learned from the local hansom cab stand. "I spoke to 'alf a dozen hansom cab drivers this afternoon, but none of 'em recalls bringing anyone to or from Princess Gate Gardens between four yesterday afternoon and when the body was discovered."

"Which could imply the killer was either already in the house or walked there," Mrs. Jeffries said. "Did you have time to question anyone at the local pubs?"

"Nah, I went to see another source, but 'e didn't 'ave much to tell me. All 'e knew was that Marcella Blakstone's late husband owned the majority of shares in a bank that went under. Fellow died of a 'eart attack soon after."

"Do we know if he left his widow anything?" Mrs. Goodge asked.

"I can answer that," Luty interjected. "I had a chat with a banker friend of mine, and he said Henry Blakstone died broke. She isn't from a wealthy family, and the only thing she got from her late husband was a run-down house in an expensive neighborhood. The Blakstone house is in Kensington, about a quarter of a mile from Princess Gate Gardens."

"That's interesting," Mrs. Jeffries murmured. She glanced at Smythe. "Anything else?"

"No, but I'll pay a visit to the local pubs tomorrow. But this is all I've got for now."

Betsy patted his arm. "Not to worry, sweetheart, you'll

have a better time of it tomorrow or the next day. If it's all the same to everyone, I'll go next." When no one objected, she continued speaking. "I went to Lanier's shop, and you'll all be pleased to know that Nanette is doing wonderfully well. She knew exactly who Ellen Swineburn was and said that Mrs. Swineburn was at her shop yesterday afternoon. But she wasn't there for a fitting, which is what she told the inspector. She was there to beg Nanette to give her more time to pay her bill. She claimed she'd be coming into money soon and that she could pay then."

"Coming into money soon," Mrs. Jeffries repeated softly.

"Did Nanette agree to this?" Ruth asked.

"She doesn't really have a choice," Betsy explained. "Nanette says that many of her customers are friends and acquaintances of Mrs. Swineburn, and if she presses her for payment, she might lose them."

"Nells bells, that's no way to run a business," Luty exclaimed. "What the dickens is wrong with her?"

"But she's right," Ruth argued. "If someone like Ellen Swineburn started gossiping about Nanette's shop, claiming that the clothes weren't well made and the service was terrible, she would lose business. It's not fair and it's not right, but it happens. What's more, from Nanette Lanier's point of view, extending credit until Mrs. Swineburn comes into money, if indeed that turns out to be the case, will cost far less than a lawsuit."

"That's exactly what Nanette said," Betsy agreed. "Now that we've confirmed Mrs. Swineburn's whereabouts yesterday afternoon, tomorrow I'll go to the British Museum and see what I can find out about Reverend Wheeler's movements."

"You'll need a ticket to get into the Reading Room," Hatchet pointed out.

"I can get you one," Ruth told Betsy. "I know Sir Richard Craddock. He's on the Board of Trustees."

"That would be wonderful," Betsy agreed.

"I'll send a note to Sir Richard tonight," Ruth said. "He's quite reliable. Now, if it's all the same to everyone, I did find out a bit of background information today." She told them what she'd learned from Octavia Wells. She took her time, making certain to repeat everything she'd heard. "And that's it for me. Wait a moment, before I forget . . ." She looked at Mrs. Jeffries. "Would you ask Constable Barnes to see if he can get a look at the police report for Mrs. Royle's death?"

"I will. The fact that the Royle family managed to hush up the suicide is a bit alarming."

"You think it might have something to do with Mrs. Andover's murder?" Phyllis asked. "But how? Mrs. Royle's death was a year ago."

"We've no evidence it has any bearing on the matter, but nonetheless, I think it's worth asking the constable to take a look at the report."

"Let's 'ope he can." Wiggins helped himself to another slice of bread.

Mrs. Jeffries turned her attention to Luty. "Did you find out anything else from your banker source?"

"Not a danged thing, but I've got a better source I'm goin' to see tomorrow. Wait, wait a minute, I tell a lie—the old feller did pass along a bit of gossip after I asked how Harriet had got her start in business. He told me he didn't know all the details, but he'd heard that some old relative of hers sent her and each of her sisters a big chunk of money when they got engaged."

"But she already 'ad money when she married Jacob Andover," Wiggins pointed out, "so was she married before? Cor blimey, someone shoulda told us that."

Luty shook her head. "Let me finish, will ya? She was engaged to some fellow, but he died before they married, and she kept the money and started investing."

"It must have been a lot of money," Phyllis murmured. "I wonder if her relative wanted it back."

"He probably didn't know." Luty chuckled. "It was some old relation who lived overseas. How would he know her fiancé died? But whatever happened, within a few years of using her stake, she had plenty of money of her own."

"Or at least enough to attract Jacob Andover's attention," Mrs. Goodge muttered. "Well, it's not much, but every little bit helps, and you've found out more than I did. The only thing I found out today was that Ellen Swineburn's coat reeks of smelly, oily soot. At least that's what the laundry boy claims, and he was the only person in this kitchen today that knew anything about the Andover family."

"Don't feel bad, Mrs. Goodge," Wiggins said. "I didn't learn much, either. But I did find out a few bits and pieces." He told them about meeting Angela Evans. Like the others, he took care to tell them every detail of the encounter.

"Sounds to me like your housemaid was just complaining because Reverend Wheeler wasn't paying much attention to her," Phyllis said.

"You're just sayin' that because you didn't find out anything," he shot back. She'd announced she'd learned nothing as soon as they'd all sat down. "At least I found someone who'd talk to me."

"Don't be mean, Wiggins," Mrs. Goodge scolded. "Phyllis will find out plenty tomorrow. It's not her fault that the shop clerks in that neighborhood are a tight-lipped bunch."

"Mrs. Barnard." Constable Barnes caught the woman as she started up the back stairs. He'd finished interviewing the servants and was on the way up himself to meet with the inspector. "May I have a word with you?"

"Will it take long, Constable? We're getting the house ready for Mrs. Andover's funeral reception."

"It shouldn't take long at all. There's just a couple of details I need clarified." Barnes looked over his shoulder at the kitchen. Angela Evans, the scullery maid, was at the sink peeling potatoes; Mrs. Fell was at the cooker, adding salt to a pot of something; and two other housemaids were at the dumbwaiter stacking plates, glasses, and silverware onto it. No one was paying them any attention; nonetheless, he didn't want his questions overheard. "Could we step back in there?" He pointed toward the servants' dining hall.

"Of course." She hurried toward him, and a few moments later, the two of them were sitting across from each other. "What is it?"

"This may seem an odd question, but I assure you, it's very important. As I'm sure you're aware, it was Mr. Andover's dressing gown sash that was used to murder his wife."

"That's what I've heard," she replied.

"Mr. Andover told us his dressing gown was taken to be laundered on Saturday and returned on Monday morning."

"Yes, that's correct."

"Do you know if the sash was taken with the dressing gown and laundered?"

"It was."

"You're certain?"

"Constable, why don't I just explain our laundry day procedures?" she offered.

He realized then that she knew why he was asking the question, and he appreciated the fact that he didn't need to explain every single detail to get her to understand. "That would be best."

"As you know, we're a fairly large household. The servants wash their own laundry, but the clothing for the Andover family and their guests is sent out. We have a procedure so we can be certain that each person's items are properly laundered. Colleen Murphy is the upstairs maid and she's in charge of collecting the laundry on Saturday morning. She would have made sure that Mr. Andover's sash was collected along with the dressing gown itself. Many clothing items come with more than one part—there are strings for petticoats, corsets, ties for stockings, detachable shirt collars, and all manner of garments that have more than one piece. All those items must be washed properly."

"You're sure that the maid wouldn't have accidentally left the sash here in the house?"

"I am, I trained the girl myself." Mrs. Barnard crossed her arms over her chest. "And I made sure I trained her thoroughly."

"I've no doubt about that, ma'am," Barnes replied. "What about when the laundry is returned?"

"The laundry basket is brought into the back hall. It's

quite large, and Mrs. Fell gets annoyed if it clutters up the kitchen, so the maids and I unload it there."

"What time did it arrive on Monday morning?"

"It generally is brought between eight and eight fifteen. On Monday it was here right after eight o'clock."

"Was it unpacked immediately?" Barnes wanted to find out if the basket had been left unattended for any length of time.

"It was. Both of the upstairs maids helped, and between us, we unloaded everything, and the maids took it all upstairs to be distributed to the rooms."

"Thank you, Mrs. Barnard, that was what I needed to know."

"I can confirm that the sash was with the dressing gown. I remember because I checked that it was there." She shrugged. "I check that every garment that has more than one piece is complete. We've had instances in the past where the laundry has lost something, but if you don't complain immediately, they won't bother to look for it."

Witherspoon wasn't too late getting home that evening, and as usual, Mrs. Jeffries was at the front door when he arrived. She took his hat and hung it on the coat stand. "Mrs. Goodge has made a wonderful beef stew for dinner."

"I can smell it from here." He sucked in a deep breath as he slipped off his coat and handed it to Mrs. Jeffries. "Do we have time for a sherry?"

"Of course, sir." She slung his coat onto the peg under his bowler and followed him down the hall to his study. Within a few minutes, she had poured both of them a glass of his favorite sherry, handed him his drink, and then taken her chair across from him. "Now, sir, do tell me everything that happened. You know how I love hearing about your investigations."

Witherspoon took a sip. He was so glad he'd started this habit with Mrs. Jeffries. Telling her the details of his day always helped him to think more clearly. "Well, it was quite a day." He started his narrative by telling her what he'd learned from Constable Barnes' interviews with the Andover servants. "So even though one doesn't like to make too many early assumptions, it appears that the servants all felt that Mrs. Andover treated them decently and fairly."

"And like yourself, Constable Barnes is very perceptive. Both of you are very adept at reading between the lines," Mrs. Jeffries murmured. "If that was his impression, I'm quite certain it must be correct."

"I agree." The inspector took another quick sip. "My own day started off with another interview with Percival Andover." He gave her a quick synopsis of Percy's statement, all the while saving the best for last. "And then he begged me not speak to his employer to confirm his whereabouts on the afternoon of the murder, as he'd been sacked months ago. What's more, he's hidden that fact from his family."

"He's what?"

"Lied to his family, mainly his father and stepmother, about being gainfully employed." Witherspoon told her the rest of their conversation. "From what he said, it was quite obvious that it was Mrs. Andover who he was most afraid of finding out about his employment situation."

"Didn't he realize that could be a motive for murder?" She drained her glass and contemplated pouring another.

"Not until it was too late." Witherspoon finished his

sherry, looked at her, and said, "It's been a long day, let's have another."

"Absolutely, sir, but do keep on, you've such a wonderful way of telling things that it's utterly fascinating."

He chuckled in delight. "Thank you, Mrs. Jeffries. After I spoke to Percy Andover, I finished taking Reverend Wheeler's statement."

She listened carefully as she poured the sherry and returned, handing him his glass and taking her seat. She wasn't just trying to bolster the inspector's confidence—he really had developed into a very good narrator.

"When I'd finished with him, I spoke to Marcella Blakstone." He told her everything about that conversation, including the names of shops she'd visited, and the fact that she'd then gone to check on the repairs to her home. "After that, she came back to the Andover house for tea." He sighed heavily.

"What's wrong with that, sir? At least now you can track her movements."

"But that's just it—tea in the Andover household is served at four fifteen. But when I asked her what she did between teatime and dinner, which is when Mrs. Andover was murdered, she claimed to have gone for a walk. Honestly, Mrs. Jeffries, with so many of our suspects out 'walking,' it will be jolly difficult to verify their movements in the hours preceding the murder."

"But don't you just need to know where they were when the murder was committed?"

"That's the most important, but experience has taught me that one can never learn too much when someone has been murdered."

"True, sir. You've often realized who the actual killer might be because of something he or she did prior to committing the crime."

"I think that's very important. Still, the problem is that even with the postmortem report, Dr. Procash wasn't able to be very definite about the time of death. The best he could come up with was what we already knew—she was murdered between four in the afternoon and eight fifteen that night."

"I see, sir."

"That's why my timeline for each member of the Andover family and their guests is so important." He frowned. "They do help me enormously. But this time, I suspect it will be difficult to verify their movements. Everyone was either shopping or walking, except for Reverend Wheeler, who was at the British Museum."

"You've confirmed that, sir?"

"Oh yes, I sent Constable Miller, and the librarian confirms Reverend Wheeler was there all afternoon. We also verified that Jacob Andover was indeed at his club from five thirty in the afternoon until he returned home at seven." He told her about his conversation with Jacob Andover.

"You'll have this murder solved before Christmas, sir. I know it."

"Thank you, Mrs. Jeffries, one does one's best." His smile faded. "But I do have some very dispiriting news. There's a rumor that Inspector Nivens is back."

Alarmed, Mrs. Jeffries said, "Back where?"

"On the Metropolitan Police Force." Witherspoon sighed heavily. "We don't know for sure it's true as yet, but the current gossip is that he might be doing night duty at Bethnal Green Police Station."

CHAPTER 5

Mrs. Jeffries sat at the kitchen table and stared across the room at the window over the sink. The illumination from the gas lamp across the road cast just enough light to see the street outside. It was past midnight, and everyone, including her, had gone to bed. But she'd barely unbuttoned her dress before she knew she couldn't sleep. So instead of lying in a soft, warm bed tossing and turning, she was sitting here in the chilly kitchen wrapped in a heavy woolen shawl.

She had too much on her mind to get a decent night's rest. The investigation was worrying enough—no one wanted their Christmas ruined—but her real concern was Inspector Nigel Nivens. When Inspector Witherspoon told her Nivens might be back on the force, she'd been stunned. It was a shocking turn of events, but it was obvious from what the inspector said that if the rumor was accurate, nothing could be done about it. If this was the truth, Nivens had won this battle and, by winning, had sent a strong message to those at the top of the Metropolitan Police Force who wanted to be rid of him. He had power, and now she was afraid he was going to use that power to come after Inspector Witherspoon. But she couldn't worry about that right now; they had a case to solve. For the time being, Nivens and the havoc he might cause needed to be pushed aside so she could concentrate on their current case. The rumor hadn't been confirmed as yet, so she would hope for the best.

She took a deep breath to clear her mind. It was too early to see any useful patterns or connections between the members of the Andover household and the murder—she knew that as well as she knew her own name. But it wouldn't hurt to examine the information they'd learned thus far, she told herself. As long as she didn't come to any conclusions, it could prove useful to marshal all the facts into some semblance of order in her own mind.

She thought about Jacob Andover first. The inspector said that today he wasn't quite the sorrowing widower he'd been yesterday evening. Don't read anything into that, she told herself. The man might have been in shock last night, so of course his behavior would be different once he'd adjusted to today's reality. It didn't mean he'd had anything to do with his wife's murder.

On the other hand, she thought, now that his late wife's sister was dead, Andover was the heir to what was believed to be a substantial estate, and as many of their other cases had proved, money was perhaps the most common motive for murder. Perhaps Jacob Andover hadn't been as shocked by his wife's murder as he appeared last night. Perhaps he was merely a good actor.

But he wasn't the only member of the family to behave suspiciously. Ellen Swineburn, Harriet's stepdaughter, told Nanette Lanier she was "coming into money" soon. What did that mean? But the question was, was that the truth, or was she merely saying it to Nanette to get more time to pay her bills? It was impossible to know one way or the other, but they'd keep an eye on Mrs. Swineburn as well as her brother, Percival Andover.

She found herself smiling when she thought of Percy. The man had pulled off a rather spectacular deception. She knew she shouldn't find it amusing. It meant he was dishonest. But she couldn't help herself. It was very funny, but from another point of view, having to lie about his employment could easily be a motive for murder.

It was Harriet Andover who'd forced him to find a job instead of allowing him to live the life of a gentleman, a life that he felt entitled to by birth. What's more, if she'd had that kind of influence over her husband's son to begin with, Percy's assertion that his father wouldn't have allowed his wife to toss him out of the house rang a bit hollow. If his stepmother had found out he'd been sacked, she could well have insisted he leave the family home. Percy had made it clear to Inspector Witherspoon that he'd tell his father the truth as soon as the funeral was over. So now that she was gone, he wasn't concerned about losing the roof over his head.

Then there was Marcella Blakstone. What did they know of her? She was Mrs. Andover's best friend and a houseguest. They also knew that her husband had left her with nothing but a run-down house in an expensive London neighborhood. So if she was left with nothing, where did she get the money to make the repairs to her home? That was suppos-

edly the reason she was spending Christmas with the Andover family. But was there more to this situation than met the
eye? They needed to know more about her.

Lastly, there was the Reverend Daniel Wheeler. He was
the only blood relative of the victim, but he was also a
stranger. Mrs. Jeffries pulled her shawl tighter against the
night air. What did they know of him? He claimed to be
doing research at the British Museum, and they had no reason to think he was lying. But Mrs. Jeffries was glad that
Betsy would be confirming the good reverend's statement
tomorrow. Some of their previous cases had taught them to
leave no stone unturned. They also knew that he'd been in
England only a few weeks before moving into the Andover
home. But was that all there was to the man? Had he perhaps
expected to be so warmly welcomed into the bosom of the
family that he thought he might be in the running for an
inheritance? But the only way that idea made sense was if he
knew his aunt had changed her will, and until the inspector
spoke with her solicitor, they had no idea what the woman
might have done. Sighing, she realized the truth was they
needed to know more—not just about him; they needed to
know more about everyone.

Constable Barnes put his cup down on the kitchen table. "So
as you've guessed by now, the servants all thought that Mrs.
Andover was the one who treated them right. Mrs. Fell, the
cook, claimed that it was Mrs. Andover who insisted the
staff be fed decently. She also reported that until the mistress
married Jacob Andover, the house was fallin' down around
their ears."

Mrs. Goodge snorted faintly. "They'd not be the first gentry to go broke. Do we know how the Andover family got so poor?"

Barnes shrugged. "Not specifically. But both the housekeeper and Mrs. Fell certainly hinted that prior to Harriet Andover's arrival, the family was barely keeping a roof over their heads. But you've raised a good point—it might prove interesting to find out what happened to the family wealth. They're not aristocrats, but I had the distinct impression that at one time they might have been more than just jumped-up gentry. That house alone is worth a fortune."

"Yet prior to Mrs. Andover's arrival, they let it go to rack and ruin," Mrs. Jeffries mused. "I think you're right, Constable. Someone should find out when and how the family fortune was lost."

"I'll see what I can learn." Barnes drained his cup and put it down. "But our biggest problem right now is confirming Mrs. Swineburn's and Mrs. Blakstone's statements as to where they were that afternoon."

"Why is that so urgent?" Mrs. Goodge asked. "Mrs. Andover wasn't killed until after four that afternoon."

Barnes chuckled. "Come now, Mrs. Goodge, you know as well as I do that our inspector relies on his 'timelines.' He always wants to know and confirm what suspects were doing, not just at the time of the murder, but in the hours prior to the crime as well."

"And that has been a very successful policy," Mrs. Jeffries added. "Often it's activities in the hours before the murder that point to the killer."

"I suppose that's right," the cook admitted grudgingly.

"But why will it be so hard to find out what those two women were doing? Both of them claimed to be visiting friends or shopping. Someone should remember them."

"But they were in crowded shops or on crowded streets," Barnes pointed out. "So there's a good chance no one's going to remember either woman. If that's the case, we'll not be able to prove their whereabouts one way or another."

"Perhaps there's a way, Constable," Mrs. Jeffries said. "Ask the housemaids what both of those ladies were wearing Monday afternoon."

"What they were wearing?"

"Yes, believe it or not, it might prove helpful. Shop assistants frequently recall what women wear, especially if they're rich and well-known to the shop. When you send the constables to the shops to verify their statements, the constables will be able to describe their clothes."

"Well, it can't hurt." Barnes looked doubtful. "And when we come home from church on Sunday, my good wife frequently mentions what other ladies are wearing."

Mrs. Goodge, who'd been staring off into space, suddenly spoke. "Did you and the inspector search Mrs. Andover's study or her bedroom?"

"Not yet," he admitted. "It's taken so long just to get proper statements from everyone that we didn't think of it. Between the household and the servants, we've had to speak to twelve people. But I'll put a flea in the inspector's ear about it. The truth is, we were both so startled by yesterday's news."

The cook interrupted, "You mean findin' out his nibs might be back on the force."

Barnes made a face as he nodded. "Neither of us could believe it, but if it's true, the gossip I heard was that there's nothing that can be done about it. Someone at the very highest level must have intervened to get him back on the force."

"That's what Inspector Witherspoon said last night. If nothing can be done, then let's hope for the best," Mrs. Jeffries said. And prepare for the worst, she thought.

The carriage clock on the sideboard chimed the half hour. Barnes shoved away from the table. "I'd best get upstairs. We've a lot to do today."

"Before you go, Constable, do you think you could do something for us?" Mrs. Jeffries asked. Even though the constable was considered a close ally, she was still uncomfortable asking him to do some things.

"If I can, I will. What do ya need?"

"A year ago, Mrs. Andover's sister, a woman named Henrietta Royle, committed suicide on the train home from burying her husband. He was buried at Brookwood Cemetery."

"She shot herself on the Necropolis Railway? Ye gods, that's always crowded. I'm surprised I didn't hear about it."

"No, she wasn't on that train. She'd stayed late at the cemetery to watch her husband being buried and came home on an express train. She was alone in a first-class compartment and shot herself with a derringer as the train pulled into Waterloo Station. The Royle family supposedly hushed everything up to avoid a scandal. But surely there would have been a police report about the incident?"

"There would have been," he replied. "Do you know when this happened?"

"We don't know the exact date, but Lady Cannonberry's source said it was sometime in December of last year. Is it possible for you to read the police report?"

He thought for a moment. "You think it might have something to do with the Andover case?"

"I don't know, but I did think it an odd coincidence. Two sisters, both of them dead a year apart."

"I'll see what I can find out, but it might take a few days to track it down." He rose to his feet. "Time's a-wastin', I'll get on upstairs. I hope searching her rooms won't take too long. We have to verify as many statements as we can today and try to fit in a visit to Mrs. Andover's solicitor."

"You're going to find out the contents of her will?" Mrs. Jeffries stood up, as did the cook.

"Jacob Andover said he was her heir." Barnes raised his eyebrows. "But one thing I've learned in life, just because he thinks he's inheriting doesn't mean he is—especially as she appears to be so fond of her nephew."

Everyone was on time for their morning meeting. Mrs. Goodge put a fresh pot of tea on the table and took her seat next to Wiggins. Mrs. Jeffries poured and Phyllis handed around the cups.

Mrs. Jeffries waited till everyone was quiet before she spoke. "I'm afraid I've some unsettling news to tell you."

"Unsettling, my foot." Mrs. Goodge snorted. "It's just plain bad news, Hepzibah, and that's that."

"Cor blimey, Mrs. Jeffries, what's wrong?" Wiggins exclaimed.

"Are you alright?" Phyllis asked, her expression worried.

"Oh dear, this can't be good," Ruth murmured.

"It's not good," Mrs. Goodge snapped. "It's ruined my morning and it'll probably ruin all yours as well. Stop beatin' around the bush, Hepzibah, and tell them."

Mrs. Jeffries didn't think she'd been beating around any bush, but she agreed with the cook that before everyone got hysterical, it was best to just come out with it. "Inspector Nigel Nivens might be coming back on the police force."

There was a moment of shocked silence. Then everyone spoke at once.

"Blast a Spaniard, he's resigned. 'Ow can he be back?" Smythe snapped.

"That can't be right," Ruth cried. "Surely there's been a mistake."

"Nells bells, I thought Scotland Yard had better brains than to let that varmint back inside," Luty yelled.

"I don't believe it," Betsy moaned. "We just got rid of him."

"Now, now." Mrs. Jeffries held up her hand. "Thus far, it's only a rumor, but if true, it's a terrible situation. Still, we can't worry about what he's going to do right now. It's even more important that we help Inspector Witherspoon get this case solved as quickly as possible."

"That's the only way we can protect our inspector, isn't it?" Phyllis asked, her expression glum. "If Inspector Nivens has the power to get back on the force after what he did, he's got more power than any of us ever thought, right?"

Mrs. Jeffries wasn't going to make light of the situation. "Yes."

"And if the rumor is true, Nivens is going to come after our inspector, isn't he? He blames him, doesn't he?"

"Yes. It was on our inspector's last murder case that got him into so much trouble, but the best way we can help Inspector Witherspoon is by solving this case as quickly as possible. No matter what Nivens tries to do, our inspector has solved more homicides than anyone in the history of the Metropolitan Police Force. That matters. I don't think even the Home Secretary would countenance any action against Inspector Gerald Witherspoon. But we mustn't waste any more time. This case is now the most important case we've ever investigated. Now, everyone take a breath and a sip of tea," Mrs. Jeffries ordered, "and we'll get back to work."

She waited a brief moment and then told them what she'd learned from Witherspoon. When she'd repeated every point, she glanced at the cook, signaling that she was to tell them the additional bits and pieces they'd heard from Constable Barnes.

Mrs. Goodge took her time and reported what they'd heard from the constable. Their past experiences had taught them never to leave out a detail, no matter how insignificant it might seem.

When the cook had finished, Ruth said, "The fact that the household staff liked Mrs. Andover better than the Andover family says volumes about her character. Yet it seems to me that we don't know much about her at all. Surely she didn't spring into existence ten years ago after marrying Jacob Andover. Even my source, the one who told me about Henrietta Royle's death, didn't know much about either woman."

"You think her past might have something to do with her death?" Mrs. Jeffries asked.

"We've often found that to be the case, so I think it's possible," Ruth replied. "If no one has any objection, I'd like to pursue that line of inquiry."

"That's an excellent idea, Ruth."

"Someone in our Women's Suffrage Society should know

something about Harriet Andover," Ruth continued. "It might even be possible to learn something about Marcella Blakstone and Ellen Swineburn."

"Not tryin' to steal yer thunder, Ruth, but my source might know somethin' interestin' about them women," Luty offered. "She's a good friend and she loves gossip more than breathin'."

"Then by all means, see what she can tell us." Ruth laughed and then looked at Betsy. "That reminds me—last night I sent that note to Sir Richard Craddock, and gentleman that he is, he replied early this morning. He'll have a ticket for the Reading Room waiting for you at the reception desk."

"Thank you, that's wonderful." She looked at the housekeeper. "I'll make sure I speak to Nora Barlow. That was the name Daniel Wheeler gave to our inspector, right?"

"Correct. The inspector sent a constable to verify Daniel Wheeler was there Monday afternoon, which he did. But I think it might be useful to speak to the lady herself. Reverend Wheeler might have made comments to her about the Andover household that could prove useful. I've a feeling the more background information we can gather, the better."

Betsy glanced at her husband, who was staring off into space. She nudged him. "Are you listening? Honestly, you've been woolgathering since yesterday. I might be home later than you, depending on when I can find this Miss Barlow."

"Sorry, love." He grinned. "I was plannin' out what I'm goin' to be doin' myself today. I'm seein' a source this mornin' and then tryin' the local pubs. But I should be back in time for our afternoon meetin'."

"I might be late," she warned. "If I am, you'll need to

fetch Amanda from upstairs and make sure you pay Lilly for minding her today." She turned to the others. "I'll do my best to get here this afternoon, but I don't want to miss speaking to Miss Barlow."

"Of course," Mrs. Jeffries said.

"I'm not sure what to do." Phyllis frowned. "The local shop assistants weren't very chatty yesterday, and if we're going to have this case solved by Christmas and help our inspector, I need to do my fair share."

"Don't worry, Phyllis, we'll get it sorted." Wiggins smiled sympathetically. "We always do. This time's not goin' to be any different. Now stop yer frettin'. Just because you ran into a bunch of tight-lipped shop assistants yesterday doesn't mean the same thing's goin' to 'appen today."

"I know, but it's so discouraging when it does happen."

"Then why don't you do something a bit different?" Mrs. Jeffries hesitated for a brief moment before plunging ahead. "There's something that Constable Barnes mentioned this morning that I think needs looking into. It's going to sound silly, but it's been bothering me all morning."

"What would that be?" Mrs. Goodge demanded. "Did I miss something?"

"No, no, not at all," the housekeeper hurried to reassure her friend. She knew that the cook was concerned she was getting forgetful or failing to understand when something was or was not important. "As I said, it's just one of those odd facts that stick in the back of your mind and won't stop poking at you. It's been bothering me since Constable Barnes told us what the housemaid complained about."

"What is it, Mrs. Jeffries?" Phyllis asked eagerly.

"You'll have to speak to more shop assistants, but there's

very specific information I'd like you to find out. Apparently, there was a time recently when the Andover household didn't get their newspaper delivered for three days in a row. See if you can find out exactly when that was and what newspaper it might have been."

"That sounds easy enough."

"There's two newsagents in that neighborhood," Smythe reminded her.

"I'll walk with ya," Wiggins offered. "I'm goin' to talk to either another Andover servant or someone from the neighborin' homes. If that don't work, I'm goin' to try the local pub." He looked at Smythe. "You don't mind, do ya?"

"Nope, if I go in one and you're sittin' there, I'll 'ead to another one," he said. "There's plenty of pubs 'round that area, enough for the both of us."

"I'm seeing my friends the Manleys'," Hatchet volunteered. "That might be helpful in learning more about both Harriet Andover and the Andover family's background. As Ruth has pointed out, the victim didn't spring into existence ten years ago when she married Jacob."

"You want to search Harriet's study?" Jacob Andover stared at the two policemen with a horrified expression.

"We were given to understand she spent a great deal of time in her study," Witherspoon replied. "And as it's right next to her bedroom, we'll be searching in there as well." He tried to frame his response as if he assumed there would be no objection. The truth was, he wasn't sure if he could compel Mr. Andover into letting them search. "Mr. Andover, I assure you, we're not going to violate your late wife's privacy, but we do need to search the areas that belonged exclusively to her. Our task here is to see if there might be something in her business papers or her personal papers that might help us find her killer."

Jacob frowned irritably and then looked away. "I doubt you'll find anything of significance, but go ahead." He walked over to the bellpull and gave it a yank. "I'll have Mrs. Barnard take you up to her rooms."

A few minutes later, the housekeeper opened Harriet Andover's bedroom door and ushered them inside.

The walls were papered with bright yellow diamonds against a white background, heavy gold curtains hung at the two windows, and the double brass bed was covered with a white-and-gold-striped coverlet. A tall mahogany chest of drawers stood between the windows, and a mirrored dressing table with a matching chair was in the corner. A small fireplace topped with a wood-framed mirror hung on the wall opposite the windows, and there were two closed doors, one on each side of the bed.

Witherspoon pointed to the doors. "Where do they lead?"

"The one on the left is the connecting door to Mrs. Andover's study," Mrs. Barnard explained. "And the one on the right leads to her bathroom. She converted what was a small sitting room into a modern bath several years ago."

"Did Mrs. Andover spend a lot of time in her study?" Witherspoon realized the housekeeper could tell them details of how Harriet Andover spent her day.

"She did, Inspector." Mrs. Barnard turned to leave.

"Just a moment, Mrs. Barnard," Witherspoon said quickly. "May I ask you something else?"

She stopped, her hand on the doorknob. "Of course, Inspector."

"How did Mrs. Andover spend her time? She doesn't appear to have been concerned with social activities."

Mrs. Barnard said nothing for a moment. Then she smiled. "She wasn't. Mrs. Andover thought most social functions boring, and I once heard her tell Mr. Andover it was a silly waste of time. As to how she spent her days, she concentrated on working."

"Could you elaborate further?" the inspector said. "I want to get a picture of how she lived her life on a daily basis."

"Will that help catch her killer?"

"It might," he replied.

"That's good enough for me, sir. Mrs. Andover rose early and spent an hour or so reading in her room. She was fond of novels, and once a week she went to Mudie's Lending Library for books. She'd then join the family for breakfast—"

Barnes interrupted, "What time did they eat?"

"Eight o'clock. When the meal was over, Mrs. Andover would read *The Times* and that generally lasted till nine or nine fifteen. Then she'd go about her day. She was very busy. She'd come in here and go over her business affairs, and quite often—at least once or twice a quarter—she'd go out and have a look at a company she thought might be worth investing her money in."

"She'd have a look at them? How so?"

"I meant it quite literally—she'd go to their premises, look them over from the outside, and then she'd speak to the employees. She wasn't shy, Inspector. She'd speak to the workers as they left. It didn't matter if it was a ship's chandlery or a furniture manufacturer, she'd find out what she needed to know. Then she'd go inside and have a good look at the company equipment, the manufacturing processes, and who were their suppliers. That's the main reason she was such a successful businesswoman, Inspector. She was very thorough."

"Thank you, Mrs. Barnard, you've helped enormously," Witherspoon said.

"Has anyone been in here since Mrs. Andover died?" Barnes asked.

"Not as far as I know. The maids cleaned that morning, of course, but since then there's been no need for anyone to come inside," Mrs. Barnard replied.

"Has the door been locked?" Witherspoon was annoyed with himself for not having searched Mrs. Andover's rooms immediately. A good, thorough search of the victim's private rooms was basic police procedure, but he'd been too distracted by the circumstances of the murder to ensure it was done properly. Thank goodness Constable Barnes had brought it up this morning.

She seemed surprised by the question. "No, but I hardly think anyone other than Mr. Andover would dare to come in here, especially now. Certainly none of the servants would have come in here without reason."

Witherspoon started to remind her that there was a killer, possibly here in the house, who might have had reason to search the victim's room, but then the inspector changed his mind. "Did you see Mr. Andover entering this room?"

"I didn't say that. He wasn't in here, but he was in her study for several hours yesterday. As I was serving luncheon yesterday, I overheard him tell Mrs. Swineburn that he was going to go through his wife's papers, and then I saw him go inside when I was bringing up some clean sheets for the up-stairs linen cupboard."

"I see." The inspector glanced at Barnes. "Was that the only time you've seen Mr. Andover in either of these rooms?"

"It was. Now, if you'll excuse me, I've got matters to at-tend to in the kitchen."

"Of course, Mrs. Barnard, and thank you for your as-sistance."

The two policemen waited till she was gone before speak-ing. Then Barnes said, "Seems to me that Mr. Andover didn't waste any time having a snoop around his wife's study."

"And that's my fault," Witherspoon said. "I should have insisted on searching both her study and her bedroom much earlier. Who knows what he was looking for—or even more importantly, who knows what he might have found?"

"Maybe he was just having a general snoop to suss out how much she was worth? It sounds like the late Mrs. An-dover was tight-lipped about her business affairs, and he's already told us he thinks he's her heir. Besides, sir, we've a lot on our minds. Especially with the rumor that Nivens is showin' up again."

"Indeed, that was a shock. Nonetheless, we'll get on with doing our duty."

Barnes gazed around the room. "Compared to the rest of the house, her room is simple, sir. The only decoration on the walls is that set of framed wildflower prints on each side of the fireplace, and there's nothing on the top of her dress-ing table but a jewelry box, a hairbrush, and a comb. The only photograph is on her chest of drawers." He started to-ward the drawers. "Should I begin there, sir?"

"Good idea. I'll take the dressing table." Witherspoon walked to it. The dressing table was plain, with a tilting mirror supported by two arms, beneath which were four small drawers with plain wood knobs. A rosewood jewelry box sat on the left side, and a silver-plated hairbrush with matching hand mirror was on the right.

Witherspoon opened the top-left drawer. Inside he found a gold bracelet and two broaches—one of pearl, and one with dark blue sapphires and diamonds in a starburst pattern. He picked up the sapphire-and-diamond broach. "Goodness gracious, this jewelry looks expensive, yet Mrs. Andover had it sitting in an unlocked drawer. I wonder why it isn't in the jewelry box?"

Barnes closed the top drawer he'd just searched. "Nothing in here but Mrs. Andover's undergarments. How many pieces are in there, sir?"

"Three—a gold bracelet and two nice broaches."

"Maybe she meant to put them away and forgot. My wife does that sometimes. Not that she has much expensive jewelry, but she does have a nice pin and matching earrings she inherited from her aunt. She keeps them in a pretty ceramic box. Sometimes, she puts them on the dresser and they sit there for ages before she remembers to put them away."

Witherspoon nodded. Despite his deepening relationship with his beloved Ruth, being a bachelor, he wasn't as familiar with female habits as the constable. He took a closer look at the jewelry box. "This is almost identical to the box my late aunt Euphemia had." He opened the lid of the jewelry box. Inside was an assortment of pins, necklaces, and earrings spread across the shallow green velvet interior. "It's exactly the same. There's two parts to it. But unlike my aunt's box, this one isn't locked. Perhaps that explains why Mrs. Andover kept things in her dressing table drawer." He lifted the green velvet top half and laid it on the tabletop then looked inside. "Same sort of jewelry here, several nice broaches, three strings of pearls, and quite a few pairs of earrings. But I don't see a key."

"Perhaps she lost it, sir," Barnes muttered.

"I'll see if it's in one of these drawers." He put the top half back on and closed the lid. Witherspoon reached toward the next drawer when there was a knock on the door. A second later, Daniel Wheeler stuck his head inside the room.

"I do hope I'm not disturbing you, Inspector, but I was wondering if I could speak with you a moment."

"Of course, please come in." Witherspoon turned. "What can I do for you?"

Daniel winced slightly. "This is a bit delicate, Inspector, but the family is getting very anxious about the funeral. They didn't come right out and request that I speak to you, but I could tell from the conversation at breakfast that Mr. Andover is worrying about when my aunt can be buried."

"The postmortem has been completed, so I'm sure your aunt's body will be released sometime today. Mr. Andover will be contacted by the morgue. If no one contacts him, please let me know and I'll see to it. Will you be officiating?"

Daniel shook his head, his expression somber. "I'm helping with the arrangements, Inspector. The household isn't very devout so Jacob asked me to pick out the readings and recommend the hymns. But I doubt if I'll be doing the service itself. Jacob was saying that they've a family friend who is a bishop. He's not said anything definite, but I expect the bishop will be officiating."

Constable Barnes closed the drawer he'd been searching and looked at Wheeler. "Will you be staying on here?"

"Again, Jacob hasn't said anything, but without my aunt here, it might be awkward." He shrugged. "Still, we shall see what happens. I can always go back to the Pennington Hotel. It's not as nice as here, of course, but it's comfortable and close to the museum."

"Have you thought more about who your aunt might have meant when she told you she was concerned about someone here in the household?" Witherspoon asked.

"In truth, Inspector, I have thought about it." Daniel clasped his hands together. "The only thing I can think of is something my aunt said to me last week. At the time I didn't think much of it, but considering what has happened, I do believe you need to hear it."

"And what would that be, sir?" Barnes opened another drawer and looked at Wheeler.

"It was after dinner," he began. "I don't recall the exact day, but after we finished dining, Aunt Harriet and I went into the drawing room. Jacob had gone to his club to visit an old friend. Ellen and Percy had both gone to their rooms."

"Where was Mrs. Blakstone?" Witherspoon asked.

"She was dining with friends that evening and wasn't home," Wheeler replied. "Aunt Harriet and I settled down with our coffee and then she asked me if I'd noticed anything odd about Ellen or Percy. I was a bit confused, so I asked what she meant, and she said that at various times during the past weeks, she'd noticed that each of them had come home unduly excited."

"Unduly excited," the inspector repeated.

"Those were her words exactly. I asked her to elaborate,

but the truth is I knew what she was talking about, because I'd noticed the very same thing." He stopped and dragged in a deep breath. "Both Percy and Ellen had come home on separate occasions noticeably exuberant. Last week, it was very obvious when Mrs. Swineburn came in; her cheeks were flushed, her hair disheveled, and she was giggling like a schoolgirl. The same thing had happened earlier in the week with Percy. I think it might have been last Tuesday, but Percy arrived home right before dinner, and like his sister, his cheeks were rosy, his tie askew, and he was in a very silly, happy mood. I told Aunt Harriet that I'd also noticed this behavior, but I'd thought it was probably due to the holidays. You know, there's lots of merrymaking, quick trips to pubs, parties, and that sort of thing."

"Did your aunt agree with you?" Barnes asked.

"She didn't say one way or the other. She merely said that she thought both their behaviors strange." He shrugged. "Then she changed the subject. But I could tell that she was concerned about her stepchildren. Aunt Harriet wasn't one to worry about social conventions, but she wasn't the sort of woman to let a family problem go unaddressed, either."

"Did she ever bring the matter up again?" Witherspoon asked.

"Not with me. She might have said something to Jacob."

"You're closer to both their ages than their stepmother," Barnes said. "Do you have any idea where either Mrs. Swineburn or Mr. Percy Andover might have been?"

"No, Constable, I don't. I hope it was something such as an innocent drink with friends and not anything untoward. As a clergyman, I know that it's very easy for lambs to be led astray." He stared at Witherspoon for a long moment and then sighed. "I realize this sounds quite silly, but my aunt was honestly upset about the matter."

"When they came home in that state," Barnes said, "did anyone ever ask them where they'd been?"

"Not as far as I know."

"That's unfortunate," Witherspoon said. "But as both Mrs. Swineburn and Mr. Percy Andover are adults, it might have been awkward to ask too many questions."

"Yes," he agreed, and sighed again, "but perhaps someone should have."

Myra Manley handed her husband, Reginald, a cup of tea, and then turned her attention to Hatchet. The three of them were sitting in Myra's morning room. The Manleys were seated close together on an ivory-and-blue-striped love seat across from Hatchet, who was in an overstuffed chair.

The room was both welcoming and festive. Evergreens and holly branches were artfully arranged on top of the white marble fireplace. Red vases—the same shade as the holly berries and overflowing with ivy—stood at each end of the mantelpiece. A potted evergreen the size of a five-year-old and decorated with painted ornaments; strands of woven red, gold, and silver ribbons; and unlighted candles stood in the far corner. Several of Reginald's landscapes hung on the cream-colored walls, and the polished oak floor was covered with a dark-blue-and-red Oriental rug.

"I've met the Andover family a number of times," Myra said. "But I haven't seen much of them in recent years. Miriam Andover, Jacob Andover's first wife, was very sociable. But she died years ago, and I don't believe his second wife was quite as outgoing. Though I have heard that Harriet

Andover was a very intelligent, strong-willed business-woman."

"Darling, I've told you, you should spend more time listening to gossip." Reginald grinned at his wife. He was a middle-aged man, but still handsome as sin with his blue eyes, black hair, and high cheekbones. "I do, and I know a lot about the Andover family, most of it salacious."

Hatchet loved a visit to the Manley house, as he adored them both.

Myra was a slightly bucktoothed woman with brown hair threaded with a few gray strands, a longish face, and deep-set chocolate eyes. She wasn't a beauty in the conventional sense, but her face was compelling. She was from one of the wealthiest families in England; he was a bohemian artist who specialized in portraits of "slightly vapid upper-class twits," as he put it.

Yet the two of them—who should have never married, according to both their immediate social circles—nonetheless amazed his artist friends and her aristocratic circles with their undying devotion to each other. Even better from Hatchet's point of view, they were both dedicated to the cause of justice, and had helped him with very useful information on a number of other occasions. Myra knew everyone important in England, and Reginald loved gossip almost as much as he loved his wife.

"Do tell, Reginald," Hatchet urged. "I'm all ears."

"One hates clichés, but I'll start with the most obvious one, of course." Reginald grinned broadly. "Jacob Andover was flat broke when he married Harriet Tichner—that was her maiden name—and if he'd not convinced her to marry him, he'd have lost the family home."

"She'd never been married before?" Hatchet took a sip of his tea. "How old was she?"

"From what I've heard, she was in her early forties, and not particularly enamored of the male of the species. Jacob asked her a number of times before she said 'yes,' and even then he had to guarantee she'd be left alone to manage her finances herself."

"That's right." Myra put her cup on the side table. "Now I remember, I heard that as well. The rumor was that she made him give her a half share in the house before she'd agree to the marriage. Katherine Parkhurst was furious when she found out Jacob was remarrying, because she had her eye on him as well."

"I take it she didn't have as much money as Harriet?"

"That's right, but she thought herself a much better match. Katherine was widowed, upper class, attractive, and socially well connected. Supposedly, she and Jacob had been involved in a relationship while his first wife was alive." She tapped her fingers against her chin. "Oh my goodness, it's all coming back to me now. When Katherine found out Jacob was marrying Harriet, she was so furious, she tossed a glass of whisky in his face, and she did it in full view of the guests at her dinner party."

"Did she expect him to be faithful to her?" Reginald sneered. "Silly woman, if a man cheats on his wife, he'll cheat on his mistress, especially if said mistress has far less cash than the one he wants to marry."

"You do have very old-fashioned views about fidelity," Hatchet teased his friend. He knew that Reginald took his marriage vows seriously and had nothing but disdain for people who didn't.

"My views aren't old-fashioned, they are simply correct." Reginald took a sip of tea. "And from what I've heard, good old Jacob hasn't changed his philandering ways."

"What do you mean?"

"There's rumors that he's involved in an affair. Though I've no idea who the new lady in his life might be. Apparently, after the fiasco with Katherine Parkhurst, Jacob has learned to be discreet. Though I am surprised that Harriet Andover put up with him. I mean, before she was murdered."

"Perhaps she didn't know," Myra suggested. "From what I've heard of the late Mrs. Andover, she wouldn't have allowed him to make a fool of her."

"That may be why she's no longer in the land of the living." Reginald shook his head, his expression disgusted. "I never liked Jacob Andover, and I firmly believe that once a cheater, always a cheater. But that's not the only gossip I know." He glanced at his wife. "Cover your ears, darling, I'm about to tell something that might make you blush."

"Nonsense, I want to hear, too, and I haven't blushed since I was twelve." She laughed. "So do your worst, and don't skip any of the details."

"Right then." He chuckled. "Percy Andover visits a . . ." He hesitated. "I suppose the nicest way to put it is 'a house of ill repute.' It's in Soho and is one of the more expensive brothels in London. Which is odd, really, considering the man lost his job back in September."

As soon as Reverend Wheeler left, Barnes looked at Witherspoon. "Don't you think that's strange, sir?"

"What? That Mrs. Andover was upset because her stepchildren were excited, or the fact that she told her nephew her concerns?"

"Both, sir. Seems to me that no matter how formal a household, if someone came home in the state Reverend Wheeler described, someone would ask where they'd been."

"One would think so." Witherspoon continued going through the drawers of the dressing table. But thus far, he had found only a small tin of rouge, lavender water, hair-pins, extra corset laces, and a stack of old calling cards. "But then again, Mrs. Andover might have felt it was her husband's responsibility to ask questions of his children, not hers. Nonetheless, something in her stepchildren's behavior must have caused her alarm enough to discuss the matter with her nephew."

"Should we ask Mr. Andover about it?"

Witherspoon closed the last drawer and looked at the constable. "Not yet. Let's see if he brings it up. If not, we'll ask."

"Right, sir. Shall we start on her study?" Barnes asked.

"Yes, and after that, we'll pay a visit to her solicitor."

Barnes picked up the framed picture from the top of the chest of drawers. "This is an old one, sir, probably from the late fifties."

"What is it?" Witherspoon walked across the room and stared at the sepia-tinted photograph. Three little girls wearing old-fashioned dresses stared out at him from somber faces. "I wonder if this is Mrs. Andover and her sisters," he mused. "They were sweet-looking little girls, weren't they?"

"And now they're all gone." Barnes put the photograph back and glanced around the room. "It's the only likeness in here, sir. You'd think she'd have a picture of her husband, at least."

"I've a feeling Mrs. Andover wasn't very sentimental when it came to the Andover family. We've found nothing here—let's hope we have better luck in her study."

Harriet Andover's study was much like her bedroom: plain enough to be considered austere, yet fully functional as a business office. The walls were painted a deep forest green, simple ivory curtains hung from the windows, and the polished wood floor was bare of rugs. On each side of the door was a bookcase filled with ledgers and books. A mahogany desk and chair stood on the far side of the room. The top of the desk was bare.

The two policemen crossed the room, their footsteps loud against the wooden floor. The desk had two shallow drawers along the top with three deeper drawers on each side. Witherspoon took the drawers on the left and Barnes took the ones on the right.

"Excuse me, sir." Constable Griffiths stepped into the room. "I wanted to let you know that I had a word with Colleen—the upstairs maid—and she confirmed Mrs. Barnard's statement. The sash was with the dressing gown when she took them up to Mr. Andover's room on Monday morning."

"Thank you, Constable," Witherspoon said.

"Constable Dunlop and I are off to those shops, sir, to verify Mrs. Swineburn's and Mrs. Blakstone's statements."

"Did you check to see what outfits the ladies were wearing?" Barnes asked.

"I did, sir. We have quite good descriptions for both ladies. Let's just hope the shop assistants remember them." Griffiths nodded politely and then quickly left.

Witherspoon opened the top drawer. Inside were neat stacks of stationery, a shallow box of pencils, and a sheaf of writing paper. Closing that one, he opened the one beneath it. That drawer contained an old-fashioned envelope seal, a tin of wax, and a stack of envelopes.

"At least we know why Percy's cheeks were flushed. He'd probably spent the afternoon drinking in a pub." Barnes riffled through his drawer. "Nothing here but office supplies, sir. Extra ink bottles, three brand-new pens still in their boxes, and two blank ledgers."

The two policemen spent the next half hour searching the room. But all they discovered were stacks of business correspondence, household invoices, receipts, prospectuses from half a dozen companies, and canceled checks.

"Not much here except her business papers." Barnes closed the bottom drawer and grimaced as he got to his feet. "I wonder what Mr. Andover was looking for."

Witherspoon was searching one of the bookcases by the door. "Perhaps he was just having a look around. From what we've been told about Mrs. Andover, she kept the business affairs very private, and he might have just been curious. Just a moment, here's something." Witherspoon pulled a stack of papers from behind the row of books on the top shelf of one of the bookcases.

"What is it, sir?" He hurried over to the inspector.

Witherspoon put them on top of the bookcase and gave them a closer look. "It's letters. They're not in envelopes." He picked up the top paper and squinted to read the tiny, spidery handwriting. "Ye gods, it's dated 1862 and it appears to be from Helen Wheeler—at least it's signed 'From your loving older sister.'" Witherspoon chuckled as he read the letter. "She's written to let her sister know she's just had a son, and they've named him Daniel."

He picked up the next one. It, too, was a letter, but this one was written by her other sister, Henrietta. He leafed through the stack and saw that they were all from her two sisters, and that most of them had been written years ago. "I'll have Constable Griffiths go through these, just in case there might be something useful in them. But they're from so many years ago, it's doubtful." But just as he grabbed the stack, another sheet, this one made of much heavier paper, slipped from the center of the pile and drifted to the floor.

Witherspoon knelt down and picked it up. Straightening, he stared at the date on the top of the page. It was typed and dated December fifteenth, three days before Mrs. Andover's murder. It didn't take long to read.

"What is it, sir?" Barnes tried to read the small print over Witherspoon's shoulder, but it was impossible without his spectacles.

"Gracious, Constable." Witherspoon turned and looked at Barnes. "This letter is from Hamish McGraw, Mrs. Andover's solicitor. He's confirming an appointment for December nineteenth, and in it, he tells her he'll have witnesses available as well as everything else ready for her to change the terms of her will."

CHAPTER 6

Phyllis dashed under the canvas awning of the newsagent's and gave her umbrella a shake before closing it. She peeked into the narrow shop window and saw that, except for the elderly woman reading a newspaper behind the register, the place was empty. Good, people's tongues tended to loosen if they didn't have an audience. She wished she'd remembered that earlier at the other newsagent's, instead of being so excited to have something useful to do that she'd barged in without thinking. That place had been so crowded, she'd not been able to ask her questions.

Opening the door, she stepped inside.

"Good day, miss." The clerk put her paper aside. "May I help you?"

"Yes, thank you." Phyllis hurried to the counter. "Isn't it a miserable day out?" She'd found that getting people chatting tended to work well when one was seeking information.

"Yes."

"Uh, do you carry *The Times*?" This wasn't going as well as Phyllis had hoped. The clerk was not in the least friendly.

"We do. Do you want one?"

"Well, not precisely." Phyllis swallowed uneasily. "I've a question about the services you might be able to provide. Do you have delivery on a daily basis?"

The woman stared at her for a moment and then crossed her arms over her chest. "We do, but it's morning papers only."

Phyllis wished she had worn one of her good dresses under her jacket instead of her black maid's uniform. From the way the clerk was looking her up and down, she knew the woman had realized she was only a housemaid. Drat. What could she do now? She had no idea why Mrs. Jeffries wanted this specific information, but she was certain it must be important. Perhaps the shopkeeper would be more responsive to a different approach? She gave the woman what she hoped was a timid smile. "Oh dear, this is rather awkward, but I must ask it. My employer specifically instructed me to ask you if your service was reliable."

"It is."

"Well, actually, the reason Mr. Makepeace wanted me to ask is because we've only moved into the neighborhood, and one of our neighbors said that they get their newspapers delivered from here and, oh dear, I don't know how to ask this."

"Try using words."

"Our neighbor claimed that you didn't deliver his newspapers properly."

"That's a bloomin' lie." The woman's eyes flashed fire as

she got off her stool. "It was that Andover household, wasn't it? I'll have you know that we deliver our papers every day, and on time as well. Now you can just turn around and trot right out of here. I'll not have the likes of some housemaid comin' in 'ere and pesterin' me with stupid nonsense. We delivered those papers and even gave them extra copies when they tried to say we didn't."

"I apologize." Phyllis began backing away. "I wouldn't normally ask such a thing, but Mr. Makepeace insisted." Reaching the door, she shoved her hand behind her, fumbled till she found the knob, and twisted hard and fast to get the ruddy thing open.

"Just get out of 'ere and don't be comin' back. I don't want your Mr. Makepeace's business," the woman shouted. "And you can tell the Andovers they can take their custom elsewhere, too. I'll not put up with them blackenin' my good name."

Phyllis turned and fled. The rain hammered her as she dashed across the road. She dodged hansom cabs, loaded wagons, and an omnibus as she raced for the other side. Water flooded into her shoes as she hit one puddle after another before almost falling as she skidded on the mud on the far side. Taking shelter under the awning of an ironmonger's, she stopped to catch her breath.

Well, drat, once again she'd have to show up at their afternoon meeting with nothing to report. Tears flooded her eyes, because she desperately wanted to contribute to their efforts to catch this killer. "Blast a Spaniard," she muttered to herself, "it isn't fair!" Wiggins was going to show up with all sorts of useful information, and she was going to look a fool.

She sucked in a deep, calming breath, blinked her tears back, and told herself not to be such an idiot. There was still plenty of time on this case, and she'd figure out a way to do her part. She refused to give up and become the silly, cowardly girl she used to be. She owed too much to Inspector Gerald Witherspoon to quit now.

Before she'd come to his household, her life had been a misery. From the time she'd lost her grandmother and had gone into service at the age of thirteen, every waking moment of her life had been filled with backbreaking work, constant hunger, and fear. She'd spent her days terrified she was going to be tossed into the street and being treated by her previous household's servants as the lowest of the low.

But when she'd started working for the inspector, everything had changed. The inspector had been so kind, so decent, that she'd stopped being frightened of not having a roof over her head. Losing *that* fear had been a turning point in her life. Because it hadn't just been the inspector who had helped her—the others in the household had treated her with consideration and respect. Everyone worked hard, but she hadn't been singled out because she was the newest or the youngest servant. Mrs. Jeffries and the others made certain she wasn't given the nastiest tasks in the household, and most important, they listened to her when she spoke. It hadn't been long before she'd gained enough confidence in herself to start helping them on the inspector's cases. It was the only way to pay him and them back for all they'd done for her. That decision had changed her life. She had a future now, and she wasn't going to turn away from it. She'd been saving her wages, and one day, she'd have enough to open her own business. She already had the name picked out:

"Thompson's Private Inquiries." Beneath that would be the words "Assisting Ladies Is Our Specialty."

She lifted her umbrella, intending to open it when she saw a skinny, dark-haired young lad who looked to be no more than twelve or thirteen running toward the newsagent's shop. She could see he was a newsboy from the empty burlap bag he had slung over his shoulder. She watched him go inside the shop. Throwing caution to the winds, she raced across the street again and found a spot by the shop next to the newsagent's, a fishmonger's, where she could peek into the shop without the harridan from hell catching sight of her.

The boy was gesturing with his hands, obviously trying to explain something that the harridan didn't want to hear because she was glaring at the poor lad as if he'd stolen her last bite of food. Finally, the harridan went to the cash register, punched a couple of keys, and the drawer sprang open. She took some coins out and handed them to the newsboy.

Phyllis stepped back to the edge of the fishmonger's, barely staying underneath the awning while she waited for the lad. A few moments later, he came out and stopped on the top step, his expression grim as he contemplated the pouring rain.

Phyllis raced across the road, no longer caring if the harridan caught sight of her. "Excuse me." She smiled brightly. "But if you've a few moments, I'd like to speak with you."

The lad's mouth opened in surprise. "Me? Why do ya want to talk to me?"

This close, she could see he was thin, malnourished, and pale. The boy should have been in school, but like so many of the poor, he'd had to leave and come out into the world to make a living.

"We're both soaking wet," she said, "and there's a nice café up the road. If you've a few minutes to spare, I'll buy you a hot cup of tea and a bun. I'll also pay you a shilling. You might have some information that's important to me." She jumped as thunder cracked overhead.

His eyes narrowed suspiciously. "You're goin' to buy me a cuppa tea, a bun, and give me a shilling? Why would ya do that?"

"Because I'm a private inquiry agent"—she fixed him with a hard stare, the kind she thought a proper private inquiry agent might use—"and you might have something useful to tell me about a case I've been hired to look into."

"But you're a lady," he protested. "Ladies can't be private inquiry agents, and you're wearin' a maid's dress."

"There's no law against a woman or a maid bein' a private inquiry agent, so of course I can." She gave him what she hoped was a reassuring smile. "Look, it's a public place so you'll not be in any danger. I just want to ask you a few questions."

He rubbed his nose. "What kind of questions?"

"I'll tell you that when we get to the café," she replied. She decided to try another tactic. "You interested or not? There's lots of lads around here I could be talkin' to—"

"I'm interested," he interrupted. "I could do with a cup and a bun. All we had for breakfast this morning was the end pieces of a loaf of bread."

"Right then, come along." She opened her umbrella, motioned for him to get under it, and the two of them hurried off down the road. Less than five minutes later, they were seated at a small rickety table in the front window of Jemma's Café.

Phyllis knew what it was like to be hungry. She didn't speak while the boy ate his bun and drained his tea. Then she got up, went to the counter, and ordered another cup of tea and three more buns.

His eyes widened when he saw her bringing the food to the table. She put them in front of him. "Do you have brothers or sisters?"

He didn't take his eyes off the food. "I've a little brother. He's six."

"Take these buns home for the two of you." She pulled a clean handkerchief out of her jacket pocket, laid it flat on the table, and scooped two of the buns into the center.

He met her gaze. "Why you doin' this? I'm nothin' to you and that's a nice handkerchief. Why you givin' it to me?"

"But you're someone to your brother, aren't you? Don't worry, lad, I'm doing this because I've been hungry myself," she replied, "and I've plenty more handkerchiefs. Besides, it'll make a nice present for your mum. Now, let's get to my questions. First of all, do you deliver *The Times* to the Andover household at Number One Princess Gate Gardens?"

"I know where the Andovers live." He took a sip of tea. "I've been takin' them their morning papers for two years now. But not just *The Times*. I take 'em *The Daily Telegraph* every day as well."

"Was there a time when they claimed you hadn't delivered them?" Phyllis took a sip of her tea.

He made a face. "Them bastards almost cost me my job. It's not much of a job, but it's all I've got an' I'm helpin' to take care of my family. Me mam's a washerwoman and she don't make much, so we need every penny."

He looked so miserable, she impulsively reached across

the rickety table and patted his hand. "I know. I've been in the same position. Just tell me what happened."

"Nuthin' happened. I took them newspapers to the Andover house every single day. I've never made a mistake with my deliveries, it ain't like it's hard. But for three days that week, someone from the household showed up at the shop and claimed the paper hadn't been shoved through their ruddy front door." He leaned across the small table, his expression now angry, not sad. "The first time it happened, I thought I might 'ave made a mistake, so I was extra careful the next few days, but blow me down if that housemaid didn't show up on them days, too, claimin' they'd not got their *Times*. But they had. Because she didn't say they'd not got *The Daily Telegraph*, just *The Times*. Now I ask ya, why would I deliver the one and not the other?"

"This happened in the same week? You're sure of it?"

He nodded. "'Course I'm sure."

"What week was it?"

His narrow face creased in thought. "I don't know the exact dates. I think it was in the end of October or maybe the first part of November."

Hamish McGraw's office was located on the ground floor of a two-story redbrick building just off the Kensington High Street.

"Mr. McGraw will see you now, Inspector." The thin, black-haired clerk stood by the open door on the far side of the room and motioned them forward.

They stepped between the wooden railing separating the reception area from the three clerks' desks and followed him to an open door. The clerk stuck his head inside McGraw's office. "Here's the police, sir." He nodded at the two men and stepped back.

Witherspoon and Barnes stepped into the office. The room was large with an elaborate globe and brass chandelier hanging from the high ceiling. Directly opposite the door was a pale pink fireplace topped with a huge, wood-framed mirror and bracketed by floor-to-ceiling bookcases filled with law books, ledgers, and file boxes. A bearded white-haired man stood up from behind the massive desk in the center of the room.

"Good day, gentlemen. I'm Hamish McGraw. I've been expecting you." He gestured at the two chairs in front of the desk. "Please have a seat."

They took their seats as McGraw sat down. The constable took out his pencil and notebook and then flipped to a blank page.

"Thank you. I'm Inspector Gerald Witherspoon, and this is my colleague, Constable Barnes," the inspector said.

"And you're here to question me about Harriet Andover," McGraw said. "I couldn't believe it when I heard the news about Mrs. Andover. This is a dreadful business, Inspector, absolutely dreadful."

"Murder is always dreadful," Witherspoon replied. "How long have you represented the late Mrs. Andover?"

"Twenty-five years." He smiled sadly. "After all these years, Inspector, she has become more of a friend than a client."

"Of course, Mr. McGraw. I'm sorry for your loss, sir. Do you mind telling me the details of that first meeting with Mrs. Andover?"

McGraw's white eyebrow rose. "Is that relevant? It was

a long time ago, so I hardly think it is pertinent to the matter at hand."

"It's relevant in the sense that it might help us to understand her character," Witherspoon explained. "When conducting homicide investigations, we've discovered that the more we know about the victim, the more likely we are to catch the assailant. It's difficult to put it into words—"

McGraw interrupted, "I understand, Inspector. Not everything that is useful can be articulated factually." He smiled slightly. "I'm well aware of your reputation, sir, and frankly, when I heard you were in charge of Mrs. Andover's case, I was very relieved. Harriet was a force to be reckoned with, and though she didn't suffer fools gladly, she was a good friend and, most importantly, a decent person. I want her killer caught."

"And we'll do our best to ensure that happens as quickly as possible."

"Twenty-five years ago, Harriet Tichner, as she was then, came to me for two reasons. She was purchasing a small commercial building opposite the Nine Elms Locomotive Works and she wanted me to do the conveyancing for the purchase. I didn't think it a very good investment, especially for a single woman. I shared that opinion with her." He chuckled. "She listened politely and then informed me she wasn't hiring me for investment advice." He leaned forward, resting his elbows on the desk. "The other matter was a bit more unusual."

Barnes stopped writing and looked up from his notebook. "Unusual, sir? In what way?"

"She asked me whether she was under a legal obligation

to return something that could have been designated as a dowry."

"A dowry?" Witherspoon was genuinely confused. "But I was under the distinct impression that Mrs. Andover wasn't from the social class where such things were done."

"She wasn't. Harriet was from a very modest background. But apparently she had a wealthy uncle who lived overseas and gave her and both her sisters the sum of five thousand dollars upon their engagements."

"Dollars? Five thousand of them?" Witherspoon repeated. "I take it this relative was in the United States."

He nodded. "That's right, he was her mother's brother, and apparently, Harriet and her two sisters were the only family he had left, so he was quite generous. But unfortunately for Harriet, her fiancée died of smallpox before they married. She wanted my opinion as to whether or not she was legally obligated to return the money."

"Was she?" Barnes asked, his expression curious.

"I am not an expert on American law, much of which I understand is determined by the state where her uncle resided. Theodore Stone, her uncle, lived in California and so I was unable to comment on whether or not she was required to return the money under that state's laws. However, I was able to tell her that, under English law, if the money had been conveyed as a gift, then she could keep it."

"Do you remember how she reacted?"

"She was relieved and said it was her understanding that it was a gift. She was the one who had labeled it a 'possible dowry.' She then admitted to me that she was using the money from her uncle to buy the building in Nine Elms. But the fact that she'd even brought the subject up led me to believe she was an ethical and moral person. In all these years, Inspector, I've not changed my opinion of her character."

"I understand she had an appointment to meet with you on December nineteenth, the day after she was murdered."

"That's correct. The appointment was for three that afternoon, but of course, the meeting never took place."

"And the purpose of the meeting?"

His expression changed to one of concern. "I'm not certain I ought to say, Inspector. I don't want to inadvertently give you the wrong impression about her intentions."

"Mr. McGraw, I've seen the correspondence between the two of you. Your letter confirming the appointment specifically stated that you'd have everything ready so she could change her will, including having witnesses present."

"And that's precisely why I hesitate to speculate on what she was actually planning. Our conversation about the matter was quite casual at that point."

"But she was going to change the terms of her will?" Barnes put in quickly.

"That's what she indicated to me."

"Did she give you any idea of what those changes might be?" Witherspoon persisted. "This is important, Mr. McGraw. When it comes to money, you know as well as I do that some people will do anything, including murder, to make sure they don't get cut out of a rich person's will. The Andovers have no money; she was the one with the wealth. Someone in the household could have easily learned she was going to make changes and decided to kill her before she could."

"I know that, Inspector." He closed his eyes for a brief

moment. "I've been agonizing on what to say about the matter. I don't know for a fact *exactly* what she was going to do. But she did make several comments about her plans." He sighed. "Oh, drat and blast, I might as well tell you the gist of my conversation with her. I want whoever killed her caught, and if it was one of the Andovers, so be it."

"Thank you. I assure you, Mr. McGraw, we're not in the habit of making an arrest unless we've substantial evidence, so don't be concerned that anything you tell us will lead to an innocent person being charged."

"She told me she was changing her heir. Harriet was one of three sisters. Her older sister, Helen Wheeler, died four years ago in San Francisco before Harriet made her first will. When she finally did one, she left the bulk of her estate to her surviving sister, Henrietta Royle. But Mrs. Royle died last year and so Harriet changed her will, leaving the majority of her estate to her husband, Jacob Andover."

"Mr. Andover has told us he knew she'd made him her heir," Barnes said quickly. "Is that correct? Had she told him what she'd done?"

"She had. She saw no reason not to tell him. But that wasn't the only change she made. She increased the amount of money she was giving several charities and set up a scholarship fund for young women. Additionally, she added both of her stepchildren as well."

"How much did she leave them?" Witherspoon shifted on his seat.

"Five hundred pounds each," McGraw replied. "She also left substantial legacies to several of her friends. But something must have happened recently. Because last Thursday, December fourteenth, she stopped in and told me she was

changing her will again. I asked if it was going to be a substantial change or a minor one we could handle with a cod-
icil. That's when she told me she was cutting Jacob Andover
and his children out of her estate. As per an agreement they
made when she married Jacob, he'd be able to keep the house
and she was obligated by that agreement to provide a small
yearly stipend for the upkeep of the house, but that's all he
was getting."

"Do you have any idea what might have happened to
make her come to this decision?" Witherspoon asked.

"I can't say conclusively, but she was furious when she
stopped in here. That wasn't the only change she made. She
canceled one of the legacies she had left to a friend."

"Do you know the friend's name?"

"I do. It was Marcella Blakstone."

"How much was Mrs. Blakstone to inherit?" Barnes
looked up from his notebook, his pencil poised over the
page.

"Harriet was murdered before these changes could be
made." McGraw's mouth flattened into a thin, grim line.
"So Mrs. Blakstone will inherit as will Jacob Andover. He'll
get the bulk of the estate, but Mrs. Blakstone will get five
thousand pounds."

Betsy reentered the Reading Room at the British Museum
and smiled brightly at the librarian. He was a nice, rather
shy young man with pomaded black hair, spectacles, and a
slight lisp. She'd taken a good look around the circular room
and then slowly wandered along the edge of the perimeter in
front of the shelves. But she'd not seen the woman she'd come
to find; in truth, the only other female in the room had been

a very elderly lady. The other patrons were all men. But Betsy wasn't going to give up. She knew whom she wanted to talk with and that had prompted a trip back to the librarian. While meandering around the perimeter of the round room, she'd come up with a good story about wanting to consult with a woman researching medicinal plants.

"You mean Miss Barlow?" he'd asked.

"Yes, that's her. I understand she's an expert and I'd love to meet her. I'm interested in medicinal plants myself and I'm hoping she can help me get started with my own research." Betsy wasn't sure whether it was her flirting with the lad or whether it was the fact that the Reading Room ticket had been left for her by one of the trustees, but nonetheless, he'd been very helpful.

"Miss Barlow won't be in until after luncheon," he'd stammered as a blush crept up his cheek. "She comes in around one thirty and she sits at the end of that table." He'd pointed to one of the long tables that arced across the room like the spokes of a wagon wheel. She'd thanked him for his help, told him she'd be back later.

She held her head high as she hurried across the room to the table where Nora Barlow usually sat. Betsy put her notebook on the tabletop, pulled out a chair, and hung her umbrella on the back before sitting down. Within a few moments, she had her pencil out and was busy writing a list of plants she knew something about: the poisonous ones!

A few moments later, she heard footsteps and looked up to see a well-dressed middle-aged woman. Her graying reddish-brown hair was tucked beneath a simple hat, her face round, her lips thin, and her eyes hazel. She carried a huge book, an umbrella, a notebook, and a handbag. Betsy gave her a bright smile and rose to her feet. "Are you Miss Barlow?"

She stared at Betsy warily as she put the volume down and hung the umbrella on the back of her chair. "I am. Have we been introduced?"

"We haven't." Betsy took care to pronounce her words properly and keep her voice low. She saw the way Miss Barlow was looking at her and was glad she'd worn her blue-and-gray herringbone suit and the blouse with the fancy lace on the neck. "But I do hope you'll forgive me for being presumptuous. Sir Richard Craddock, one of the trustees of the museum, mentioned that you were doing research here on medicinal plants. I took it upon myself to make your acquaintance."

"You're a friend of Sir Richard's?" Some of the frost left the woman's expression.

"I am. He's a dear man and he obtained my entry ticket." Betsy glanced around, making certain that their low-voiced conversation wasn't being overheard or bothering another researcher.

"Sir Richard knows about my work? That's surprising, but very flattering." Nora Barlow smiled as she sat down. "Why did you wish to make my acquaintance?"

Betsy took her own seat. "I've heard about the research you're doing on medicinal plants." Again, she glanced around and saw that the only other person near them had just gone into the stacks. "And I was hoping you could help me."

"You're interested in medicinal plants?"

Betsy had learned that sticking to the truth as much as

possible was always best. "My area of interest is poisonous plants. I've a friend in America, she's studying medicine at the University of California near San Francisco, but she's very interested in the medicinal properties of poisonous plants. She's convinced that some poisonous plants contain properties that can be used to treat certain illnesses. She asked me to help with her research."

"She's studying medicine? How marvelous." Her long face broke into a wide smile. "I wanted to become a doctor, but my parents wouldn't hear of it. I expect things must be different in America. Women seem to have an easier time of it there."

This was the opening Betsy needed. "You've been there?"

She gave a negative shake of her head. "No, but I've an acquaintance, a gentleman who was born here but raised there, and he's told me a lot about America. Especially the American West. As a matter of fact, he's doing research here on the life of Saint Matthew. We usually sit together."

"Is he here now?" Betsy looked around the room, her expression contrite. "Oh, do forgive me if I've taken the gentleman's seat."

"Don't worry, he's not here today." Her expression clouded and she leaned across the table. "I'm afraid he's in the most unfortunate of situations. His aunt was murdered."

Betsy gasped and hoped that she looked shocked. "My gracious, how awful."

Nora's voice dropped even further. "It is awful. Poor Reverend Wheeler had only just met his aunt recently. Perhaps you've read about it. Her name was Harriet Andover, and she was strangled to death in her own home."

"How dreadful. I do recall reading about it in the papers. That poor woman. Have they caught the assailant?"

"Not yet, but I'm certain they will," Nora said. "I'm sure that Reverend Wheeler is heartbroken. He'd become very fond of his aunt."

"How terrible for him."

"She was one of the few relatives he had left. I'm sure he must be feeling guilty for staying here so late on Monday. We both left at closing time. I do hope he managed to get home to see her before it happened."

"Let's hope that was indeed the case," Betsy murmured. At least now she had confirmation that he was here that afternoon. But as they didn't know precisely when Mrs. Andover had been killed, he was still in the running as a suspect.

"I doubt he'll be here for some time now." Nora suddenly broke off as an elderly gentleman took a seat farther down the table, took off his hat, and nodded politely in their direction.

"Oh dear." Nora grimaced. "Mr. Swann's arrived. Usually, he only comes on Tuesdays but he wasn't here yesterday. We must be quiet now. Mr. Swann is easily distracted and I've my own work to do." She swiveled to her left and pointed. "The poisonous plants are shelved over there. *Philpott's Guide to Poisonous Plants and Herbs* is there; he's the leading authority on the subject. I'm sure you'll find it helpful." With that, she opened her notebook, pulled the huge book closer, and flipped it open.

Mrs. Goodge put the plate of currant scones next to the teapot and took her seat. Everyone was there for their afternoon meeting, and she was quite pleased with herself as she had found out a few bits and pieces.

"I'm glad everyone is here on time," Mrs. Jeffries said. "I've a feeling we've much to cover today."

"Not from me," Wiggins complained. "My day was right miserable. I couldn't get anyone to talk to me for more than ten seconds."

"Mine wasn't very good, either," Phyllis agreed. "But I did find out about the missing newspapers." She told them what she'd learned from the delivery lad.

"He didn't know the exact date the papers went missing?" Mrs. Jeffries clarified. "Just that it was sometime in the last part of October?"

"Or the first few weeks of November," Phyllis added. "The poor boy did his best, but that was all he could remember."

"Why are the newspapers important?" Wiggins asked.

Mrs. Jeffries wasn't certain how to explain her reasoning. "I don't know they are, but I do think that when we hear of something even slightly odd happening in a household with a murder, it's worth looking into."

"But the newspapers were missing over a month before the murder," Hatchet pointed out.

"True and it probably means nothing. Still, I'm glad Phyllis found out what she did." She looked around the table. "Who would like to go next?"

"I found out that there's gossip surrounding Jacob Andover." Hatchet told them about his meeting with the Manleys. "According to Reginald, Jacob Andover wasn't faithful to his first wife, and there's rumors he wasn't faithful to his second one, either."

Mrs. Jeffries put a scone on her plate. "Did you get any names?"

"No, Reginald simply said there were rumors about Andover, or as he put it, 'once a cheater, always a cheater.' But he didn't know who Andover's current lady might be." He cleared his throat. "Uh, that wasn't the only thing I learned. It seems that Percy Andover, uh, he, er . . . he frequents a house of ill repute."

"He goes to a brothel?" Mrs. Goodge snickered. "He'd not be the first and I doubt he'll be the last."

"Yes, but the point is, he doesn't have a job so how can he afford it?" Hatchet asked. "It's an expensive one in Soho."

"That's a very good question," Mrs. Jeffries murmured. "Perhaps we should be sure and let Constable Barnes know so he can ask Percy Andover directly. But time's moving along . . ."

"I'll go next," Ruth offered. "I don't have much to report. I spoke to several of the women in our suffrage group, one in particular who lived very close to Henrietta Royle."

"She's the sister who died last year, the one who committed suicide?" Mrs. Goodge asked.

"That's right. Both of my contacts said the same thing, that they were shocked Mrs. Royle used a gun to end her life. She hated guns; they terrified her."

"Yeah, but if she were plannin' on endin' it all, she probably just decided to do it quick and easy," Smythe said.

Betsy gave him a quick assessing glance. This was the first time he'd spoken except for a peck on her cheek when he'd first come inside. He'd been moping about for two days now. Something was on his mind and she was worried. "But that would mean she already had the gun, and if she hated guns, where did she get it?" Betsy asked.

"Maybe it belonged to her late husband?" Hatchet suggested.

"Wasn't she supposedly killed with a derringer?" Luty

snorted. "That ain't a man's weapon; that's somethin' a woman would carry."

"People can act out of character when they're grief stricken." Mrs. Jeffries wanted to move the meeting along. It was late and she didn't want the inspector coming home and finding everyone here. "Betsy, what did you find out today?"

"To begin with, the Reading Room is quite amazing and I did manage to make contact with Nora Barlow." She told them the details of her visit to the British Museum. "It appears Daniel Wheeler was exactly where he said he was, in the Reading Room until closing time or close to it. They left together."

"That don't mean he didn't kill his aunt." Luty snorted. "He was back at the Andover house in time for dinner, and the inspector said they don't know exactly when she was murdered."

"We might know more about the time of death once the inspector gets the postmortem report," Mrs. Jeffries murmured. "But Luty's correct, we don't know *exactly* when she was killed."

"If it's all the same to everyone, I'm goin' to send a telegram to a friend of mine in Reno and ask him to find out if this reverend feller is genuine. For all we know, he could just be pretendin' to be a preacher so he could wiggle into Harriet Andover's good graces."

Hatchet raised an eyebrow. "Really, madam, I'm sure the police have already verified his credentials."

"I doubt that," Mrs. Jeffries added quickly. "The inspector hasn't mentioned it. I think Luty's right. We should check everyone."

"Good, I can send it on my way home."

Mrs. Jeffries looked at the coachman. "You've been very quiet, Smythe. Bad luck today?"

"I've 'ad better ones." He'd stopped in to see Blimpey but he'd not been at his pub. "I spoke to 'alf a dozen 'ansom drivers, and none of 'em reported taking anyone to or from the Andover 'ouse on the evening of the murder."

"Did you go to the local pubs?" Betsy asked.

"I managed to get to one of 'em, The Cat and the Canary, but the only thing I found out was that none of the Andover family goes there and it's too posh for the servants. But there's a workingman's pub a quarter of a mile away and I'm goin' there tomorrow."

Mrs. Jeffries nodded in approval. "Good, then with that, it seems we're finished—"

"Not so fast," Mrs. Goodge interrupted. "I've got something to report." She had deliberately wanted to go last because she was fairly sure her information was important.

"Oh, I am sorry, please tell us."

"It turns out that Marcella Blakstone isn't having any work done on her home."

"What? But wasn't that the reason she's at the Andovers'?" Ruth exclaimed.

"Supposedly, but according to my source—"

Mrs. Jeffries interrupted, "Who is your source?"

"Tommy Sooner, the butcher's delivery boy. Mrs. Blakstone stopped work on the house the very day she moved into the Andovers'. Now Tommy knows what's what because his sister is the housemaid to Jonathan Brownsley. He's the builder Mrs. Blakstone hired to make repairs to the house, and accordin' to Tommy's sister, while she was still livin' at her home, Mrs. Blakstone had Brownsley fix a leaky roof and replace the window frames on the ground floor. But when she went to stay at the Andover home, she told Brownsley his services weren't required."

"She's a widow, isn't she?" Phyllis murmured.

The cook nodded. "And from what we've heard, the late Mr. Blakstone didn't have an estate. All he had was the house, which now belongs to her. She told the builder she was going to be selling her home 'as it was.'"

Mrs. Jeffries met the inspector at the front door when he arrived home. "I'm glad you've managed to get here at a decent hour, sir." She took his hat, hung it up, and then hung his coat up as well. "Mrs. Goodge has done a lovely roast pork."

She had spent the previous hour peeking out the front window for him because she wanted to judge the sort of mood he might be in before she brought up Inspector Nivens. The truth was, she wanted to see if he was as worried as she was about Nivens possibly being back on the Metropolitan Police Force. Last night, they'd discussed the matter after he'd finished dinner, but he'd not given any indication he was unduly upset. Still, she would tread carefully before mentioning Nivens again. Inspector Witherspoon didn't need any additional concerns on his mind when he had a case.

"We had a very busy day, Mrs. Jeffries, and frankly, I'll admit I've been looking forward to having a glass of sherry with you. I've so much to tell you." He hurried down the hall to his study.

The inspector seemed just fine, she thought as she followed him. Nonetheless, she'd have a word with Constable Barnes tomorrow morning before she brought Nivens up again.

They went into the study, and within minutes, she had both their drinks poured and had taken her seat across from him. "Now do tell, sir. You've made me very curious."

He grinned and took a quick sip from his glass. "When the day started out, I was a tad doubtful that we'd make much progress on this case, but honestly, today we found out so much information that I'm feeling more hopeful about getting it solved."

"Especially by Christmas, sir," she added. They'd found out some useful information as well, but she either had to come up with a way to drop enough hints to nudge the inspector in the right direction or simply to take the easy way out and tell what they'd learned to Constable Barnes. She'd wait to make up her mind once she'd heard what Witherspoon had to say. If he gave her an opening, she'd take it.

"I can't guarantee that," he replied. "But we'll do our best. Before we went to the Andover home, Constable Barnes and I stopped in at Ladbroke Road and went through the statements from the neighbors. The constables did a proper job, but unfortunately, no one saw or heard anything useful. However, there was one neighbor who wasn't home and Constable Barnes is having a constable interview her tomorrow."

"Perhaps that will prove fruitful, sir." She took a sip of sherry.

"Then we went to the Andover home. Jacob Andover gave us permission to search Mrs. Andover's study and bedroom."

"Did you find anything useful?"

"Indeed we did." He took another quick sip. "But before I tell you what we found, I had a word with Mrs. Barnard, the housekeeper."

"Really? I thought she'd already been interviewed."

"She had been, but it suddenly occurred to me that one of the problems with this case was that we simply didn't know enough about Harriet Andover. We knew the servants thought well of her and that she wasn't close to her step-children, but that wasn't enough. I wanted to find out how she spent her days. She wasn't the typical upper-class house-wife; she wasn't interested in London's social life and was a better businessperson than most men."

"What did she tell you, sir?"

"She supplied a very accurate picture of how Mrs. Ando-ver spent her time. She worked very, very hard." He told her everything he'd learned from the housekeeper. Mrs. Jeffries listened carefully, occasionally interrupting to ask a question or to get a detail clarified.

"And after we spoke to Mrs. Barnard, we searched both Mrs. Andover's bedroom and study as I said," Witherspoon continued.

"Did you find anything helpful, sir?"

"Indeed we did, but just as we began to search, Reverend Wheeler came in and asked about when Mrs. Andover's body was going to be released as the family was getting con-cerned. He's helping them to plan her funeral. Luckily, just before we left the house, a messenger arrived from the morgue. I overheard Mr. Andover making arrangements for the undertaker."

"That was good of Reverend Wheeler," she murmured.

"But that wasn't the only thing we heard from him." He repeated what the reverend had told him regarding Harriet Andover's worries about Ellen Swineburn and Percy Andover.

Mrs. Jeffries frowned in confusion. "Are you saying that Mrs. Andover was upset because her stepchildren came home 'excited'?"

"That was what she conveyed to Reverend Wheeler. But I don't think that was quite what she meant. Constable Barnes and I discussed it on our way to meet with Mrs. Andover's solicitor, and the constable agrees with me. I think it was more a case that both Mrs. Swineburn and Percy Andover were behaving out of character. I think that must have been what was concerning Mrs. Andover, because otherwise, it doesn't make sense, does it?"

"Not really, sir. I've never been alarmed because someone looked excited, but if Mrs. Goodge suddenly announced she was moving to Paris to study ballet, that would concern me."

Witherspoon laughed. "And me. I don't fault Reverend Wheeler for mentioning the matter, but I think it's likely he didn't understand what his aunt was really trying to tell him."

"That sounds quite possible, sir."

"I also asked Reverend Wheeler to look at the jewelry we found in her dressing table drawer. He confirmed one of the broaches, the sapphire-and-diamond starburst pin, was the one he'd given to her from his mum. He'd never seen the other two pieces."

"What were they, sir?" she asked. "The pieces, I mean."

"A gold bracelet and a pearl broach. I only asked him to have a look because those items weren't kept with the others in Mrs. Andover's jewelry box and I thought there might be a reason."

"Perhaps she simply forgot to put them away."

"That's what Constable Barnes said." He drained his glass. "Do we have time for another? I've so much more to tell you."

"Of course, sir." She took his empty glass along with hers, refilled his, and topped hers up. "Here you are, sir. Now, I'm all ears."

"The most interesting thing we found in Mrs. Andover's study was hidden in a stack of old letters from her sisters."

"Something was hidden? Oh, do tell, sir." Mrs. Jeffries put her glass down.

"Indeed it was." He paused dramatically. "We found a letter from Hamish McGraw."

"Harriet Andover's solicitor?"

"That's right, and it confirmed an appointment she'd made for December nineteenth. An appointment which the victim had specifically requested so she could change the terms of her will."

"December nineteenth was the day after she was murdered."

"Right again, Mrs. Jeffries. Luckily, we had time today to interview Mr. McGraw and what he told us might change our entire approach to this murder."

CHAPTER 7

Betsy tucked the half-asleep Amanda into her bed and pulled the covers over her. The child immediately rolled onto her side, drew up her knees, and fell deeply asleep. "Sleep well, my darling," she whispered to her daughter. "There's a surprise coming on Christmas Eve." She moved silently to the bedroom door and quietly closed it.

She went into the parlor and Smythe looked up from his newspaper. "Is she asleep?"

"She was almost asleep before I put her to bed." Betsy crossed the room and sat down on the settee next to her husband. "Are you going to tell me what's wrong?"

"Nothin's wrong." He raised his newspaper but she was having none of that. She grabbed it from the top and slashed it down. "What are you doin'?" he cried.

"Getting your attention," she snapped. "And don't try

giving me that nonsense that there's nothing wrong. You've been brooding for two days now and I want to know what's the matter."

Smythe knew he had to tell her the truth. He and Betsy didn't keep secrets from each other, but blast a Spaniard, this was a conversation he didn't want to have. He knew it was going to upset her, and even worse, for the first time in their marriage, he felt like he'd failed her. That was the worst feeling of all. He wondered if he could bluff it out.

"Don't try to pull one over on me." She crossed her arms over her chest. "I can read every thought you have on your face. Just tell me why you've been so upset."

He knew he had to tell her but he couldn't think of a way to say it that wouldn't break her heart.

"Is it about my mum and my baby sister?"

Surprised, he blinked. "Uh, yeah, you could say that. Betsy love, this is goin' to be hard to hear, but—"

She interrupted, "They're buried in a mass grave."

He said nothing for a moment and then he nodded. "That's one of the reasons it's been so 'ard to find out anything. The parish church that buried your family lost most of their records in a fire and my source 'ad to track down the old verger. But we found 'im and 'e told us. Look, I don't want ya thinkin' I'm not willin' to pay for gettin' it done—"

She interrupted again. "I don't think that but I don't want those other people's graves disturbed. They were like my mum and sister. They were poor, too, and they deserve to rest in peace."

"But I know how much this meant to you," he persisted. "I know how much you loved 'em."

"I did love them and I love you all the more for everything

you've done. But Mum and little Emma are long gone, Smythe. Here's what I'd really like for you to do."

"What? You know I'll do anythin' to ease your mind about this."

"I want the headstone put over the spot where they're buried, and if it's possible, for every person who is buried in that grave, every person who was considered so poor that it was worthless to remember their names, I want those names carved on a headstone."

Mrs. Jeffries put her mug of tea on the end table, grabbed the edges of the heavy velvet drawing room drapes, and shoved them open. It was half past five in the morning, but she'd finally given up on getting any sleep and had come downstairs. Staring out into the darkness, she fixed her gaze on the skeletal branches of a distant tree. She'd tossed and turned for hours trying to make sense of everything they'd learned. But despite all the new information she'd heard from Inspector Witherspoon tonight, she was still in the dark when it came to figuring out the identity of the killer. Everything the inspector had reported might eventually prove useful, but they were running out of time if they were going to get this one solved by Christmas Eve.

But she was certain of one thing now—the murder was committed by someone in the household. According to the statements the constables had taken from the neighbors, no one had seen or heard anything that pointed to an outsider getting into the conservatory. The door had been locked and there was no evidence of a broken pane of glass or anything else that would indicate someone had gotten into the room without a key.

Considering everything Harriet Andover's solicitor had told Witherspoon, perhaps it was time to go through the Andover household again. She reached for her teacup and took a sip.

The servants who had been in the household before Jacob Andover married Harriet said that she'd improved their situation, and the newer servants all said she'd treated them decently and fairly. So unless there was something strange going on belowstairs, she was confident the staff could be eliminated.

Which left Harriet's family and her friend.

Jacob Andover admitted to the inspector that he knew he was the heir. Hamish McGraw had confirmed that Harriet had changed her will, making him the heir when her sister had committed suicide. McGraw had also implied that Harriet's estate was substantial. So if Jacob Andover suspected she was going to change her will again and cut him out, wouldn't that be a motive for murder?

Of course it would. But there was no firm evidence he knew what his wife had been planning. On the other hand, he'd been in Harriet's study going through her papers the day after the murder. The inspector had found that letter from McGraw, so wasn't it possible that Jacob had found it as well? If he'd seen the letter, he would have known about the appointment with McGraw and her plan to change the terms of her will. But if her husband had seen it, why leave it in that stack of old letters to be found by the inspector? Why not destroy it? Surely that would have been the wisest course of action.

Then, of course, there was Marcella Blakstone. She was going to be cut out as well. But was she even aware that Harriet had left her a legacy of five thousand pounds? When Harriet's sister died, she'd made her husband her heir and, apparently, had told him that's what she'd done. Had she told Marcella Blakstone as well? It was possible that as she'd mentioned it to her husband, she might have told her stepchildren and her friend about their legacies as well. If that was the case, perhaps she also found out about Harriet's new plans?

Mrs. Blakstone was desperate for money. Her husband had left her destitute and she had stopped work on the one financial asset she had left, her home. Being cut out of Harriet's money would be a killing blow. Mrs. Jeffries realized it was important they learn what had happened to make Harriet Andover cut her and the others out now.

Hatchet had found out that Andover had been unfaithful to his first wife and there were rumors he'd been cheating on his second. If it was true that Andover was a philanderer, that might have something to do with Harriet's decision. But rumors were one thing; proof was another. Yet if Hatchet's source was correct, the proof might be easily obtained. She'd ask Wiggins to look into that situation.

And there were still others she needed to look at again as well. Percival Andover had no great love for his stepmother. He'd practically admitted to the inspector that she was the reason he'd had to take a position at an insurance company and then lie about it when he got sacked. His own actions implicated that he had a good reason to want his stepmother dead, especially if he knew his father was her heir and dear old Papa wouldn't toss him into the streets. Furthermore, he stood to inherit five hundred pounds. Not a huge fortune to someone of his class, but enough to ease some of the pain of his present situation. Additionally, he frequented a brothel, and from what they'd learned of Harriet Andover, she wasn't one to turn a blind eye to immorality. Yes, she was going to ask Phyllis to take a good, hard look at Percy. Perhaps a chance meeting with someone from the insurance company where he previously worked might be in order.

Mrs. Jeffries took a deep breath. What of Ellen Swineburn? How did she fit into the household? She and her step-mother weren't close, but they had little evidence there was any genuine animosity. Like her brother, Mrs. Swineburn stood to inherit five hundred pounds. Again, not a fortune to someone of her class but enough to pay off her bills. Despite Nanette Lanier giving the woman more time to pay, at some point Nanette would demand payment even if it cost her customers. Perhaps Ruth and Hatchet could take a closer look at Ellen Swineburn.

The only other member of the household was the newest, Reverend Daniel Wheeler. She took a sip of tea and grimaced as it was now cold. She was sorry now that she'd encouraged Luty to send off that telegram to America. From what the inspector had learned from Harriet Andover's solicitor, Daniel Wheeler was the only one without a motive to murder his aunt. She'd died before she could change her will.

But did the good reverend know that? Did what he know or didn't know even matter? Wheeler had met his aunt only six weeks ago. So why would he have assumed she was going to leave him anything at all? Nonetheless, just to be thorough, he needed to be examined a bit more closely, and Luty was just the one for that task.

Mrs. Jeffries' eyes unfocused as she continued staring off into the distance. Thoughts, ideas, and snippets of conversations drifted willy-nilly through her mind. She let them tumble around as they would, no longer trying to keep any semblance of rationality.

She heard Mrs. Goodge saying, "*The only thing I found out today was that Ellen Swineburn's coat reeks of smelly, oily soot,*" and right afterward, Luty saying, "*The old feller did pass along a bit of gossip after I asked how Harriet had got her start in business. He told me he didn't know all the details, but he'd heard that some old relative of hers sent her and each of her sisters a big chunk of money when they got engaged.*"

Mrs. Jerffries jumped, almost spilling what little tea she had left in her mug, as she heard footsteps coming down the back stairs. Time to get moving. There was much to do today.

She hurried down to the kitchen and found that the footsteps belonged to Phyllis. The maid was setting the table for breakfast while Mrs. Goodge was cutting slices off a slab of bacon.

"You're up early," the cook said. "Couldn't sleep?"

"Not really. I kept thinking about the case so I finally just got up and came downstairs." She took her empty mug to the sink, turned on the water, and gave it a quick rinse.

"Do you think we're making progress?" Phyllis put down the stack of plates and went back to the pine sideboard for the cutlery. "I know I've not found out much."

"You've done your fair share and it's early days yet. Besides, I've come up with some ideas that I want to discuss with everyone at our morning meeting."

Breakfast was cooked and served and the morning chores done before Constable Barnes arrived. After a brief chat with the cook and the housekeeper, where he filled in a few minor details about the case, he went upstairs to get Witherspoon.

Within minutes of the two policemen leaving, everyone was gathered around the kitchen table. Mrs. Jeffries gave them a quick, but thorough, report on what she'd heard from Witherspoon and then Mrs. Goodge added the details supplied by the constable.

"Sounds like Jacob Andover and that Mrs. Blakstone both 'ave a reason for committin' murder." Smythe put a wiggling Amanda down, who immediately dashed around the table to Luty. "Gama, want up, Gama." She pointed to the elderly American's lap. Hatchet reached down and scooped the little one safely up.

"Indeed it does," Mrs. Jeffries said. "But we have a difficulty here. We've got to find out if Jacob Andover or Marcella Blakstone knew that she was changing her will."

"But Andover searched his wife's study the day after the murder," Betsy said. "Perhaps he found the letter."

"Then why not destroy it?" Mrs. Jeffries said. "Only a fool would have left it there to be found by the police."

"That's true," Betsy murmured.

"Finding out what they might or might not 'ave known isn't goin' to be easy," Smythe said. "But I've got a source that might be able to help us." He'd been planning on seeing Blimpey this morning, and he was good at finding out bits like this.

"Excellent. The more information we have, the better." Mrs. Jeffries looked at Phyllis. "I've a task for you today and it might be arduous. I'd like you to make contact with someone from the Banker's Insurance Trust. They've offices on the High Street in Knightsbridge. I want you to find out anything and everything you can about Percy Andover."

"But didn't they sack him in September?" Phyllis looked confused.

"They did and that was months before the murder, but someone who once worked with him may be able to give us some valuable information."

"Right then, I'll do my best." Phyllis grinned. "At least it'll be more interesting than chatting up grumpy shop clerks."

Mrs. Jeffries looked at Wiggins. "We need to find out why Mrs. Andover was going to cut her husband and her best friend out of her will. I'd like you to find some of the workmen who were working at the Blakstone house." She glanced at Amanda, who had climbed down to the floor with the help of Hatchet and was now on the rug petting Fred, the household's mongrel dog. "Lean closer. I don't want the little one overhearing me. I don't think she'd understand what I'm about to tell you, but it's not the sort of thing that should be said in front of children." She told him what she needed.

"That should be easy enough," Wiggins said. "But it might take a few hours to track down the actual men who were there that week."

"I do hope you've something for me to do," Hatchet said.

"Actually, I've something I want both you and Ruth to do. We need to learn more about Mrs. Swineburn, and I'd like to know more about the death of Mrs. Andover's sister, Henrietta Royle."

"I can handle Henrietta Royle," Ruth offered. "Octavia Wells, she's the treasurer of my women's suffrage group, will know who was closest to Mrs. Royle."

"Excellent." Mrs. Jeffries turned to Hatchet. "Then if you wouldn't mind, I'd like you to see what we can find out about Mrs. Swineburn."

"I've a few sources I can tap." Hatchet took a sip of tea.

"Good, there's something odd about her."

"Did the inspector send someone to Liberty's and those other shops to verify Mrs. Swineburn's and Mrs. Blakstone's statements about their movements the afternoon of the murder?"

"Mrs. Swineburn's friends, the Jenningses, confirmed she visited them that day, but as yet, the constables haven't verified either woman's presence at Liberty's or the other shops."

"Did they get a decent description of their clothes?" the cook asked.

"They did, and hopefully, by this evening, the inspector will have found out something about the matter."

"Really, Inspector, you're here again?" Jacob Andover stood in the open door of the drawing room for a moment and then stalked across the room. "We're planning Harriet's funeral and your intrusion is most inconvenient."

"I'm sorry about that, but I need to ask you some questions, Mr. Andover," Witherspoon said calmly. He and Constable Barnes had discussed the best way to handle this matter on the way here, and the constable suggested that the inspector confront Jacob Andover and Mrs. Blakstone while he went downstairs and spoke to the servants.

"What kind of questions? I've already told you I've no idea who killed my wife." He leaned against the fireplace mantle and crossed his arms over his chest. "This is getting tiresome."

"I'm sure it feels that way to you, sir, but my obligation is to the murder victim, your late wife."

Andover's eyes widened in surprise. But before he could speak, the inspector continued, "Yesterday we spoke to Mr. Hamish McGraw, your late wife's solicitor, and he told us some very interesting facts."

"He had no right to do that," Andover complained. But some of the bluster had gone out of his voice. "Now that Harriet's passed away, McGraw is supposed to work for me and take care of my interests."

"That's not true, sir. He is still Mrs. Andover's solicitor and, as such, told us the details of her estate."

"So he confirmed that I was Harriet's main heir."

"Yes, he did. But he also told us that your wife had an appointment to see him on December nineteenth. Were you aware of that?"

Andover straightened away from the fireplace. "No, I wasn't aware of it. But Harriet wasn't one to seek my advice about business matters."

"You've no idea why she wanted to see Mr. McGraw?"

"I imagine it had something to do with her business."

"Actually, from what she told Mr. McGraw, she made the appointment to see him because she wanted to change her will."

"That's ridiculous!" Andover scoffed. "She'd never do such a thing. I knew my wife better than anyone, and family was always important to her. When her sister Henrietta died, she had no one else to leave her money to except me. McGraw doesn't know what he's talking about. He must have misunderstood her."

"I doubt that, sir," Witherspoon said. "Mr. McGraw has

been her solicitor for over twenty-five years, and he told us he considered her a friend as well as a client."

"That doesn't mean he knew everything. For God's sake, my wife loved me and would have wanted me to be taken care of after she was gone."

There was no delicate way to say this so the inspector was blunt. "Nonetheless, she had decided to make substantial changes. Mr. McGraw confirmed that Mrs. Andover was going to cut you and Mrs. Blakstone out of her estate. Mr. McGraw is adamant that those were her intentions and that had she not been murdered, she'd have done so."

The blood drained out of Andover's face. "Surely you're not suggesting . . . uh . . ."

"I'm not suggesting anything, Mr. Andover, I'm merely asking questions. Were you aware your wife was going to change her will?"

"You think I did it, don't you?" Andover stalked across the room and stopped right in front of Witherspoon. "But I knew nothing about this, absolutely nothing."

Downstairs in the servants' dining hall, Constable Barnes would have kicked himself if he could. But he couldn't as he'd just asked Mrs. Barnard an important question and she was taking her sweet time answering. This morning, Mrs. Jeffries and Mrs. Goodge had told him an interesting tidbit about Marcella Blakstone, but for the life of him, he'd not been able to think of a way to convey the information to Witherspoon that sounded reasonable. Usually he would say an "informant" had passed along gossip, but as the inspector had been with him, he'd know that the constable wouldn't have had time to speak to any of his "sources." In desperation, the constable had suggested to the inspector they send Constable Griffiths to the Blakstone home in hopes of finding the "day laborer" she'd spoken to on Monday afternoon. He didn't hold out much hope, but he had put a flea in Griffiths' ear to speak to the neighbors and see if they knew anything. Now he needed to concentrate on Mrs. Barnard. He didn't hold out much hope for anything useful from her, either. Nonetheless, he'd asked her the most important question. "Did you understand, Mrs. Barnard? Was Mr. Andover aware that Mrs. Andover had an appointment with her solicitor and that the meeting was specifically to cut him out of her estate?"

"I understood it." She exhaled heavily. "I'm sorry, I wasn't deliberately trying to avoid answering but I don't know what to say. This puts me in a very difficult position."

"I realize that. You don't want to lose your employment."

"I'm not worried about getting sacked," she interrupted. "Now that Mrs. Andover is gone, I was going to give my notice right after the funeral. I'm retiring, Constable, but that's not the reason I said nothing about the matter."

"So you do have something to tell me?"

"I do, but I didn't speak up earlier because I wasn't sure about what I overheard. My interpretation of the situation could easily be wrong."

"Why don't you tell me what happened? Any information you have might help us bring Mrs. Andover's killer to justice."

"That's what is important," she murmured. "It was last week. Thursday, yes, that's correct, right after luncheon had been served. I was upstairs and I'd just gotten the towels out of the linen cupboard and taken them into Mrs. Andover's bathroom. You've been upstairs, Constable, so you know the bathroom is just off her bedroom, as is her study."

Barnes nodded. "Yes, I know the layout."

"I'd just taken the towels into the bathroom when I realized that Mr. and Mrs. Andover were in her study and that they were having a rather heated discussion."

"Could you hear what they were saying?"

"I could hear some of it, but not everything. That's one of the reasons I hesitated to mention the incident. I didn't hear their whole conversation, and frankly, I could easily have misunderstood . . ." She broke off and looked away. "But I don't think I did misunderstand."

"What were they arguing about?" Barnes asked.

"The morning post. Mrs. Andover's post was always taken directly to her study, and as soon as breakfast was over, she'd go upstairs and read everything. She always put her correspondence away. She never let any of her letters, even the personal ones, sit out on her desk. Nor did she ever leave her business correspondence out—everything both private and business was put away in one of the file boxes in her bookcase or in the files in her desk drawer."

"Several other members of the household have confirmed that Mrs. Andover kept her business affairs private," Barnes told her. "Who took the post up to her office that morning?"

"I did. Usually Kathleen, the upstairs maid, would do it, but I was standing by the front door when the post dropped in through the slot, and as I was going up anyway, I took the letters addressed to Mrs. Andover up to her study and left the rest on the hall table. So I know that morning she received a letter from her solicitor, Hamish McGraw."

"You're certain?" Barnes wanted to be sure. This could be very important.

"I'm positive. Mr. McGraw has sent letters here for years. His address is on the back of the envelope and he uses a very distinctive stationery." She waved her hand in the air. "That wasn't the only letter that arrived that morning for her, but it was the one they argued over. I am getting ahead of myself." She paused and took a breath. "As I said, I was in the bathroom putting the towels out when I heard Mrs. Andover yell out that 'she wasn't having it.' Frankly, it startled me as Mrs. Andover can have a sharp tongue on occasion, but she rarely raises her voice and I don't think I've ever heard her yelling. She was speaking to Mr. Andover and he mumbled something that I didn't catch. But I could hear her quite plainly, and her next words were that she wasn't going to put up with him sneaking into her office and going through her letters. Then he said he'd only come in to borrow a bottle of ink, and she yelled that if that was the case, why was the letter from her solicitor out on her desk?" She stopped briefly. "She said she'd put it away in her drawer and that she knew he'd taken it out to snoop into her affairs."

"What happened then?"

"By this time, I was concerned as I didn't wish either of them to think I was deliberately eavesdropping, so I very quietly left. I had to walk across Mrs. Andover's bedroom, and just as I got out into the hall, I saw Mrs. Blakstone running for the stairs."

"Do you think she overheard their argument?" Barnes asked.

"Of course." Mrs. Barnard smiled cynically. "Mrs. Blakstone's always skulking about listening at closed doors, especially if Mr. and Mrs. Andover were talking privately."

"But we were told that Mrs. Blakstone was Mrs. Andover's best friend?"

Mrs. Barnard snorted faintly. "That's what Mrs. Andover thought, too."

"Is there a reason you're followin' me?" The burly workman took off his flat cap, laid it on the bar, and glared at Wiggins.

He decided that rather than risk upsetting the fellow further, he'd simply tell as much of the truth as he could. "There is. I'd like to buy you a pint and ask a couple of questions. I'm a private inquiry agent and I think you've got some information that might be helpful to my client. My name is Albert Jones."

The man's blue eyes narrowed suspiciously. "You ain't dressed like one."

Wiggins shrugged. He'd worn his usual clothing because he knew he'd be hunting down a workingman who wouldn't be impressed with a suit and tie. "When you're out on the job, you dress so that you blend in with people. Now, do you want that pint or not?"

"I do. There's no work for me today so you buyin' a pint saves me a bit of coin." He waved at the barman. "Two pints here, Mick." Turning back to Wiggins, he said, "My name is Tony Somers. What kind of questions you wantin' to ask?"

"You work for Brownsley and Son, don't you?" Wiggins was fairly certain he did. After the morning meeting, he'd gone to the builder's office in Kensington. He'd loitered outside until he saw a workman coming out, and within a few minutes and a bit of coin, he'd found out that one of the day told you, right?" He and Constable Griffiths stood in the open drawing room door. Jacob Andover had stalked off in a huff, and the inspector was waiting to have a word with Mrs. Blakstone.

"It was actually Constable Barnes that suggested I do it, sir," Griffiths admitted. "I spoke to two of the neighbors, and both of them confirmed it. Doesn't quite make up for us not being able to verify Mrs. Swineburn's or Mrs. Blakstone's bein' at the shops, but even with the description of what the ladies were wearin' Monday afternoon, no one could recall them being either at Liberty's or the other shops."

"Well, that doesn't mean they weren't there." Witherspoon had been disappointed this morning when Constable Griffiths reported that none of the shop assistants at any of the establishments could confirm either of the women had been there. "It's Christmas so all the shops are busy. But be of good cheer; what you found out this morning helps enormously. Now, even though I'm certain the neighbors were reporting what they saw, I'd still like you to confirm this information with the builders, Brownsley and Son."

"Right away, sir, I know where their offices are."

"And after that, I'd like you to go to the White Horse Pub in Islington. According to Percy Andover, he was there till afternoon closing on the day of the murder. Go and have a chat with either the barman or the barmaid."

Griffiths looked confused. "I thought we already did that?"

"The constable only confirmed that Percy Andover was there. He didn't find out as many details as I'd like."

"Yes, sir." Griffiths grinned. "And now that we've learned

one of our suspects has lied to us, you want me to make certain that Percy Andover was telling the whole truth about his whereabouts that day."

"That's right." Witherspoon smiled approvingly. "That pub is a good place to start. Ask the staff if Percy spoke to anyone or did anything out of the ordinary. Make sure you confirm the time he arrived, when he left, and how much he'd had to drink."

"Yes, sir." He nodded respectfully and headed for the front door just as Marcella Blakstone came down the front staircase.

She was dressed to go out in a navy blue day dress with a matching jacket and a gray-and-navy marquis hat adorned with a black feather. "Jacob says you wish to speak to me. How long is this going to take? I've an appointment."

"Not long, Mrs. Blakstone," Witherspoon assured her. "Let's go into the drawing room."

"Can't you just ask me here?" She stopped in front of him and put her hands on her hips. "I've just told you, I have an appointment and I'm in a hurry."

"And your best friend is dead. I should think helping to find her killer would take precedence over any appointment you might have, Mrs. Blakstone."

Her mouth gaped open in surprise, but she caught herself. "Alright, then, we'll go to the drawing room." She exhaled sharply and stalked through the open door, not stopping until she'd crossed the room and sat down on the settee. "What's this about, Inspector? I've told you everything I know."

"Have you, Mrs. Blakstone?" He smiled faintly as he took a seat across from her. This morning Barnes had suggested sending Constable Griffiths to the Blakstone home to

She closed her eyes and slumped against the cushions. "It's true. Once the initial work was done, I ran out of money. But Harriet had already invited me to stay here and I didn't want to spend Christmas alone. I let what few servants were left go and came here." She broke off with a self-deprecating laugh and stared at the floor. "I'd no idea that poor Harriet was going to be murdered."

"Did you know that Mrs. Andover had left you a substantial legacy in her will?"

"Harriet told me she was going to leave me money but she didn't say how much." She looked up at Witherspoon. "I know this looks bad, but she was my friend and I wouldn't have hurt her. I didn't kill her."

"Why didn't you tell us the truth?" Witherspoon asked.

"Tell you what? That my finances were in such a mess, I couldn't even pay to get my house repaired, that my friend had left me money in her will, that I have a motive for murder because my husband lost everything except the house?" She laughed harshly. "Really, Inspector, I'm not a fool."

"But surely you had to realize it would all come out?"

"You were on the case. With your reputation, I hoped you'd have it solved and the killer caught before anyone found me out."

"Was Mrs. Andover aware of your financial situation?" Witherspoon watched her carefully. He was no expert when it came to reading expressions but sometimes people weren't as clever as they thought and their faces gave them away.

"She never said anything, but I suspect she knew. We were friends, but she wasn't a sentimental woman, so the only reason I can think that she left me anything is because she knew."

"Were you also aware that Mrs. Andover planned to cut you out of her will?"

Her head jerked up and she stared at him with a shocked, horrified expression. "What are you talking about?"

"Her solicitor told us that she planned on cutting you and Mr. Andover out of her will. Do you have any idea why she'd take such a step?"

"That can't be true," she whispered. "It can't be."

"I assure you, it is," Witherspoon said. "However, Mrs. Andover was murdered the day before she could make any changes, so it appears you still have a substantial amount of money coming to you."

Lavinia Carey and her sister, Alice Emerson, were both widows and both dressed in black from head to toe. They were staunch members of the London Society for Women's Suffrage, and Ruth had met them on a number of occasions. But she didn't know them well.

Right after the morning meeting, she'd stopped in to see Octavia so she could find out who in the group had been friends with Henrietta Royle. Octavia had not only supplied her with their names, but also sent her footman here with a note requesting a brief meeting. The sisters had quickly agreed to see her, but now that she was here, Ruth wasn't sure how to go about bringing up the dead woman's name.

"It's very good of you to see me on such short notice." Ruth looked around the room. Like the widows, it, too, was dressed in mourning: heavy wine-colored drapes closed against the December day, old-fashioned brown-and-green-patterned wallpaper, portraits of somber men and unsmiling women in muted gold frames, and an overhead chandelier laborers who had worked at the Blakstone home came in most days to see if there was work for him that day. Once Wiggins had learned that interesting tidbit, it was just a matter of waiting and he'd done that at the café across the road.

"Sort of. I'm a day laborer. But I work for a couple of builders, not just Brownsley. Sometimes one of 'em has work for me, sometimes they don't." Tony nodded his thanks as the barman brought their pints.

Wiggins paid him and waited till the barman had moved off to serve someone else before he spoke again. "You worked at the Blakstone house?"

"The one in South Kensington?" He took a sip as Wiggins nodded. "Yeah, I worked there. But it was only for a couple of days. Once the lady of the house left, she stopped the work. From what I've heard, she's bein' right picky about the work we did, but Mr. Brownsley thinks it's because she's not wantin' to pay up."

"Mrs. Blakstone was there when you were working?" Wiggins clarified.

"She was, spent half the day complainin' we was too noisy, but you tell me, 'ow the 'ell are we supposed to replace window frames or fix that leaky roof without makin' noise?"

"While she was there, did she have any visitors?" He was going to lead up to his real question slowly. Asking it was going to be embarrassing enough; he didn't want to just blurt it out.

"Only one." Tony snickered. "And she wasn't entertaining him in the drawing room, if you get my meaning."

"Well done, Constable. You've shown real initiative in thinking to speak to the neighbors. They were sure of what they told you, right?" He and Constable Griffiths stood in the open drawing room door. Jacob Andover had stalked off in a huff, and the inspector was waiting to have a word with Mrs. Blakstone.

"It was actually Constable Barnes that suggested I do it, sir," Griffiths admitted. "I spoke to two of the neighbors, and both of them confirmed it. Doesn't quite make up for us not being able to verify Mrs. Swineburn's or Mrs. Blakstone's bein' at the shops, but even with the description of what the ladies were wearin' Monday afternoon, no one could recall them being either at Liberty's or the other shops."

"Well, that doesn't mean they weren't there." Witherspoon had been disappointed this morning when Constable Griffiths reported that none of the shop assistants at any of the establishments could confirm either of the women had been there. "It's Christmas so all the shops are busy. But be of good cheer; what you found out this morning helps enormously. Now, even though I'm certain the neighbors were reporting what they saw, I'd still like you to confirm this information with the builders, Brownsley and Son."

"Right away, sir, I know where their offices are."

"And after that, I'd like you to go to the White Horse Pub in Islington. According to Percy Andover, he was there till afternoon closing on the day of the murder. Go and have a chat with either the barman or the barmaid."

Griffiths looked confused. "I thought we already did that?"

"The constable only confirmed that Percy Andover was there. He didn't find out as many details as I'd like."

"Yes, sir." Griffiths grinned. "And now that we've learned

one of our suspects has lied to us, you want me to make certain that Percy Andover was telling the whole truth about his whereabouts that day."

"That's right." Witherspoon smiled approvingly. "That pub is a good place to start. Ask the staff if Percy spoke to anyone or did anything out of the ordinary. Make sure you confirm the time he arrived, when he left, and how much he'd had to drink."

"Yes, sir." He nodded respectfully and headed for the front door just as Marcella Blakstone came down the front staircase.

She was dressed to go out in a navy blue day dress with a matching jacket and a gray-and-navy marquis hat adorned with a black feather. "Jacob says you wish to speak to me. How long is this going to take? I've an appointment."

"Not long, Mrs. Blakstone," Witherspoon assured her. "Let's go into the drawing room."

"Can't you just ask me here?" She stopped in front of him and put her hands on her hips. "I've just told you, I have an appointment and I'm in a hurry."

"And your best friend is dead. I should think helping to find her killer would take precedence over any appointment you might have, Mrs. Blakstone."

Her mouth gaped open in surprise, but she caught herself. "Alright, then, we'll go to the drawing room." She exhaled sharply and stalked through the open door, not stopping until she'd crossed the room and sat down on the settee. "What's this about, Inspector? I've told you everything I know."

"Have you, Mrs. Blakstone?" He smiled faintly as he took a seat across from her. This morning Barnes had suggested sending Constable Griffiths to the Blakstone home to see if they could find the "day laborer" she claimed she spoke to on the day of the murder. But Griffiths had come back and said the place was deserted. But for good measure, he'd gone to the neighbors and been told that no workmen had been at the Blakstone home since the day Mrs. Blakstone had gone to the Andovers'.

"How dare you ask such a question." She started to get up, but he waved her back into her seat.

"I dare because we know you've lied to us."

Her eyes widened in surprise but she quickly got herself under control. "I've no idea what you're talking about, Inspector."

"Mrs. Blakstone, you told us that on the day Mrs. Andover was murdered, you went to your home to check on the workmen. Do you recall that?"

She drew back slightly, her expression wary. "There's nothing wrong with my memory, Inspector. I know what I told you."

"Then you admit you were lying when you said that?"

"I admit nothing."

"Mrs. Blakstone, there haven't been workmen at your property since the day you came here," Witherspoon said.

"That's not true," she exclaimed. "I don't know who has told you such a tale—"

"Your neighbors," he interrupted. "But I've sent Constable Griffiths to the Brownsley and Son office to confirm the matter."

"You had no right to do that," she protested. "No right to invade my privacy."

"We have every right, Mrs. Blakstone, so please, just tell me the truth."

She closed her eyes and slumped against the cushions. "It's true. Once the initial work was done, I ran out of money. But Harriet had already invited me to stay here and I didn't want to spend Christmas alone. I let what few servants were left go and came here." She broke off with a self-deprecating laugh and stared at the floor. "I'd no idea that poor Harriet was going to be murdered."

"Did you know that Mrs. Andover had left you a substantial legacy in her will?"

"Harriet told me she was going to leave me money but she didn't say how much." She looked up at Witherspoon. "I know this looks bad, but she was my friend and I wouldn't have hurt her. I didn't kill her."

"Why didn't you tell us the truth?" Witherspoon asked.

"Tell you what? That my finances were in such a mess, I couldn't even pay to get my house repaired, that my friend had left me money in her will, that I have a motive for murder because my husband lost everything except the house?" She laughed harshly. "Really, Inspector, I'm not a fool."

"But surely you had to realize it would all come out?"

"You were on the case. With your reputation, I hoped you'd have it solved and the killer caught before anyone found me out."

"Was Mrs. Andover aware of your financial situation?" Witherspoon watched her carefully. He was no expert when it came to reading expressions but sometimes people weren't as clever as they thought and their faces gave them away.

"She never said anything, but I suspect she knew. We were friends, but she wasn't a sentimental woman, so the only reason I can think that she left me anything is because she knew."

"Were you also aware that Mrs. Andover planned to cut you out of her will?"

Her head jerked up and she stared at him with a shocked, horrified expression. "What are you talking about?"

"Her solicitor told us that she planned on cutting you and Mr. Andover out of her will. Do you have any idea why she'd take such a step?"

"That can't be true," she whispered. "It can't be."

"I assure you, it is," Witherspoon said. "However, Mrs. Andover was murdered the day before she could make any changes, so it appears you still have a substantial amount of money coming to you."

Lavinia Carey and her sister, Alice Emerson, were both widows and both dressed in black from head to toe. They were staunch members of the London Society for Women's Suffrage, and Ruth had met them on a number of occasions. But she didn't know them well.

Right after the morning meeting, she'd stopped in to see Octavia so she could find out who in the group had been friends with Henrietta Royle. Octavia had not only supplied her with their names, but also sent her footman here with a note requesting a brief meeting. The sisters had quickly agreed to see her, but now that she was here, Ruth wasn't sure how to go about bringing up the dead woman's name.

"It's very good of you to see me on such short notice." Ruth looked around the room. Like the widows, it, too, was dressed in mourning: heavy wine-colored drapes closed against the December day, old-fashioned brown-and-green-patterned wallpaper, portraits of somber men and unsmiling women in muted gold frames, and an overhead chandelier with half a dozen of the globes broken. Heavy claw-footed chairs and settees upholstered in browns, blacks, and deep green were grouped together by the fireplace. The rest of the room was crammed with even more furniture. There were tables with fringed purple-and-cream crocheted runners, and four curio cabinets filled with knickknacks, china dolls, and Dresden shepherds stood along the wall catty-corner to the huge slate-colored fireplace. Straight-backed chairs, lumpy love seats, and three different-sized bookcases took up the rest of the space. A portrait of Queen Victoria as a young woman held pride of place over the mantelpiece.

"It's our pleasure, Lady Cannonberry." Alice Emerson pointed at an overstuffed brown chair positioned across from the settee where the two women sat. "Please have a seat. We were quite curious as to why you'd want to see us. But you are most welcome. Would you care for tea?"

"Don't be absurd, Alice." Lavinia frowned at her sister. "It's far too early for tea." She looked at Ruth. "Would you care for coffee?"

"Thank you, no, I'm fine," Ruth said. "I'm so sorry to have barged in on you like this, but I've been tasked with finding out some rather delicate information. I was told the two of you might be able to help me."

"Delicate information." Alice stared at her over the rim of her spectacles. "I've never heard of such a thing. Do you mean gossip?"

"Well, um, I suppose one could call it that," she began only to be interrupted.

"Gracious, that's wonderful." Alice grinned broadly and then looked at her sister. "I told you it would be something interesting. Octavia's friends are always such fun."

"Hmmm, we'll see." Lavinia looked at Ruth skeptically. "Go ahead, then, tell us why you're here."

"A friend of mine has asked me to make inquiries about Henrietta Royle."

"Why does your friend want to know about her?" Lavinia demanded. "She's been dead for a year."

"I know, but there's been some questions about the manner of her death," Ruth explained. "And her death may have something to do with another death recently."

"Now Lavinia, don't jump down Lady Cannonberry's throat. I'm sure she has her reasons." She stared at Ruth. "What are those reasons?"

Ruth decided it would be best to be honest. She didn't know why she felt that way, but she did and she long ago learned to trust her feelings. "Alright, I'll tell you, but you must promise not to tell anyone that I was here asking you questions. I'm so sorry, I don't mean to be mysterious, but I do assure you, it's very important."

Lavinia looked at Alice, who nodded. "We promise," Lavinia said. "Octavia Wells is no fool and she'd not send you to see us without a good reason. So go ahead, ask your questions."

"Thank you." Ruth breathed a sigh of relief. "Mrs. Royle supposedly committed suicide—"

Alice interrupted, "She did no such thing. Henrietta Royle was murdered. She was our best friend, and we were devastated when she died. We told the police that she couldn't have killed herself; she simply wouldn't take her own life. But you know the police—they insisted she was alone in that rail carriage."

"And they found the gun on the floor by the door," Lavinia added. "But that means nothing. The killer was the one that must have dropped it."

"You think she was murdered? Why do you think that?"

"Because she wasn't alone in that railway carriage. We were there that day. We went to Phillip Royle's funeral. He was buried in Surrey, at Brookwood Cemetery. Surely you've heard of it; one must take the train there."

"The London Necropolis Railway train," Alice volunteered. "And that's an important point."

"Why is that important?"

"Because you see, Henrietta didn't come back on the Necropolis Railway to Waterloo like everyone else. She stayed to see her husband buried while the rest of the mourners, except for the two of us, got on the train immediately afterwards."

"Let me explain what happened." Lavinia frowned at her sister. "You always tell things too fast and you end up confusing people."

"I do not, but you go on and tell it your way." She sniffed disapprovingly.

Lavinia turned to Ruth. "Phillip Royle's funeral was at noon so it was over with by half past one that afternoon. Henrietta's family and friends left for London but Henrietta insisted on staying to see Phillip buried. That sounds very odd, but despite Phillip being a bit of a martinet, they were very devoted to one another and Henrietta didn't want to leave him. Now, Alice and I have family in Woking and that's only a few miles from the Brookwood Cemetery so after the service we went to visit our cousins."

"It was a dreadful visit," Alice added. "They've plenty of money but they served a paltry luncheon and then an even worse tea that afternoon. There was nothing but a few biscuits and some rather pathetic brown bread."

"Lady Cannonberry isn't interested in what kind of tea it was," Lavinia snapped.

"But that's important," Alice argued. "The reason we were late to the station and missed the train back to London that afternoon was because Thomas—he's our cousin—took us to the train station in that old trap of his, and that horse is so old, it could barely walk."

Lavinia nodded. "That's true." She looked at Ruth. "My sister is correct. We got to the station just in time to see the train pull away, and just as it did, a man leapt into the only first-class carriage. That's the one Henrietta would have taken back to London, and we know she was going in that carriage because we overheard her telling her sister she'd be just fine as there was a first-class carriage on the train."

"But there wasn't a Ladies Only car," Alice added. "That's what we overheard her tell her sister. That was the train we were going to take back, too. So we were stuck there with our penny-pinching cousin for another hour."

"You're sure this man got on the first-class carriage?" Ruth wanted to be certain.

"We are." Lavinia leaned forward. "My eyesight is still good and I could plainly see the words 'First Class' on the outside of the carriage."

"What did this man look like?" Ruth asked.

Lavinia shook her head. "We only saw him from the back. It was December so he was wearing a black overcoat and a hat, of course."

"We didn't get a good look at his face," Alice said.

"Did you tell the police what you've told me?"

"We did but nothing ever came of it," Lavinia replied.

"That's because Phillip's family wanted everything hushed up," Alice snapped. "They didn't want the scandal of a suicide in their midst. But I know she didn't kill herself. Henrietta wouldn't have done that."

"What makes you so sure?" Ruth asked. "She'd just lost her husband, and from what you two have told me, she was very devoted to him. Perhaps she was simply overwhelmed by grief. That does happen."

"We know that," Lavinia replied. "But Henrietta was different. She'd been raised as a Quaker."

Ruth finally understood. "And that meant she believed that only God had the right to take a human life."

"That's right. She believed it with every fiber of her being. It was one of the few times she ever stood up to that old tyrant she married. He tried to stop her from signing a petition to end hanging here in this country. But she refused and signed it anyway," Lavinia said. "And this happened just a few weeks before she died. I don't care what anyone says; Henrietta Royle didn't kill herself."

CHAPTER 8

"If you've no more questions, Inspector, as I've already told you, I've an appointment." Marcella Blakstone stared at him coldly. "Furthermore, I resent your implication. I had nothing to do with Harriet's murder. She was my friend."

"Yet she was going to change her will," Witherspoon reminded her. "And you've no idea why she'd do such a thing?"

Marcella shrugged and got to her feet. "Perhaps she'd decided to leave it to her nephew. He certainly did everything he could to ingratiate himself to her."

"In what way?"

"Every way, Inspector." She smiled cynically. "He bribed his way into the house with a broach supposedly from his dead mother, and if the gossip from the housemaids is to be believed, that wasn't the only present he gave her. But it wasn't just Harriet he buttered up; he set his sights on Ellen

Swineburn as well. Now, if you'll excuse me . . ." She headed for the door.

"Could you ask Mr. Percival Andover to come here?" he called. But she ignored him and kept walking, closing the door firmly behind her as she left.

Witherspoon sighed, got up, and followed her out into the hallway. Constable Barnes was at the far end; he'd just come up the servants' stairs.

The inspector leaned against the doorjamb. Marcella Blakstone's parting comments could have just been an attempt to divert him from examining her too closely or they might have some merit. There was only one way to find out. "Constable, if you've a minute, there's something you need to do."

"Sorry I wasn't 'ere yesterday, but I got called away on another bit of business." Blimpey nodded at the stool across from him. "But I'm 'ere now and I've got plenty to tell ya."

Smythe sat down. "Good. I can use some decent information. But before ya begin, I want to tell ya about what we've decided."

"That means you've sorted it out with your lady." Blimpey smiled. "I'm glad. I know it was worryin' ya."

"She took the news better than I thought she would," he admitted. "We talked about it and Betsy said she didn't want the grave dug up. She said it was disrespectful to everyone else who'd been buried with her mum and sister."

"That's understandable. So what does she want?"

"She wants a proper headstone, a big one, and she wants the names of every person buried in that grave to be on it, not just her family," Smythe replied. "Can ya do that?"

Blimpey's eyebrows rose. "I think so, but we might 'ave a problem if the others are from the same parish as Betsy's family. Those records were lost, remember. That's why it took so long to find out exactly where her family ended up."

"What about the cemetery? Don't they keep the names of the dead?"

"They do if you've paid a packet of money and put up a fancy headstone," he said, his expression cynical. "And to give them credit, I think they try to keep proper records, but they're paupers' graves, mass graves, and half the time, even the parish that's payin' for the burial sometimes don't know the names of the dead. If you drop dead at the local churchyard, the parish has to pay even if no one knows who the 'ell ya are."

"Can you at least try to find out?" Smythe asked. "I can't go back to Betsy and tell her it can't be done. She's got 'er 'eart set on it."

"It can be done," Blimpey assured him. "But it may take a bit of time to track down everyone in that grave."

"We've waited this long; we can wait a bit longer if need be. Will the cemetery object to the raising of the headstone? I mean, it's been years since they buried Betsy's family and the others."

"I'll find out."

"Bribe 'em if you have to," Smythe said. "I don't want Betsy upset by some snooty little clerk sayin' it's too late to put up a headstone. There's somethin' else you need to know. With the headstone, Betsy knows what she wants written on it."

"I thought she wanted the names of the dead on it."

"She does, but she also wants a bit more than that and

she doesn't want that usual nonsense about angels lookin' down from heaven. She wants to tell the truth, that people were buried in a mass grave not because they were traitors or criminals or even bad people. They were shoved in one because they were poor."

"The stonemason won't care what you put on the headstone as long as he gets paid, and I doubt anyone from the cemetery will bother to come read the headstone, so they won't care. Now, if we've finished that bit of business, let me tell ya what I found out about your case," Blimpey said. "First of all, Percy Andover frequents a very expensive brothel in Soho."

"Yeah, we already found out about that."

"Did ya find out that Percy owes them a lot of money? Billy Ross runs that place and he's one mean bugger. My people found out that Ross gave Percy until the end of the year to pay what 'e owes, or they'll take it out of his hide. Those are Billy's exact words."

"Was your source able to find out 'ow much Percy owes?"

"Over three hundred pounds." Blimpey shrugged. "Apparently, Percy's tastes are expensive, they run to dressin' up—"

Smythe interrupted, "Ya don't need to give me the details, I understand. That information could be important. What else did ya find out?"

"Daniel Wheeler was in France before he came to England."

"We know that. 'E was there for two weeks doin' research."

Blimpey shook his head. "Nah, it weren't for just two weeks. Reverend Wheeler was there for over a year."

*   *   *

A housemaid stuck her head into the butler's pantry. "I'm Colleen Murphy. Mrs. Barnard said you wanted to speak to me."

Barnes, who'd been reading her original statement, looked up and smiled at the young woman. She had light brown hair, blue eyes, and regular, even features. She'd been one of the two servants interviewed by Constable Griffiths on the night of the murder, so Barnes hadn't met her. When he'd read through her statement the first time, he'd not seen anything that indicated a second interview should be done. But the inspector had told him Marcella Blakstone implied that Daniel Wheeler had somewhat shady motives for coming to see his aunt. Her comments seemed to indicate he deliberately ingratiated himself, presumably either to get invited to stay or to worm his way into her estate. The constable wasn't sure there was anything to Mrs. Blakstone's remarks. In his experience, carping like that, especially as Mrs. Blakstone was now one of their main suspects, usually meant a feeble attempt to muddy the waters and turn their attention to someone else. But he'd do as the inspector wished and find out if this lass was as big a gossip as Mrs. Barnard said when he'd asked which of the maids had the loosest tongue.

"Yes, please come in." He gestured to the chair across from him.

"Why do you want to speak to me?" She sat down. "I've already told everything I know to that nice young Constable Griffiths."

"Yes, I know. I've got your statement right here." He tapped the sheet of paper in front of him. "But there's a bit more we need to ask. Can you tell me who took Mr. Andover's laundry up to his room?"

"I brought it up and then put everything away."

"Was Mr. Andover's dressing gown visible?" Barnes needed to find out if any of their suspects had actually seen the dressing gown and, hence, knew the sash would be with it.

"It was right on the top of the basket."

"What time did you take the laundry upstairs?"

"I don't know the exact time, but breakfast had been served. I know that because the rest of the household was out and about. So it was probably eight forty-five or so."

"Did you see anyone as you took Mr. Andover's laundry up to his room?"

She tapped her finger against her lips. "Let me think now. Well, Mrs. Barnard, of course, she was unpacking the basket with us."

"I meant did you see anyone in the household?"

"I passed Reverend Wheeler as I came up the stairs. He and Mrs. Andover were on the first-floor landing."

"They were on the servants' stairs?"

"Yes, she'd come to the kitchen to have a word with Mrs. Fell and I suppose he'd come down to tell her something. When I reached the second floor, Mrs. Blakstone was coming out of her room as I went past it and Mrs. Swineburn was going into her room."

"Anyone else?" Barnes had seen the dressing gown and the sash. The distinctive pattern was such that it could have been seen by either Mrs. Blakstone or Mrs. Swineburn.

"I don't think so."

"What did you do after that?"

"I put the clothes away and took the basket back to the dry larder and hung it up. Then I went up to do the upper floors. I start at the top and work my way down."

"Did anything odd or unusual happen while you were up there cleaning?" Barnes asked. "Anything that set that day apart from other days?"

She looked down at her hands, which were folded neatly in her lap. Then she raised her head and glanced at the closed door. "Well, I don't like to talk out of turn, and I don't want to lose my position . . ."

"We don't share what witnesses say to us with anyone. The only way it would be made public is if you had to testify in court about it." He hoped his words would reassure her.

She hesitated, but then said, "Right then, when I went upstairs to start the cleaning, Mrs. Blakstone was listening at Mrs. Andover's bedroom door. She and Mr. Andover were in there talking. I kept on going and pretended I didn't see her."

"You pretended you didn't see her?"

"She's got a sharp tongue, Constable, and she likes to point out our mistakes to Mrs. Barnard, so yes, I pretended not to see her. It wasn't the first time I'd seen her listening at a door, either. Mind you, she's not the only one. I've seen Mrs. Swineburn with her ear to a closed door more than once."

"I see. Did anything else happen that morning?"

"The only other thing that morning was Reverend Wheeler getting a telegram."

"And you brought it up to him?"

"Oh no, he went downstairs to get it," she replied. "Normally Marlene or Mrs. Barnard would bring it up, but the reverend happened to be coming out of his room; it's on the second floor, not the first floor or the ground floor, but the way sound carries when you're at a certain spot, you can hear everything from the foyer. He heard the telegraph lad announce he had a telegram for Daniel Wheeler so he hurried down and got it himself. That is just like Reverend Wheeler, always lookin' to save us girls from having to go up and down the stairs all the time."

Witherspoon opened the door and came face-to-face with Constable Reed. "Oh, hello, Constable, did you need to speak to me?"

Reed was a tall, brown-haired lad with ivory skin, brown eyes, and a baby face. "Er, excuse me, sir, I don't like to interrupt, but Constable Griffiths said I should tell you what I found out this morning."

"Not to worry, Constable, I've not started the next interview as yet. What is it?" Witherspoon noticed a rim of moisture on Reed's forehead. The lad was new to the Ladbroke Road Station and the inspector didn't know him very well, but the young man seemed both willing and capable. "Constable Reed, are you feeling ill?"

"I'm fine, sir." Reed swallowed so heavily, his Adam's apple bobbed up. "I'm just a little nervous. You see, everyone knows your reputation, sir."

The inspector was surprised that anyone would be nervous of him. He wanted to put the lad at ease. "That's very kind of you to say. But everyone on this case is working hard and doing their best. Now, what is it you wanted to tell me?"

The constable yanked a white handkerchief out of his pocket and swiped his forehead. "Well, sir, as you know, we'd finished doing interviews with the neighbors except for one of the homes across the road. That's one of your methods, sir. You have us out there talking to everyone no matter how long it takes."

"Thank you, Constable, again, that's kind of you to say, but I'm certainly not the only inspector that follows that policy." He heard a clock from somewhere in the house strike the hour and knew that time was getting on. "Now, what did you find out?"

"Actually, sir, now that I'm here, I'm not certain it has anything to do with this case, but Constable Griffiths insisted I tell you. He said that one never knows what might or might not be relevant."

"Yes, yes, that was good of Constable Griffiths." Witherspoon tried to hurry the lad along. There was a lot to do today. In addition, he was concerned they might be summoned to Chief Superintendent Barrows' office at the Yard for a progress report.

"It was a statement from Mrs. Pinchon, sir. She's the housekeeper at the house across the road. She told us that beginning in October, she saw an elderly man who appeared to be watching the Andover home."

"An elderly man?" Witherspoon repeated. He wondered if it was the same person whom Daniel Wheeler said he'd seen on the morning of the murder.

"Yes, sir. But she claimed he wasn't an old man at all; she claimed he was wearing a theatrical costume."

"A theatrical costume?"

"It sounds strange, sir, which is why I hesitated to mention it, but Constable Griffiths insisted and he's been on the force far longer than I have," Reed said. "And the lady did seem confident in reporting what she'd seen."

"She saw this person in October?" Witherspoon asked.

"She saw him a number of times, sir," Reed said. "The first time she spotted the fellow, he was too far away for her to get a decent look at him."

"Was she watching him from the window?"

"No, sir, she was outside. She said she enjoyed sweeping the stoop, that the fresh air was good for a woman of her age and that exercise was essential if one was to live a long and healthy life. Her words, sir, not mine."

"She saw this man while she was outside sweeping the stoop? Did she mention what specifically he'd done to make her notice him? This neighborhood has a lot of foot traffic."

"She did, sir. Mrs. Pinchon said she noticed him because he made a gesture that is common to actors wearing a false beard or mustache. It was this one, sir." He lifted his fingers to his upper lip and mimed smoothing a nonexistent mustache. "She said that actors always did it before goin' on the stage, sir. They wanted to make certain their false mustaches and beards were attached properly."

For a moment, Witherspoon wasn't certain he'd heard correctly. "Did she say why she thought he was wearing a theatrical costume?"

"She did, sir. It turns out that she was the wardrobe matron for the Strand Theater for twenty years before she became a housekeeper."

"Really? Did she say anything else about this man?"

"She did, sir. She said he got out of the cab and walked up and down the street several times before disappearing around the corner. She claimed he never went inside a house and that he always, always seemed to have his attention on the Andover home."

"Did you ask her exactly when in October she noticed the man?"

"I did, sir, and she thinks it was the first two weeks, then the fellow simply disappeared and she never saw him again," Reed said.

Witherspoon was suddenly intrigued. "I'll have a word with her when I've finished questioning the rest of the household. You didn't happen to see Percy Andover, did you?"

"He's in his father's study. Shall I send him in, sir?"

"Yes, thank you."

"Nell's bells," Luty muttered. She folded the telegram that had just arrived and tucked it into her fur muff. "Turns out I was dead wrong. That Reverend Wheeler feller is real. My friend Braxton confirmed that he was the preacher at Saint Peter's Episcopal Church in Carson City two years ago."

"Well, at least we know he wasn't lying." Hatchet helped Luty into the carriage and then climbed inside himself. They were going to the afternoon meeting at Upper Edmonton Gardens.

"But I had me a feelin' about him." Luty adjusted her peacock blue cloak around her knees and grabbed the hand-hold as the carriage pulled away. "My feelin's are almost always right."

"Almost doesn't mean always." He grabbed the heavy blanket they kept in the carriage and draped it over Luty's lap before taking his own seat across from her. "Besides, madam, let's be honest here. You don't like men of the cloth. You get positively giddy with delight when you read a salacious or negative newspaper article about one of them."

"That ain't true. I just don't think they walk on water like you people do."

"You people?" Hatchet raised his eyebrows. "Forgive me, madam, but you've lived in England for so long that you now qualify as 'you people' as well. What's more, we don't revere Church of England priests or Nonconformist pastors unless they earn it by taking care of their parish properly or by good works in the community."

"Humph." Luty snorted. "Seems to me that most preachers take care of themselves first and foremost. But let's not argue about it. That Reverend Wheeler really is a preacher so I wasted my time, and we've got to get this case solved. Christmas is only a few days away."

"You did not waste your time," Hatchet declared. "No more than I did. I spent most of today talking to everyone I know who might have had information regarding Mrs. Swineburn. The only thing I learned was what we already knew but I'm not giving up—I've a plan in mind for tomorrow. Now come on, don't look so glum. We'll do our part to help find this murderer."

"Let's hope someone has found out somethin' useful today," Luty muttered. "My baby is old enough to really enjoy Christmas now and I don't want the holiday spoiled because that killer is still out there."

"I'm afraid I've no idea what you're talking about." Percy Andover looked confused. "What will?"

"Your stepmother's will," Witherspoon explained patiently. "Were you aware that Mrs. Andover was going to make some substantial changes to her estate?"

"Why would I know anything about that? She wouldn't have discussed such a subject with me."

"She didn't tell you that she had left you and your sister a legacy?" Witherspoon wasn't sure this was the best method for finding out if the two Andover stepchildren were aware they were each being left five hundred pounds. It wasn't a fortune, but considering that Percy was unemployed and Mrs. Swineburn was concerned about the bills from her dressmaker, even that sum could be a motive for murder. The inspector had decided that Percy was a bit less intelligent than his sister and he might be the best one to question first.

"Not directly." Percy leaned against the mantel, much like his father had earlier. "Why would she? I'm sure she didn't expect to get murdered."

"People rarely do." Witherspoon wanted to get him talking, but the day was getting away from them and he also wanted to have a word with the housekeeper from across the street.

"Especially someone like her," Percy exclaimed. "She was always bragging about the longevity in her family, which I thought was ridiculous. Both of her sisters are dead, but if one mentioned that fact to her, she'd point out that her elder sister foolishly allowed herself to catch pneumonia and that her younger one committed suicide. She was most unreasonable about the subject just because she has some old uncle in California who's well into his nineties and still very strong."

"What about her parents?" Witherspoon asked, just to keep him chatting.

"They died years ago and neither of them was particularly old, but if one brought them up, Harriet always said that she'd advised them not to take that ship as it was the middle of winter and the seas were dreadfully rough. That's how they died, you see; the ship they were on sank just off the coast of Ireland. Harriet thought she would live forever, and frankly, I was fairly certain she would as well . . . so it wasn't as if I expected to inherit that five hundred quid anytime soon . . ." He broke off as he realized what he'd said. "Uh, er, I mean—"

"You knew she was leaving you and your sister a substantial amount of money," Witherspoon interrupted. "Correct?"

Percy's lips flattened to a thin, angry line. "What if I did? Yes, I'll admit it. I knew about the legacy."

"Did Mrs. Swineburn know?"

"She did. I told her."

"How did you find out?"

"I overheard her discussing the matter with her solicitor."

"You were eavesdropping?"

An ugly flush climbed Percy's pale cheeks. "That's a rather offensive accusation, Inspector. It's hardly my fault that her solicitor has a loud voice. It was last year, only a day or two after her sister's funeral. She'd asked Mr. McGraw to come here as she had a cold. I happened to be out in the hallway when the two of them were discussing the new terms for her will and I overheard it."

"Were they upstairs in Mrs. Andover's study?"

Percy's face got redder. "They were, but as I said, Mr. McGraw has a very loud voice and I could hear every word he said."

Witherspoon nodded as if he understood. Apparently, Marcella Blakstone and Ellen Swineburn weren't the only ones who eavesdropped.

"So you knew she'd left you money but you claim you

didn't know she was planning to make changes again. Changes that would essentially cut all of you out of any share of her estate?"

"Of course not. I swear she never said a word to any of us about that."

"But she died before she could make those changes so you, your sister, and most importantly, your father will inherit the bulk of what is a very large estate."

"That's nothing to do with me." He pushed his spectacles back up his nose. "I tell you, I knew nothing about her plans."

"Your father never mentioned them to you? He didn't tell you that he knew she was meeting with her solicitor on December nineteenth?"

"My father knew no such thing," Percy snapped. "Furthermore, your implication that he did is completely unwarranted. Everyone knows my stepmother didn't discuss her business affairs with anyone."

"We've been told that by a number of people, but I hardly think the fact she was going to change her will constitutes a 'business affair.' Furthermore, Mr. Andover has already admitted that Mrs. Andover told him he was going to be her heir when she changed her will after her sister passed away."

"That doesn't mean she told us what she was planning to do this time," he cried.

The inspector realized that they could go around in circles for hours and he didn't have time for that. "Thank you, Mr. Andover, that'll be all. Can you ask your sister to come in, please?"

Ruth was the last one to arrive for their afternoon meeting. "I hope I've not kept you waiting, but the traffic was dreadful and it took ages to get across the bridge." She unbuttoned her mantle as she crossed the room to the coat tree.

"Don't rush, Ruth," Mrs. Goodge said. "We've only just sat down. I'll pour you a cup of tea."

"Thank you, that would be lovely. It's so cold out there, I'm half-frozen." She hung up her garments and hurried to take her place at the table. She nodded her thanks as the cook passed her the tea.

"Who would like to go first?" Mrs. Jeffries asked.

"I didn't learn anything." Phyllis sighed. "Percival Andover's previous employer has a very small office. There were only two clerks that I could see and a grumpy-looking old man. I followed one of the clerks to the café down the road, but I couldn't make contact with him."

"Why not?" Wiggins stared at her curiously. "You're good at gettin' fellas to talk to you."

Phyllis gave him a sharp look, not sure whether to be flattered or insulted. She decided on flattered. "Thank you, I think. But the young man met a young lady and they had lunch together."

"So tryin' to horn in on that would be awkward," Luty pointed out. "That's just plain bad luck."

"That's what I thought," Phyllis exclaimed. "I went back to see if I could find the other clerk but it was too late. He was gone. But I'm going back tomorrow and trying again."

"I think I've already found out what we need to know about this Percy fella," Smythe said. He looked around the table, his expression anxious. "But it's the sort of thing that isn't to be said in mixed company."

"Don't be ridiculous." Betsy frowned at her husband. "We're investigating a murder and all of us are adults."

"Amanda's not."

"She's napping in Mrs. Goodge's room. Now come on, tell us." She patted her husband's arm. "We already know that Percy goes to a brothel and it can't be worse than that."

"It can."

"I assure you, our ears won't fall off," Mrs. Jeffries said. "But if it's absolutely dreadful, just give us the gist of it and leave out the unseemly details." She wasn't sure that was a solution, but she knew that Smythe could be quite stubborn.

"Yeah, don't worry about it, Smythe." Wiggins grinned. "I found out somethin' that's a bit unseemly and I'm goin' to tell about it."

"Please, Smythe, if you're holding back on my account, I assure you, the interests of justice are more important than my sensibilities," Ruth said.

"Right then, I went to see my source and he knew all about Mr. Percy Andover," Smythe said. "It's not very nice but it could be important." He broke off and cleared his throat. "As ya know, Percy likes to frequent a . . . a . . . place where ladies of the evening . . ."

"He goes to a brothel," Ruth prompted. "Do go on."

"Well, it's not just that." Smythe could feel a blush creeping up his face. "Andover has some strange . . . uh . . . things and they're the sort of things that brothels charge extra for providin' for their customers. A lot of extra."

"I think we get the gist of it," Mrs. Jeffries said quickly.

"How can he afford it?" Hatchet asked. "He was sacked, and according to what he told the inspector, Mrs. Andover canceled his quarterly allowance because he was employed."

"And he complained to the inspector that he was usin' up his savin's," Luty reminded them.

"'E can't afford it," Smythe interjected. "Ya didn't let me finish. My source said that the brothel 'as told Andover they'll not extend any more credit and he's got to pay what 'e owes or things might get nasty for 'im."

"He's being threatened with physical violence?" Mrs. Jeffries wanted to be sure she understood.

"'E is, and the owner of the establishment 'as a reputation for bein' a brutal bas—" He broke off. "Uh, you know, a really nasty sort."

"Wasn't 'e supposed to inherit five hundred pounds from his stepmother?" Wiggins asked.

"He is now that she's dead," Mrs. Goodge said. "And it sounds to me like 'e's the one with the real reason for wantin' her gone."

"That's what it sounded like to me as well," Smythe said. "On the other 'and, Jacob Andover's now goin' to get it all so 'e's got as big a motive as Percy. But I'll keep nosin' about the Andover neighborhood and see what else I can find out."

"I'll go next if it's alright with everyone," Ruth offered. She told them about her visit to the two sisters. She took her time and made certain she didn't leave anything out of her narrative. "They insisted that Mrs. Royle would never commit suicide and that she firmly believed only God had a right to take a human life."

"She was raised Quaker?" Luty asked, her expression thoughtful. "I knew a family of Quakers, or Friends as they called themselves, when I lived in Cripple Creek. The Perkins family. They were right good people. They didn't own guns, wouldn't even have 'em on their property. They were brave, too. Jeff Perkins and his two sons faced down a lynch mob and stopped a bounty hunter from bein' hung. Not that they had any great love for the bounty hunter, but they believed in the law and the feller hadn't even had his trial yet."

Mrs. Goodge looked at Mrs. Jeffries. "Let's remind Constable Barnes tomorrow morning about having a look at the investigation report on the poor woman's death."

"Are you sayin' that one of the Andovers killed Mrs. Royle so Mrs. Andover would change her will and leave them 'er money?" Wiggins frowned in confusion. "That's takin' a big risk, ain't it? How would they know that Mrs. Andover would leave 'er estate to any of them? She didn't like her stepchildren all that much."

"Don't sound like she liked her husband much, either," Luty said. "She was right contrary about her privacy, especially her business dealings. We know that about her. But we also know that 'family' was important to her. Could be whoever killed her knew that, and *if* that person also killed Henrietta Royle, they thought the risk was worth it."

"But that's a very big *if*," Hatchet warned. "We've no real evidence that Mrs. Royle was murdered."

"Sure we do," Luty argued. "We've heard two things that should cast some doubt on that suicide story. One, Ruth's source said that Mrs. Royle hated guns, and supposedly, there was a derringer on the train carriage floor by her hand. Now I ask ya, if ya hate something, do you buy one?"

"It could have belonged to her husband." Hatchet took a sip of tea.

"True, but like I said before, a derringer isn't a man's gun. Most men would carry a pistol or use a shotgun."

"And the second thing you mentioned," Mrs. Jeffries reminded her. "What is it?"

"Three, actually, the second bein' what Ruth just told us,

Mrs. Royle thought suicide a terrible sin. The third thing is that them two sisters also told Ruth that they saw someone else gettin' in that first-class railway compartment." Luty shot Hatchet a quick, triumphant grin. "Which means she wasn't alone on that train."

"That's something to think about, Luty," Mrs. Jeffries murmured. "Have you found out anything for us?"

Luty told them about the telegram she'd received. "He's a real preacher," she finished.

"Madam is disappointed because she doesn't like pastors." Hatchet chuckled.

"At least I found out somethin'," she snapped back. "You're just jealous 'cause you wasted a whole day and Christmas is comin'. We're runnin' out of time."

"I've not wasted my time, and as I told you, madam, I have a plan for tomorrow. If all goes as I hope, I should have some information on Mrs. Swineburn then."

"'Ere's what I don't understand," Wiggins said. "If Mrs. Royle was raised to be a Friend or a Quaker, wouldn't 'er sisters 'ave been raised that way, too?"

"I imagine that would be the case," Mrs. Jeffries answered. "What do you find puzzling?"

"Then why is Daniel Wheeler an Episcopal priest? Why isn't 'e a Quaker? 'Is mum would be one, so why isn't 'e?"

"Maybe his father was an Episcopalian," Phyllis suggested.

"Or perhaps, when he came of age, he was attracted to a more ritualistic spiritual tradition," Mrs. Jeffries suggested. "It does happen, Wiggins. Children don't always follow their parents' path."

"That's true, I guess. I'll go next." Wiggins looked at

Smythe. "My bit's not as good as yours, but I did find out that Mrs. Blakstone often 'ad a visitor every afternoon in the weeks before she went to the Andover 'ouse and they weren't just drinkin' tea."

"Did your source know who this visitor might be?" Mrs. Goodge asked.

"'E didn't know the fellow's last name, but he overheard Mrs. Blakstone call 'im Jacob."

"And when you say they weren't drinking tea . . ." Mrs. Jeffries deliberately trailed off.

Wiggins blushed. "'E was a workman, Mrs. Jeffries, and they was puttin' in new window frames. 'E says he accidentally saw 'em and they was in Mrs. Blakstone's bedroom."

Luty started to giggle and then it turned into a belly laugh. "Oh Lordy, Lordy, I'll lay odds that explains why Mrs. Andover was cutting her and the rest of the Andovers out of her will."

"We don't know for sure that she knew about them," Betsy pointed out as she tried to keep a straight face. She gave up after a few seconds and giggled, too. "But if you ask me, your theory makes a great deal of sense."

"Course it does. Why else would she cut them out? Sounds to me like she was madder than a wet hen and she wanted to punish Jacob. She wasn't just goin' to cut him out, she was goin' to cut his children out, too."

"Which means that any of them could have done it. They all have a motive," Mrs. Jeffries said.

"Let's not get ahead of ourselves," Betsy warned. "You've said that often enough, Mrs. Jeffries. Just because people have a reason to kill, it doesn't mean they would. We've still got time to suss this out."

"Thank you for the reminder, Betsy. Quite right. We mustn't make assumptions about guilt or innocence. We simply don't have enough facts."

Smythe patted his wife's hand. "Did you have any luck today?"

"No, I tried some of the local shops, but Phyllis was right—those clerks are a tight-lipped bunch. But like Hatchet, I've a plan for tomorrow."

Witherspoon was home on time that night. "We learned a number of facts today, Mrs. Jeffries," he said as she handed him his sherry. "But nothing is any clearer to me. It's as if the more we learn, the more of a muddle it becomes."

She could tell he was doubting his abilities again. That happened less often than it used to happen, but nonetheless, she wanted it nipped in the bud. It was true that this was a very complicated case, but so had been most of the others he'd had over the years. "Nonsense, sir, you know that's just your 'inner self' gathering information and putting it safely in the back of your mind. You'll know precisely what to do and who the culprit is when the time is right."

She silently prayed the time would be right before Christmas Eve. Luty's Christmas Eve party had become a tradition, and none of them could enjoy it properly if this case was still hanging over their heads like the Sword of Damocles.

"That's kind of you to say and I sincerely hope you're right." He took a sip of his sherry.

"I'm right," she insisted. "Trust yourself, sir. This is all part of your process and it happens on all your cases. Now, do tell me about your day."

"We stopped off at the station before going to the Andover home. Constable Barnes and I went through all the evidence again, including the postmortem report. But I will admit I saw nothing in either the report or the witness statements that pointed me in any particular direction." He took another drink. "Then we went to the Andover home." He told her everything that had transpired. He relaxed as the words came out and he began to see things in a clearer light. Taking his time, he made sure to include each and every detail he could recall. When he'd finished, he drained his glass and put it on the side table.

Mrs. Jeffries listened carefully and occasionally interrupted to ask him a question. She finished her own sherry, got up, and grabbed his empty glass. "Do you believe Mrs. Barnard's assumption is right?" She poured them each another sherry. "Because if it is, that means Mr. Andover knew his wife was meeting with her solicitor and that the meeting was to change her will."

"I'm certain she is correct," Witherspoon said. "She has no reason to lie. The question then becomes, could she have been mistaken in her interpretation of what she heard? But I doubt that's the situation. When I asked him, Mr. Andover denied it, of course, but my instincts tell me he knew about the meeting."

"When you confronted Mr. Andover, did he give you an alternative suggestion as to why his wife wanted to meet with her lawyer?"

"No, he simply kept saying that he had nothing to do with his wife's death and that she loved him." Witherspoon took a sip, his expression thoughtful. "Nonetheless, I'm beginning to think I know why Mrs. Andover was going to cut

Mr. Andover and Mrs. Blakstone out of the estate. She didn't come right out and say it, but Mrs. Barnard hinted that Mrs. Blakstone wasn't a genuine friend to Mrs. Andover. One doesn't like to jump to conclusions, but I got the distinct impression that she was hinting there was an illicit relationship between Jacob Andover and Marcella Blakstone."

Relieved, Mrs. Jeffries made a mental note to include everything Wiggins had found out from the workman when Constable Barnes came by tomorrow morning. Witherspoon was already thinking along those lines, but a bit of insurance never hurt, either.

The inspector continued speaking, telling her about the rest of his day. "I must say, we did get a bit of unsettling news." He sighed. "It appears that the rumors we've heard about Inspector Nivens coming back on the force are true."

"I don't understand how that's possible, especially considering what he's done."

"Apparently the Home Secretary has involved himself in the matter and Nivens is coming back in January. But hopefully, he's learned his lesson and he'll behave himself. On a brighter note, we found out a very interesting piece of information today. Constable Reed interviewed the housekeeper directly across from the Andover house. It seems that the lady saw an elderly gentleman keeping watch on the Andovers in October. The housekeeper claimed the 'elderly gentleman' was wearing a costume and theatrical makeup. Constable Reed had the good sense to ask the housekeeper how she could be so certain, and she said she'd been the wardrobe matron at a London theater for twenty years before becoming a housekeeper."

"Did you speak to her directly?" Mrs. Jeffries asked.

"Unfortunately, when we went to speak to her, she'd gone out. But I'm going to have a word with her tomorrow." He frowned slightly. "I'm not sure what to think about this new information. If the woman is correct, it could mean that an outsider did manage to get into that conservatory and murder Mrs. Andover."

"In which case, you'd need to focus the investigation elsewhere," she murmured.

A steady rain beat against the window over the kitchen sink. It was only half past five in the morning, and once again, Mrs. Jeffries was fully dressed. She'd given up trying to sleep and had come downstairs to make herself a pot of tea. She had gone over every single fact they had learned thus far but wasn't able to make those facts point in any particular direction.

Every member of the Andover family had the same reason to want Harriet Andover dead. Money. If Harriet had kept that appointment, all three of the Andovers would have been cut out. But they weren't the only ones with a strong motive. Marcella Blakstone desperately needed money, and if the worker Wiggins had spoken with was to be believed, she had another motive: She was having an affair with Jacob Andover.

Mrs. Jeffries glanced at the kettle on the cooker and saw it wasn't on the boil as yet so she had time to get to the wet larder for milk. She went down the hall, moving quietly so as to not wake Mrs. Goodge, stepped inside, and got the milk jug from the cold shelf. She returned to the kitchen.

Putting the jug on the table, she got to the kettle just as it boiled, grabbed a tea towel, and poured the water into the big brown teapot. She glanced at the carriage clock on the pine sideboard and made note of the time. The tea needed five minutes to make it as strong as she wanted this morning. She sat down and stared across the quiet, dimly lighted kitchen and let her mind wander.

What exactly did they know? The Andovers and Mrs. Blakstone had a motive for murder. But what about the houseguest, Daniel Wheeler? Did he have a reason to murder his aunt? It seemed unlikely. Why kill her unless she'd already changed her will? Furthermore, according to Luty's source, the man was a genuine clergyman and most Episcopal priests didn't commit murder.

But the most worrying aspect was the statement from Mrs. Pinchon. If her observations were right and someone had disguised himself as an elderly gentleman to spy on the Andover home, then perhaps they'd approached this case from the wrong angle entirely.

Perhaps Mrs. Andover had been murdered by someone they hadn't even considered.

CHAPTER 9

"We'll be havin' a word with Mrs. Pinchon today," Barnes said. "But you're right, Mrs. Jeffries, if there was someone keeping watch on the Andover house, it's possible the killer did get in from the outside."

"But how?" Mrs. Jeffries tapped her finger against the rim of her tea mug. "The doors were locked. One key was found in Mrs. Andover's pocket and the other was hanging downstairs in the kitchen."

"There's plenty of crooks out there who can get in a locked room without a key," Barnes said cynically.

"Maybe whoever did it was good at picking locks," Mrs. Goodge suggested. "Or maybe Mrs. Andover let her killer in. Maybe he or she slipped across the back garden, rapped on the door, and she, for whatever reason, unlocked the door."

Something tugged at the back of Mrs. Jeffries' mind, and then just as quickly, it disappeared.

"I suppose that could have happened." The constable looked doubtful. "But that means Mrs. Andover had to have known and trusted that person."

"But if it was someone from her household, she would have trusted them," the cook argued. "She wouldn't be expectin' that they were there to murder her, would she?"

"That's true," Barnes agreed, "but we still can't dismiss the possibility that it was an outsider."

"That will make catching the murderer more difficult," Mrs. Jeffries pointed out. "We don't know of any outsiders that can even be considered a suspect at this point. However, time is moving along and there's more we need to tell you, Constable. Wiggins found out some interesting information yesterday." She told him about the footman's conversation with the day laborer. "And then, last night, the inspector said he thought that Mrs. Barnard was hinting there might be an illicit relationship between Mrs. Blakstone and Mr. Andover."

"And that would give Marcella Blakstone a double motive for wantin' Harriet Andover dead," Mrs. Goodge added. "She wanted her money and her husband."

Barnes pulled a pencil and his little brown notebook out of his pocket, flipped to a blank page, and started scribbling. "This Tony Somers works as a day laborer for Brownsley and Sons?"

"That's what he told Wiggins," Mrs. Jeffries replied. "But he works for another builder as well."

"Not to worry, we'll track him down. I'll send Constable Griffiths along to find the fellow."

Mrs. Jeffries suddenly thought of another matter. "Constable, did you or any of the other constables read the letters from Mrs. Andover's two sisters?"

"The ones where we found the letter from Hamish Mc-Graw? We haven't as yet, we've not had time. I didn't think it a priority as those letters were written years ago." Barnes eyed her curiously. "I don't see how they could have anything to do with her murder. But why do you ask?"

"I'm not sure." Mrs. Jeffries shrugged. "But there's something bubbling in the back of my mind and the question just popped out. I've a feeling there's something right in front of my nose, but for the life of me, I can't fathom what it is."

"You'll figure it out, Hepzibah," the cook reassured her. "Now, let's finish telling the constable everything we found out."

Mrs. Jeffries was the last to take her seat around the kitchen table.

Smythe cleared his throat. "Before we start the meetin', I've got something to tell ya." He paused and dragged in a deep breath.

"And he's been fretting about it since we got home yesterday. He almost came back last night to tell you"—Betsy glanced at Mrs. Jeffries—"but I said it would be better to tell everyone at once rather than have to repeat it half a dozen times." She poked him on the arm. "Go on, then, tell them."

"This is embarrassin', but I forgot to mention somethin' important yesterday," he said. "The truth is, I was so rattled by findin' out about Percy Andover's brothel bits that this information, which is probably even more important than Percy's bits, went completely out of my head."

"You gonna tell us or do we have to guess," Luty said impatiently.

"My source told me that Daniel Wheeler was in France."

"We know that," Phyllis said. "He was there for two weeks doing research."

"But that's not true. He wasn't there just for them two weeks like he told the inspector. Wheeler was there for over a year."

"Your source was sure of this?" Ruth pressed.

"He was. But that's not all I found out. Durin' that year, Wheeler went back and forth to England at least twice and maybe even more than that. But this is the interestin' bit: When he was in France, he wasn't a preacher."

There was a moment of stunned silence, then Luty said, "But that can't be right. We know Wheeler is a real preacher."

"Priest, madam, Wheeler should be referred to as a priest," Hatchet interjected.

Luty waved her hand dismissively. "Call him whatever you want. But Braxton, he's a right good detective, and he'd not have gotten it wrong. He said Daniel Wheeler served at Saint Peter's Episcopal Church in Carson City two years ago."

"No one is saying your friend got it wrong," Mrs. Jeffries said hastily. "But this information might change everything." Suddenly, the idea that had been lurking at the back of her mind settled in and stayed instead of disappearing.

"What are you sayin'?" Luty stared at her in confusion. "I just told ya, Braxton wouldn't have gotten it wrong."

"Not wrong, Luty. But perhaps one question wasn't enough. There may be a different explanation and it would be worth sending another telegram asking for more information on the man."

Luty looked doubtful. "Alright, if you think it's worth it, I'll send another one asking him to dig a little deeper."

"Thank you, Luty." Mrs. Jeffries looked around the table. She needed a few moments to think. Daniel Wheeler had lied to Witherspoon about how long he'd been in France. Why? More important, could that lie have anything to do with Harriet Andover's murder? She had a feeling that it did, although they needed to know more. But she didn't have time to analyze the situation right now. "Smythe isn't the only one with some interesting news to share. It's about Inspector Nivens. He is coming back on the force. The rumor is he's going to Bethnal Green, but exactly where he'll end up hasn't been confirmed as yet."

"Oh no." Phyllis groaned. "That's terrible."

"That's not good news," Wiggins exclaimed.

"Why is he obsessed with staying on the police force?" Hatchet grumbled. "His family has plenty of money. He doesn't need the job."

"Let's not get carried away here," Mrs. Jeffries warned, interrupting the moaning and complaining. "As Phyllis pointed out yesterday, right now the best thing we can do is help our inspector get this case solved." She looked at Betsy. "I know you've already been to the British Museum, but I think it might be wise to have another go at finding out anything you can about Daniel Wheeler. See if you can get more information out of Miss Barlow."

"I'll try the librarian as well. He's very friendly and it's likely he's chatted with Daniel Wheeler. I've still got my ticket, so it should be easy enough," Betsy replied.

"I'm seein' my source again this mornin'," Smythe said. "He said he might 'ave more information for me."

"What do ya want me to do?" Wiggins asked the housekeeper.

"I'm not sure it's possible, but do you think you can make contact with Angela Evans again?" Mrs. Jeffries said.

Wiggins thought for a moment. "I don't know, Mrs. Jeffries, she's a scullery maid so she'd be downstairs in the kitchen. But if I do see her, what do you want me to ask?"

"Angela claimed that one of the housemaids, Colleen Murphy, had been snooping in Wheeler's desk and had passed along the contents of a telegram he'd received the morning of the murder."

"Yeah, it was about some old uncle of his going to a place called Tombstone," Wiggins said.

"We need to find out everything that was in that telegram Daniel Wheeler received on Monday morning. I've been thinking about it, and it suddenly occurred to me that we're looking at this case from the wrong angle."

"What do you mean?" Ruth asked.

"Our attention has been on Mrs. Andover and who would benefit from her death."

"Right, who is going to inherit her fortune seems to be the pertinent question," Hatchet commented.

"But what if it isn't her fortune that's important?" Mrs. Jeffries said. "I'm not sure how to explain it because we simply don't have enough facts as yet. But early this morning, two things suddenly popped into my head and I can't stop thinking about them."

"What are they?" Mrs. Goodge asked.

"Harriet Andover and both her sisters were gifted a substantial amount of money from their uncle upon their engagements, right?"

"That's what Hamish McGraw told the inspector," Betsy said. "Why?"

"Well, if her uncle had that much money twenty-five years ago, when Harriet was first engaged, what if her uncle had even more money now?" Mrs. Jeffries explained. "The second thing that bothered me was Henrietta Royle's death. Originally, we looked at the idea that someone in the Andover household killed Mrs. Royle so that Mrs. Andover would change her will and leave her estate to her husband. But what if there's another reason? I was thinking of it when I remembered what Percy Andover said to our inspector. He said that Mrs. Andover was always talking about the longevity in her family even though both her sisters were dead."

"And now she's dead," Phyllis murmured.

"But she's got an aging uncle in San Francisco who isn't," Mrs. Jeffries said. "And maybe that uncle has an even bigger fortune than Mrs. Andover."

"Do we even know his name?" Ruth asked. "I don't believe I've heard it."

No one said anything as they all thought back to every name they'd heard thus far in the investigation. After a few moments, Mrs. Goodge said, "I remember now, the uncle's name is Stone, Theodore Stone. That's what Hamish McGraw told Inspector Witherspoon."

"Gracious, you've a good memory, Mrs. Goodge." Mrs. Jeffries looked approvingly at her friend. "I'd completely forgotten the man's name."

"I don't know why I remembered it. Sometimes names stick in your mind." The cook grinned broadly, pleased with herself for recalling such a small detail.

The atmosphere in the kitchen suddenly grew serious, almost somber. They'd been down this road before, and all of them knew that Mrs. Jeffries, whether she was aware of it herself or not, was halfway to figuring out who had murdered Harriet Andover.

"What do you want us to do?" Phyllis asked.

"I want you to go to the Pennington Hotel. Find out exactly when Daniel Wheeler arrived and how long he was there. Find out as much as you can about the man." She looked at Luty. "And now that we've a name, can you contact one of your sources and send another telegram to California and find out if this Theodore Stone has any money and, if so, how much?"

"I know what I saw, Inspector." Mrs. Pinchon fixed Witherspoon with a hard stare. "As I told that nice young constable yesterday, I've spent most of my life working in the theater. I know an actor's gesture when I see it, and that person was no more an old gentleman than I'm the Queen of Sheba."

Barnes shifted his weight to his other leg. They were standing in the foyer of the house across the street from the Andover home. Mrs. Pinchon, a plump matron with gray hair and a firm, no-nonsense manner, had been on her way out to the shops just as they'd reached the front door. "How often did you see him?"

"Four or five times. He came by hansom cab and it was always close to the same time of day."

Witherspoon interrupted, "What time was that?"

"Between a quarter to ten and ten o'clock." She reached for the shopping basket she'd put down next to evergreens on the side table. "How much longer is this going to take? The family is coming back tomorrow and I need to get my shopping done."

"Not much longer, Mrs. Pinchon," Witherspoon said. "Can you show us exactly where the hansom dropped him and what the man did when he got out of the cab?"

She opened the door and stepped out onto the stoop. "Come along, then. You'll not see anything if you stand about here."

They crowded behind her in the doorway. Mrs. Pinchon pointed to the end of the street, to a spot opposite the Andover house. "There's where the cab stopped. When he got out, the first thing he did was to check to be sure his mustache and beard were still in place. As soon as the hansom pulled away, he'd cross the road and stand in front of the Andover house for a few moments. Then he'd walk all the way to the end"—she turned and pointed in the opposite direction—"cross back to this side of the road, and then he'd come back. He wasn't in the least trying to hide what he was up to."

"How do you know that?"

"Because it was obvious, Inspector. He was there to spy on the Andovers. Twice, Mr. Percy Andover came out, and both times, the old man followed him, and one time, he even followed Mrs. Swineburn. Now if it's all the same to you, I must get to the shops."

"Of course," Witherspoon said as he and Barnes hastily stepped outside. She waited for them to get out of her way before she locked the door.

"You've been very helpful, Mrs. Pinchon," Witherspoon said.

"Mind you catch Mrs. Andover's killer then," she told him as she stepped off the stoop and onto the flagstone pathway. "I liked her and I thoroughly disapprove of murder." She turned and headed down the street.

"What do you think, sir?" Barnes asked.

"She's very sure about what she saw"—the inspector

moved farther onto the walkway—"and if she worked in the theater for twenty years, she'd be exceedingly familiar with actors and their various gestures. If the house really was being watched by someone, it could well mean that no one in the Andover household had anything to do with the murder."

"If it isn't one of them, then we've no idea where to start looking next," Barnes said.

"I know, but we'll just have to keep digging." He headed down the pathway to the street.

"Speaking of digging, sir, I'd like to read those letters we found in Mrs. Andover's study. The ones from her sister. There might be some clue in one of them that will help."

"That's a good idea, Constable. It'll be faster if both of us do it."

The two policemen walked back to the Andover house. Witherspoon stopped as they reached the front door. "Let's hope there's something in those old letters that might help. Except for two very mild disputes, one with Mr. Cragan, the neighbor, and the other with Peter Rolland, her former stockbroker, Mrs. Andover was well liked and respected."

"We've not found she had any other enemies."

"That's what makes this case so difficult." The inspector's eyes narrowed in thought. "It's not that I'm completely dismissing the idea of an outsider getting into the conservatory, it's simply that there doesn't seem to be anyone other than her own family that had a reason to want her dead. What do you think, Constable?"

"In my experience, it's far more likely she was killed by someone in the household," he replied. "But on the other hand, we've now had two witnesses, Mrs. Pinchon and Reverend Wheeler, that noticed someone watching the house."

Witherspoon reached for the brass door knocker.

"Inspector, Inspector," Constable Reed shouted as he raced around the corner. "Just a moment, please. I've found out something."

They stopped and waited for him.

He was out of breath by the time he reached them. "Sorry, I didn't mean to be rude, sir," he gasped. "I wanted to catch you before you went inside, sir."

"Take your time and catch your breath," Witherspoon ordered.

Reed took in a deep breath. "Thank you, sir. I've just come from Liberty's, and this time I found two shop assistants, and both of them know Mrs. Swineburn by sight."

"Did either of them confirm that Mrs. Swineburn was there on Monday afternoon?"

"No, sir, just the opposite. Both of them said they didn't see Mrs. Swineburn at all on Monday."

"Were they certain? Perhaps they missed seeing her?" Barnes looked at Reed. "Liberty's isn't some tiny little dress shop. It's fairly large."

"I thought of that, sir, but according to Mrs. Swineburn's statement, she left the Jennings household at a quarter to four. Which means she'd have been at Liberty's by four fifteen if not sooner and she claimed she was there until closing at six. That's almost two hours, sir. That's a long time to be in a shop."

"You think one of those shop assistants would have spotted her?" Witherspoon nodded in agreement. "I think so, too. Thank you, Constable Reed, you've done very well." He glanced at Barnes. "I think it's time for another chat with Mrs. Swineburn."

* * *

"You've figured it out, haven't you," Mrs. Goodge said to Mrs. Jeffries as the two women took their seats at the table.

Mrs. Jeffries frowned slightly. "I don't know. I think I might have, but unless we get very, very lucky, we're going to have a difficult time finding any proof."

"Nonsense, Hepzibah, we'll find a way. Now, what is it you think you need to put this case to rest before Christmas?"

"Well, I'm not sure," she stammered. "I'm basing my assumption on very flimsy evidence, but honestly, it's the only thing that makes sense. But I could easily be wrong."

"You say that every time. Now what do we need to do to get this one solved?"

"The one thing I think might prove most useful is if we had *The Times* for those three days the paper wasn't delivered to the Andover home." She broke off for a moment. "Do you think your friend Ida Leacock could help with that? She owns those newsagent shops."

"She might if she was in town, but she's gone to Swindon to spend Christmas with her niece," Mrs. Goodge said.

"That's unfortunate," Mrs. Jeffries said, her expression glum. "I've a feeling about those newspapers. They might turn out to be the key to the whole thing. Unfortunately, short of sending someone to *The Times* office and trying to obtain copies that way, I don't know what else we can do."

"There's another way. We can do this, Hepzibah, because I've got the recipe somewhere. Give me a few moments and I'll get it." The cook got up and hurried out of the kitchen and to her quarters on the far side of the back stairs.

"What are you doing? What's this about a recipe?" Mrs. Jeffries shouted after her.

But Mrs. Goodge didn't answer, and from her room Mrs. Jeffries heard the cook muttering as drawers opened and closed, several ominous thumps, and a wardrobe door being slammed shut. Confused and a bit alarmed, she started to get up to make certain everything was alright, but before she could get out of her chair, the cook bustled back into the kitchen. She carried a huge hatbox. Hurrying to the table, she put it down, flipped off the lid, and began rummaging inside.

"Amanda"—Mrs. Jeffries used the cook's Christian name—"what is going on? What are you doing?"

"We need those newspapers and I've got a plan, but it's based on finding that ruddy recipe."

"Which recipe?"

"My strawberry and cream sponge cake." She pulled two cookbooks, one of which had the front cover missing, out of the hatbox and put them on the table. "Mrs. Penny across the garden, she's the cook for Colonel Tolliver, she's been after that recipe for ages."

"It is a delicious recipe, but how will that help?" Mrs. Jeffries was still confused.

"Mrs. Penny saves newspapers because her sister owns a fish and chips shop in Fulham. But the only way I can get the papers out of her is to give her my recipe. She's dying to know what my secret ingredient is, that's what makes it so good. Blast, where is it?"

She took out a stack of letters tied together by a blue ribbon, a tin of Potter's Pills, a silver belt buckle, an empty bottle of lavender scent, two crumpled cook's hats, and finally a sheaf of papers. "Ah good, it should be in this lot."

She thumbed through the papers, tossing them willy-nilly

onto the tabletop and out of her way. "Here it is! Good, this ought to help." She held up the paper, read it quickly, and then tucked it into her pocket. "Right then, I'll go over and have a word with Mrs. Penny. No, no, best to wait until later this afternoon. She always takes a rest in the afternoon when Colonel Tolliver goes to his club. I think she helps herself to a drop of his whisky as well, which will be to our advantage. I want her in a good mood. That'll give me time this morning to get my treacle pudding made so it can set properly in the wet larder." She looked at Mrs. Jeffries. "What dates do we need?"

"Try and get the newspapers from the last week in October through the first ten days in November."

"That many?" Mrs. Goodge's bushy white eyebrows rose over the rims of her spectacles. "Gracious, it looks like we'll be doing a lot of reading."

"Actually, no. If it exists at all, what we need should be on the front page."

"Mr. Andover would prefer you to use the small drawing room while you're here," Mrs. Barnard said as she ushered the two policemen down the hallway.

"That's fine," Witherspoon said as he and Barnes stepped inside the room. "Would you please tell Mrs. Swineburn we'd like to speak with her."

"Of course, sir." The housekeeper closed the door as she left.

The room was as elegant as the drawing room but on a much smaller scale. The walls were the color of ivory, coral drapes hung at the two windows, and a rich sapphire-blue-and-red Oriental rug covered the polished oak floor. Grouped around the small blue-tiled fireplace on the far side of the room were a cream-and-blue-striped love seat and two matching chairs. A large mahogany drinks cabinet was topped with a silver tray, two square-shaped decanters filled with amber liquid, and half a dozen matching cut-glass whisky tumblers.

"Mrs. Andover decorated beautifully in here, didn't she," Barnes said.

"This room is precisely the same as it was before my stepmother arrived here," Ellen Swineburn snapped as she stepped inside. "She had nothing to do with the decor or the furnishings."

But Barnes wasn't intimidated by her haughty manner. "Really? According to everything we've been told by a number of different sources, this house and everything in it were falling to wreck and ruin before Mrs. Andover started pouring money into the place."

Ellen's eyes widened in surprise as she drew back slightly. "How dare you speak to me like that!" She looked at Witherspoon. "Are you going to allow him to say such things to me?"

"Mrs. Swineburn, the constable is only repeating what we've been told. Are you saying your stepmother's money wasn't used on the upkeep of this room or, for that matter, the house?"

Witherspoon knew what Barnes was doing. It was an old street copper's trick. He was deliberately upsetting the woman, fanning the flames of anger in order to loosen her tongue. People tended to blurt out the truth when they were overly emotional.

"That has nothing to do with the reason you're here." Ellen stalked farther into the room, stopping in front of the inspector. "You're not here to make personal remarks about my family or our circumstances. I shall report your behavior to your superior."

"His name is Chief Superintendent Barrows and his office is at Scotland Yard," Witherspoon replied.

"Duly noted. Rest assured, I'll be contacting him." She stepped back and sat down on the love seat. "I shall also be asking him how much longer we have to endure the presence of the police in our home. It's dreadfully inconvenient and it is creating havoc in planning my stepmother's reception."

"Reception?" Barnes repeated. "What does that mean? The poor woman is dead."

"We're well aware of that. But the funeral won't be held until after the New Year. Yet something to mark my stepmother's passing needs to be done before Christmas, so we're hosting a reception in her honor for our family and friends. It's not just a social event. Reverend Wheeler will be doing a service with readings from the Book of Common Prayer. It's being planned for December twenty-third, and we'd appreciate the police leaving us alone for a few hours so we can mourn her decently."

"Why is the funeral being postponed?" Witherspoon asked. "Mrs. Andover's body was released two days ago and there's ample time to plan her funeral, especially as you have a priest in the family. The ground isn't frozen so she can be properly buried."

A flush crept up her face. "She isn't being buried. We have a family crypt. She'll be laid to rest there. But it's being repaired and the workmen won't have it finished until after the New Year."

"Repaired with Mrs. Andover's money, no doubt," Barnes muttered softly yet loud enough for her to hear.

Mrs. Swineburn leapt up. "This is intolerable. I won't have it, do you understand? I'll not have some police person speaking to me in such a disgraceful manner."

"Mrs. Swineburn, why did you tell us you were at Liberty's on Monday afternoon?" Witherspoon said. "We know you weren't there."

Her mouth gaped open and she froze for a moment. "That's absurd," she stammered. "I most certainly was there."

"We have it on good authority that you weren't. Mrs. Swineburn, we're not deliberately being disrespectful, we're trying to find the truth. Someone murdered your stepmother between four o'clock and eight o'clock Monday afternoon. You've not been truthful with us as to your whereabouts during part of that time period. You do understand what this means?"

She looked uncertain, almost frightened. "It means nothing," she retorted, but most of the bluster had gone from her voice. "I did not kill Harriet."

"Tell us where you were," Barnes said. "That'll go a long way to proving you had nothing to do with her death."

She closed her eyes and gave a short, soft sob. "Oh dear. If I tell you, can you be discreet? Please, I'll be ruined if anyone finds out. Absolutely ruined. I'll never be able to hold my head up in society again."

"Unless you have to testify to your whereabouts in court, we've no reason to tell anyone where you were or what you were doing," Witherspoon said, his expression sympathetic.

"Do you promise, Inspector? It's important that no one finds out."

"As long as the activity had nothing to do with your stepmother's death, there would be no need to make the information available to the public or anyone else."

"Thank you. Now that Papa is inheriting Harriet's money, we'll be rich again and I'll have a real chance at finding another husband."

Her bluntness surprised him, and Witherspoon's expression shifted from sympathy to shock. "Er, well, yes, let's get on with this. Where did you go?"

"I went to Paddington. The station, not the place."

"To catch a train? To meet someone?"

"No, Inspector, to see the trains," she explained. "The locomotives."

"The locomotives?" he repeated. "I'm afraid I don't understand."

"That's because you've never looked at them properly. They are just magnificent. Thrilling." Her face was now flushed with excitement and passion. "Such feats of engineering—all that power coming from steam. Who doesn't get excited by such things? The smell of warm damp air and the sounds of the engines bursting with energy."

The inspector was baffled. Why would a lady be so enamored of railways?

"What was there?" Barnes asked. "Anything interesting?"

"It was wonderful, Constable. I saw my first 2201 Class express locomotive—number 2212. Those come out of Swindon, I believe. Another triumph for William Dean. Honestly, the man's an engineering genius."

"You think he's an improvement on the Class 806 locomotive designed by Armstrong?" Barnes asked enthusiastically.

"Absolutely, Constable, it's a much more powerful engine. But of course, Mr. Armstrong's engines are superb in their own right."

"Did you see any of the Class 645 or 655 saddle tanks?"

"I saw both of them, Constable. It was a lovely, lovely afternoon. I've found that one has the best chance of seeing both Mr. Dean's and Mr. Armstrong's engines if one goes to Paddington late in the afternoon—before the evening express trains leave for the West. Which, of course, is why I was there between four and six on Monday." She turned her attention to the inspector. "You see now, don't you? You understand why you mustn't tell anyone about my, uh . . . hobby?"

Witherspoon simply stared at her.

"It's considered unfeminine and unseemly," she explained hastily. "And now I'm looking for a new husband."

"Did Mr. Swineburn know of your, er . . . hobby?" Witherspoon asked.

"Yes, and he didn't approve of it." She frowned heavily and crossed her arms over her chest. "He can't stop me now, but he's one of the reasons I learned to keep my activities to myself."

Witherspoon stared at his constable. He wasn't sure what surprised him more, that this refined semi-aristocratic woman loved trains or that he'd never had an inkling that Constable Barnes had such an interest in steam engines.

Phyllis stared at the Pennington Hotel. It stood at the end of a row of three-story attached buildings on Keppel Street not far from the British Museum. Black wrought-iron railings enclosed the staircase leading to the lower ground floor, and a stone facade bordered the entryway leading to the front door.

Phyllis stepped onto the wide, flat, short flight of stairs and walked to the front door. She peeked through the thick glass. A formidable-looking woman dressed in black was behind the reception desk. "Drat," she muttered, "I was hoping there would be a male clerk."

Since her altercation with the woman at the newsagent's, she'd been leery of approaching females for information. They didn't mind being rude to other women, but a young man was almost always polite and usually helpful. Perhaps she should come back later; perhaps there would be a nice male clerk on the evening shift? But she knew that was a foolish hope. It would be hours before the staff changed for the evening.

Stop being a ninny, she told herself. One rude woman isn't going to prevent you from doing what's right. You'll never be a private inquiry agent if you can't find the courage to ask questions. She opened the door and stepped inside. She stopped for a moment to give her eyes a chance to adjust to the dimmer lighting.

The lobby was large, filled with leather sofas, overstuffed chairs, and potted plants and leafy ferns. It was a comfortable place, but hardly lavish. It was precisely the sort of hotel that would cater to people using the British Museum.

"May I help you?"

Phyllis walked the short distance to the reception desk. "Good day, I'm hoping you can assist me."

"Did you wish to book a room?" The woman examined her for a quick moment, assessing her clothes, hat, and most important, her shoes.

But Phyllis didn't make the same mistake twice.

When she'd gone to the newsagent's to find out about the

Andover household's missing newspapers, she'd foolishly put her old jacket over her maid's uniform. The harridan running the shop had tossed her out without so much as a by-your-leave. But this time, she'd asked Betsy if she could borrow her lovely and expensive-looking blue-and-gray-herringbone jacket so she didn't think she'd be dismissed so easily. The shoes were her own, but they were good ones.

"You don't have any luggage," the woman continued.

"I'm not here to book a room for tonight. I'm here to make an inquiry as to your rates." Phyllis smiled brightly. "You've been recommended as an excellent hotel by one of my acquaintances, a clergyman."

"Thank you." The woman smiled back. "That's precisely what we like to hear. By any chance was the clergyman named Daniel Wheeler?"

"Why, yes, he was," Phyllis gushed. "How very clever of you. He said he thoroughly enjoyed his time here."

"We enjoy having him, even though most of his stays are brief."

Phyllis kept her smile firmly in place. "Yes, he mentioned that you're very good at providing accommodation at short notice."

"But of course, he's been here several times this past year. So much so that he's asked us to store his trunk here so he won't have to cart it to Paris and back. Now, what kind of accommodation were you seeking?"

"I was starting to get worried," Mrs. Jeffries called as she heard the back door open and then close. A moment later, Mrs. Goodge bustled into the kitchen. She had a stack of newspapers clutched against her chest. The cook had gone to see Mrs. Penny but had been away for an hour and a half. "It's almost four o'clock. The others will be here at half past."

"Sorry it took so long." She dumped the papers on the tabletop, untied the ribbons of her old-fashioned bonnet, and hurried to the coat tree. "I thought she was never going to agree to the exchange. I underestimated that woman. She drives a hard bargain."

"What happened?" Mrs. Jeffries grabbed the top newspaper. It was dated October twenty-fourth.

"To begin with, she insisted I have tea with her. Honestly, the bread was drier than a midwinter leaf, but I didn't want to offend her so I pretended I liked it. Then, when I told her what I wanted and offered to give her the recipe, she played coy."

"Played coy?" Mrs. Jeffries fixed her gaze on the front page and searched for the right column. "How so?"

"You know, all of a sudden she started pretending she'd no interest in my recipe. So I turned the tables on her and said I'd have a chat with my friend Ida, I told her, the one who owns the newsagent's." Mrs. Goodge chuckled. "That changed her tune pretty fast, and all of a sudden, I could borrow these newspapers."

"Why did you tell her you wanted them?"

"Oh, that was the easy part. I told her that I'd seen a 'Pleasure Tour to Rome for Thirteen Guineas' advertised, but that the maid had accidentally tossed out the newspaper"— she sat down at the table—"and that it was sometime between the last week in October and the first ten days in November."

"You implied you were going to Rome?"

"I always wanted to see the place." The cook snickered.

"And I enjoyed letting her think I could afford a trip like that. But she managed to best me. I've got to take these"—she nodded toward the stack of newspapers—"back to her when we're done with them. As I said, she drives a hard bargain and wouldn't give them to me outright. Now, what are we looking for?"

Mrs. Jeffries handed the cook the next newspaper from the stack. "If I'm right, it will be in the Personal column on the front page. Look for anything that has a French address and that describes lost or stolen jewelry."

For the next twenty minutes, the two women worked their way down the pile of papers, reading every word of the Personal column. They'd finished October and started on November when Mrs. Jeffries said, "Here it is, it's November third. I've found it. Thank goodness, I was so worried I had it all wrong."

"What is it?" Mrs. Goodge demanded.

"Read it for yourself. It's the fourth notice down." She handed her the newspaper then grabbed the next one off the stack and began scanning that Personal column.

Mrs. Goodge read the notice:

Substantial reward—a hundred pounds, offered for the return or information regarding three items of stolen jewelry. A sapphire-and-diamond starburst pin, a gold bracelet, and a pearl broach. Contact Mrs. Jonas Tyler, 7 Avenue Montaigne, Paris, France

Mrs. Goodge looked at Mrs. Jeffries. "This description is just like the jewelry the inspector found in Mrs. Andover's dressing table."

"That's right and the same notice is in the November fourth paper and the November fifth. This is it, Mrs. Goodge, now we know why these newspapers disappeared from the Andover home before Mrs. Andover could read them. But to prove anything useful, we'll need this woman's help."

"You mean this Mrs. Tyler?"

"That's right." Mrs. Jeffries looked at the clock. "We're running out of time. The others will be here soon. You'll have to take charge of the meeting." She got up, hurried to the coat tree, and grabbed her cloak. "I'm going to send a telegram."

"To Paris?"

"Yes." She slipped the cloak over her shoulders and fastened the top. "I'll be back as quick as I can."

"Put on your scarf, Hepzibah. It's cold outside," Mrs. Goodge said. As soon as the housekeeper was gone, the cook set about tidying up the mess they'd made. She arranged the newspapers into a neat stack, put the kettle on to boil, and set out the cups and plates.

Ruth was the first one to arrive and she was followed by Smythe, Betsy, and Wiggins, followed by Phyllis.

"Mrs. Jeffries had to send a telegram," Mrs. Goodge announced as they all took their seats. "She told me to start the meeting but we'll wait for Luty and Hatchet."

"Why'd she send a telegram?" Wiggins demanded.

"We found something, but before you start peppering me with questions, you'll have to wait and let her tell you what's what."

"There they are." Phyllis pointed to the window over the sink. "They're getting out of a hansom. I wonder why they didn't use the carriage. I'll go up and let them in the front door."

The others helped themselves to scones and tea while they waited for Phyllis to return with Luty and Hatchet.

"Sorry we're late," Hatchet said as the trio appeared in the kitchen. "But we were held up when Madam received a telegram."

"You heard back from someone?" Mrs. Goodge asked. "Who?"

"Braxton." Luty unbuttoned her bright red cloak and slipped it off her shoulders. "But I'm gonna wait till everyone's here before I say anything."

"I told them that Mrs. Jeffries had gone to send a telegram," Phyllis explained as she took her seat.

"I'm here now." Mrs. Jeffries rushed into the kitchen, untying the black ribbons on her hat as she hurried to the coat tree. Yanking the hat off, she unbuttoned her cloak, shrugged it off, and hung it up as well.

"Slow down, Hepzibah," Luty ordered. "My news can wait a minute or two."

"But then you have to tell us why you sent a telegram," Betsy said.

It took less than a minute before Mrs. Jeffries was at her seat. "You first, Luty."

"I heard back from Braxton"—she looked at the housekeeper—"and you were right. There was more to the story. It seems that the Reverend Daniel Wheeler is a real Episcopal priest, but he's also buried in the Carson City graveyard."

"Then who is it that is livin' at the Andover house?" Wiggins asked.

"Apparently it isn't the Reverend Wheeler," Hatchet said.

"But it is," Ruth interjected. "I continued my quest to find out what I could about Harriet's family. I didn't find out very much, but I did learn that the family was from Reading and they were Quakers. Apparently, they were quite conventional and the only whisper of scandal was about the eldest daughter, Helen. She ran off with a man named Paul Wheeler when she was just eighteen, and they married and had a son who they named Daniel."

"I don't understand. Are there two Daniel Wheelers?" Mrs. Goodge asked.

"It's a common sort of name," Betsy murmured. "It's possible."

"But it gets even more complicated," Ruth said. "I also found out that Paul Wheeler wasn't a fisherman; he was an actor."

"But Daniel told our inspector his father was a fisherman," Betsy said.

"Which means his father either changed professions or he's a liar," Ruth concluded.

"I think he's a liar," Phyllis blurted out. "Wait till you hear what I found out at the Pennington Hotel." She glanced at Luty. "Sorry, I didn't mean to step ahead of you."

"That's alright, you go right ahead." Luty grinned. "Mine can wait a minute or two."

Hatchet snorted. "She's just being melodramatic and hoping that Chester—he's Madam's coachman—will show up with the other telegram so she can hog the limelight. That's why we took a hansom cab and not the carriage." He shot his employer a steely-eyed stare. "She wanted Chester to make a dramatic entrance."

Luty snickered, but said nothing.

Mrs. Jeffries nodded at Phyllis to go ahead.

"I went to the Pennington Hotel and I got very lucky." She told them everything she'd learned from the lady at the reception desk.

"He's got a trunk?" Smythe shook his head. "I'd give a few bob to see what's inside it."

"As would I," Mrs. Jeffries murmured. "But it's getting late and we're running out of time. Unless anyone else has something to report, let's hear what Luty learned."

"Let me do mine first. It won't take long," Betsy said. "I wasn't able to make contact with Nora Barlow today but I had a chat with the librarian. He said that Daniel Wheeler was there until closing time on Monday but that he disappeared for several hours. He had a habit of going up to the galleries to look at artifacts."

"Did the librarian remember precisely when he went up to the gallery on Monday?"

Betsy shook her head. "He wasn't certain. It was a busy day. He saw him leave but didn't notice the time, and when he saw him next, it was almost half past five."

"It's imperative we find out if Nora Barlow knows what time Wheeler went up to the galleries on Monday." Mrs. Jeffries looked at the cook. "Remind me tomorrow morning to be sure and mention this to Constable Barnes."

"Right, along with everything else we've learned today, including that." She pointed to the stack of newspapers on the sideboard.

"Now if it's all the same to you, I'd like to tell mine." Luty paused, and when no one objected, she continued. "Like Hatchet said, we took a hansom cab here because I've got my driver waitin' at home to see if I git an answer from my contact in San Francisco. He's an old banker friend but he's still smart enough to understand what I wanted him to find out fer us."

"And if the telegram comes, he'll bring it right over," Hatchet added.

"Lucky for us you had me double-check with Braxton about the so-called Reverend," Luty said to Mrs. Jeffries. "Otherwise, we'd all still be thinkin' the Daniel Wheeler at the Andover house is a priest, and he ain't. He's a confidence trickster or an out-and-out crook."

"Did Braxton say how long ago the real Reverend Wheeler had passed away?"

"He did. The poor man died two years ago of scarlet fever."

CHAPTER 10

"If that's all, Inspector, I'm very busy." Mrs. Swineburn gave the constable a friendly smile as she rose to her feet and went to the door.

"Thank you, Mrs. Swineburn. If it's no trouble, would you please ask your father to step in for a moment."

"Of course, Inspector." She stepped out, closing the door behind her.

"What do you think, sir?" Barnes kept his voice down.

"What do *I* think?" The inspector chuckled. Now that he was over the shock, he found the situation amusing. "You're the one that knows about locomotives, Constable. What do you think? Was she telling the truth?"

Barnes smiled sheepishly. "In my opinion, she is, sir. But if you've doubts, I can always check with the station to verify those engines were there on Monday afternoon."

"I don't think that will be necessary. I doubt anyone

would go to such lengths to fabricate an alibi," Witherspoon said. "We can always check later if there's any indication she wasn't telling the truth . . ." He broke off as the door opened and Jacob Andover stepped into the room. "Oh good, you're here. We've several more questions for you."

Andover moved farther into the room. "What on earth can you possibly need to know now?" he complained. "How much longer will the police be here, Inspector? We've family members as well as friends coming tomorrow for a special reception and prayer service in honor of Harriet."

"Tomorrow? But tomorrow's the twenty-second. Mrs. Swineburn said the service was going to be on the twenty-third." Witherspoon stared at him curiously.

"Unfortunately, the twenty-third is too close to Christmas for some of our family members. That's why we've made the change. I would very much appreciate it if you could leave us alone for the duration of the reception. Frankly, having constables hanging about will just remind all of us of the dreadful circumstances of my poor wife's death."

"I quite understand, Mr. Andover, and I assure you, we'll respect your privacy during the reception," Witherspoon said. "When is it?"

"The family and guests will begin arriving at half past ten, and the service will start at eleven o'clock. After that, we'll have a reception until half past one." He turned toward the door.

"Just a moment," Witherspoon said. "As I said, I've some questions for you."

"Yes, yes, get on with it then," Andover said irritably. He went to the love seat and stopped and stood there with his arms folded across his chest. "Will this take long?"

"We'll be as quick as we can," Witherspoon said. There was something that needed to be asked and it was going to be awkward. Mrs. Barnard had definitely hinted about the matter yesterday, and this morning, when he'd mentioned it to Constable Barnes, he said he'd also heard much the same thing from the other servants. None of them had come right out and said it directly, but nonetheless, that was Barnes' impression.

"Now that Mrs. Andover is dead"—the inspector watched Andover's expression—"will Mrs. Blakstone continue staying at your home?"

Andover's lips parted and fear flashed across his face. But he quickly brought himself under control. "Our domestic arrangements aren't any of your business, Inspector. I've tolerated an enormous intrusion into my house and my life, but you go too far."

But Witherspoon had seen the flash of panic in the man's eyes. "I'm sorry you think the question intrusive. I assure you, that isn't our intent."

"I don't care what your 'intent' might be. Mrs. Blakstone is a family friend and neither of us answers to the Metropolitan Police Force."

Barnes looked up from his notebook, his pencil poised over the pad balanced on his knee. "We've heard gossip that suggests that Mrs. Blakstone is more *your friend* than she ever was to your wife."

"How dare you?" Andover's chin jutted out. "That's an outrageous lie. I don't know who you've been speaking to or what you've heard but I'll not respond to that kind of scurrilous gossip. Your superiors will hear from me." He spun around and stalked toward the door.

Barnes glanced at Witherspoon, who nodded. He knew exactly what the constable was doing, and apparently, it was effective.

"If you won't answer our questions," Barnes continued as if he hadn't heard Andover's threat, "then we'll send Constable Miller to speak to the workmen at Brownsley and Sons."

"Talk to whoever you like." Andover stopped at the closed door and whirled around, glaring at the two policemen. "I've no idea what you're trying to do, but I assure you, Mrs. Blakstone and I have done nothing wrong."

"We'll verify that with workmen who were repairing the window frames at Mrs. Blakstone's home in the days before she came here," Witherspoon said quietly. "We don't wish to take such action, but we must have the truth."

"I've told you the truth. Mrs. Blakstone is nothing more than a dear family friend. We've done nothing wrong."

"Then I'm sure that's precisely what the workmen will tell us." Witherspoon looked at Barnes. "Send Constable Miller to the builder's office."

"Yes, sir." Barnes got to his feet.

"Wait," Andover cried, his face now a mask of embarrassment, misery, and flat-out fear. "Please, don't." He looked at the inspector. "If you send the police there and start asking questions like that, it will cause even more gossip. Good Lord, Inspector, my wife has been murdered and that's caused enough talk and speculation. For God's sake, Mrs. Blakstone and I still have to live in this society. How much are we expected to endure?"

"Then answer my questions, Mr. Andover. What is the real nature of your relationship with Mrs. Blakstone?"

"We are lovers." He closed his eyes for a moment. "I know what that sounds like and I know it presents both of us in a less than noble light. But I swear, neither of us had anything to do with Harriet's murder."

"Did your wife know about the two of you?"

"Not for a long time, but I think she was starting to suspect."

"How long have you been in an illicit relationship with your wife's best friend?" Barnes asked.

Andover shot him a quick glare. "I'd not put it like that, Constable. We didn't plan for it to happen; it just happened. These things do, you know. It's no longer considered a crime in this country."

"No, but it could be a motive for murder," Witherspoon reminded him. "Especially as your wife was the one with the money."

"That's right, Inspector, she was the one with the money and she never let me forget it." He gave a cynical snort of laughter. "Do you have any idea what it's like to live like that? How slowly, over time, you realize you've made a dreadful mistake and that if you want any happiness at all, you've got to grab it for yourself?"

"Her solicitor, your servants, and the neighbors all seemed to admire your late wife."

"Yes, yes, I know she was a good and decent woman. The servants liked her, the neighbors liked her, even her damned lawyer liked her. But they didn't live under her thumb as we did. She held the whip hand when it came to finances."

"But wasn't that the agreement between you when you married her?" Witherspoon pointed out. He felt obligated to defend the dead woman's honor to some extent.

"I thought I could live with it," Andover murmured. "I

thought she and her money would save us. My father frittered away the family land holdings and my first wife spent what was left. So I courted Harriet and finally convinced her to marry me. But after we married, I couldn't make any decisions without her approval. She decided how much allowance to give my children each quarter. She decided how much could be spent on food, drink, club fees, everything. She wouldn't even let me choose the paint colors for my own study or the color of the carpet for the front hall. Do you know what that feels like, Inspector? To not be consulted or listened to about anything?"

"But Mrs. Blakstone listened to you, didn't she?" Barnes said softly.

"That's right, and I fell in love with her." He straightened his spine. "What's more, once a decent interval has passed, we're going to marry."

"So with your poor wife's murder, you end up with all her money and a woman you're in love with," Barnes said. "A bit of blessing in disguise, isn't it?"

"Of course not, you simply don't understand. I didn't hate Harriet. In our own way, we cared for each other, but she wasn't an easy woman to live with. I was unfaithful to her, but I didn't kill her." Andover once again went to the door. Putting his hand on the knob, he looked at the two policemen. "And you'll never prove I did."

As she handed Inspector Witherspoon his sherry, Mrs. Jeffries wondered if she'd made a dreadful mistake. She'd done what she could to protect the others; she'd been very vague about the details when she'd told them she'd sent the telegram to Paris. The one thing she'd not told them was that she'd given the inspector's name and the Ladbroke Road Station if Mrs. Tyler wanted to contact someone. But now that she'd done it, she realized that if he did get an answer, he might wonder who had used his name.

"Thank you, Mrs. Jeffries, I've looked forward to this. It's been a very unusual day."

"Really, sir?" She took her seat. "Do tell, you know how much I love hearing the details."

"The day started off quite well." He took a quick sip. "We had a word with Mrs. Pinchon."

"She's the housekeeper from across the road." Mrs. Jeffries knew who she was, but she took every possible opportunity to pretend she knew less than she did. "The one who claimed someone was watching the Andover home?"

"That's right. She is quite a forceful personality, and I must say, she was very sure of herself when she described what she saw." He told her about the meeting, taking his time and thinking about the encounter as he spoke.

"Do you think she was right?" Mrs. Jeffries asked.

"Right?" He looked confused. "I don't see that she'd have a reason for making up such a tale."

"I'm not disputing that she saw a man get out of a hansom cab several times," she said quickly. "What I'm asking is, do you think her interpretation of what she saw was correct?"

He thought for a moment. "Yes, I do. Someone was taking an unusual interest in that house, and she noticed him."

"She claimed it wasn't an elderly man at all, but someone pretending to be such a person. Do you think her observation was correct?"

"Actually, I do."

Mrs. Jeffries had a good idea of who this "elderly gentle-man" really was, providing, of course, that her theory of the crime was right. But that would have to wait to be proven. "What else happened today, sir?"

"We learned that Mrs. Swineburn hadn't been truthful with us when she claimed to be at Liberty's late Monday afternoon," he said. "She'd been at Paddington Station."

"Was she meeting someone?"

Witherspoon put his glass down on the side table. "No, she was looking at trains."

"Trains?"

"Yes." He laughed. "Trains, and apparently, she isn't the only person who is passionate about them." The inspector told her everything that had transpired in that interview, including the fact that Constable Barnes was also a train engine enthusiast. "I don't know what amazed me the most, the fact that this middle-aged woman was completely smit-ten with the power of locomotives or that Constable Barnes had such hidden depths to his personality."

"Gracious, sir, that is remarkable." Mrs. Jeffries was stunned as well. That explains the tidbit about Ellen Swine-burn's coat smelling like soot that Mrs. Goodge had passed along, she thought. But she couldn't believe the woman had been stupid enough to hand the inspector another reason for wanting Harriet Andover dead. "Mrs. Swineburn actually said that now that her stepmother was gone, they'd be rich again and she could find another husband?"

"Words very much to that effect." He looked at his empty glass. "I was quite shocked at her bluntness, but it's been a day of surprises. Have we time for another one? I don't want to be too late to the table and ruin what I'm sure is one of Mrs. Goodge's lovely meals."

"Mrs. Goodge made a lamb roast, sir. It's in the warming oven." She got up, grabbed his glass, and poured them each a second. "Here you are, sir."

"After Mrs. Swineburn left, Constable Barnes and I had a word with Jacob Andover." He broke off and shook his head. "Honestly, Mrs. Jeffries, I'll never understand some men." He told her what had happened, taking care to repeat every detail of the encounter. "Andover seemed astonished that he wasn't in charge. He showed no remorse whatsoever for being unfaithful to his wife and tried to justify his behavior by blaming her. What did he think he was getting when he married a rich, middle-aged businesswoman who hadn't ever displayed any inclination to be a housewife?"

"He's from the class that believe they've a right to make all the decisions regardless of whether they're competent or even capable," she murmured. "I imagine he thought that once she was married to him, she'd acquiesce to his wishes. After all, he was from the upper class, and from the way you've described Mrs. Andover and her family, they appear to be from much more modest circumstances."

"You're right, of course. But to have an illicit relationship with his wife's best friend . . ." He looked disgusted. "That's beyond the pale. He bragged that we'd never prove he had anything to do with the murder."

"Do you think he or Mrs. Blakstone did it? Mrs. Andover's death clears the way for them to marry as well as leaving him a fortune."

"Truth to tell, I've no idea who murdered that poor woman. All I know is that I won't give up until I catch the culprit."

* * *

Mrs. Jeffries spent another restless night, but by morning, she was fairly sure she was right. When Constable Barnes arrived, she had the tea ready and a mental list of everything that needed to be done.

"Sorry I'm a bit late." Barnes slipped into the chair. "But my neighbor's a widow lady and she needed help moving a settee into her parlor so she'd have enough room for her Christmas company."

"Not to worry, you're here now. But we've much to tell you and not much time." Mrs. Jeffries glanced at the clock and then handed him a newspaper. She pointed at the fourth notice down in the Personal column. "Before we say anything, read this."

Barnes read it, read it again, and then looked up. "Ye gods, this description matches the three pieces we found in Mrs. Andover's dressing table."

"I know, that's why I sent the telegram." Mrs. Jeffries swallowed nervously. She wasn't sure she ought to tell him what she'd done, but in truth, she didn't think she had much choice. Logically, she could think of a dozen reasons her analysis might be wrong and this whole situation could lead to disaster. But one part of her knew that she was right. "Constable Barnes, I've something you need to know."

"What telegram? You replied to this?"

"I did, and what's more, I signed the inspector's name, and the address for reply is the Ladbroke Road Station," she blurted out. "I didn't think I had a choice in the matter; it's the only way we can prove that he's the killer."

"You know who it is?" He stared at her for a few moments, his expression unreadable.

"Yes, I think so."

"Well then, let's hope she gets back to us promptly. Lucky for you, we're at the station today instead of the Andover home."

"Why are you at the station?" Mrs. Goodge demanded.

"Because the Andovers moved Mrs. Andover's reception up by a day and the inspector agreed we'd give the family privacy," he explained. "It works out well—the inspector and I are going to use the time to read through those letters between Mrs. Andover and her sisters. It's a good thing you reminded me of them, Mrs. Jeffries. We don't want to have missed something important here, and you never know what you can find out from background information. If we get a reply from the telegram, we'll be at the ready."

"I'm not sure I should have done it," Mrs. Jeffries admitted. "The inspector is going to wonder who sent it and that could lead to some awkward questions."

"Let me handle that," Barnes said.

A surge of relief swept through the housekeeper. "Thank you, Constable. I've another question. I'm fairly sure I'm right, but there's a chance I've knitted a whole blanket from a tiny bit of yarn."

"You do this every time, Hepzibah," Mrs. Goodge scolded her. "You doubt yourself but you're most always right."

"I've been wrong a time or two," she pointed out. Though in truth, even if she'd got some of the details wrong in their past cases, she'd always been able to pinpoint the killer. She looked at Barnes. "The key that was found in Mrs. Andover's pocket, it was taken into evidence, correct?"

"It's in the evidence cupboard at the station. What about it?"

"Is it possible to get access to it on short notice?"

"The inspector can get it." He stared at her curiously. "Why?"

"Was it ever tested? Was it ever put into the lock?"

"Of the conservatory?" He frowned. "I would hope so. Constable Griffiths was there with the inspector on Monday night; I'm sure he would have checked it."

"Can you ask him? Make sure he did, because if he didn't, then don't you think it would be useful to verify that key is the one that locks the door?"

"I'll take care of it. It's getting late. If there's nothing else . . ." Barnes put his mug down and started to get to his feet.

"There's a bit more," Mrs. Goodge said. She told him everything that Betsy had learned at the British Museum, paused long enough to take a swig of tea, then continued by telling him about Phyllis' trip to the Pennington Hotel.

When the cook had finished speaking, Mrs. Jeffries added the details Luty's source had discovered.

"Then if Reverend Daniel Wheeler is dead and buried, who is the one giving the prayer service at Harriet Andover's reception today?" Barnes muttered.

"He's a Daniel Wheeler as well," Mrs. Jeffries said. "At least, I hope so, because if he isn't, my whole theory is wrong."

"Let's hope you're not; otherwise this is going to cause all of us a problem." Barnes got up as the clock struck the hour. "You two have given me a lot to think about. But the inspector is waiting for me." He pointed at the copy of *The Times*. "Can I borrow that? It'll help me convince the inspector to send some constables to the Pennington Hotel. We need to see what's in Wheeler's trunk."

"Just try to bring it back if you can." Mrs. Goodge handed him the paper. "That Mrs. Penny across the garden wants it returned to her."

"I'll not lose it," he promised.

"If you do hear from Mrs. Tyler, can you send a street lad here to let us know?" Mrs. Jeffries asked. There were always a number of boys hanging around the police station. Ladbroke Road was close to the High Street and the railway station. A clever lad could make a lot of coin by carrying packages for the local matrons, buying tickets, and taking messages.

"I'll send someone to let you know," he agreed before disappearing up the staircase.

Five minutes after the constable went upstairs, they heard the two policemen leaving out the front door.

Mrs. Goodge put the kettle on to boil while Mrs. Jeffries set out the cups and saucers. They turned as they heard footsteps on the stairs and the sounds of crockery and silverware bashing together as Phyllis carried the inspector's breakfast dishes into the kitchen.

"I've tidied up the dining room." She hurried toward the sink. "I had time to set the table for his dinner, just in case there's something I need to do outside."

"We'll see how the day goes," Mrs. Jeffries said.

Within a few minutes, the others, save for Hatchet and Luty, had arrived. Everyone took their seats.

"What's keepin' 'em?" Smythe stared at the empty chairs where Luty and Hatchet usually sat.

"I'm sure they'll be here very soon," Mrs. Jeffries said. She wondered if they should start and then decided against it. The Andovers were having a reception and the inspector was at the Ladbroke Road Station so there would be little to no activity. "Let's give them a few more minutes."

But they didn't need more time as a few moments later the back door opened and Hatchet and Luty burst into the room. "Sorry we're late, but I had to wait and make sure these were the only telegrams comin' from my sources in San Francisco."

"Sources?" Smythe repeated. "You have more than one?"

"I sent telegrams to three different people and two of 'em have answered me." Luty hurried to her seat, tossed two telegrams onto the tabletop, and unbuttoned her peacock blue cloak.

Hatchet grabbed it off her shoulders, pulled out her chair, and then went to the coat tree, taking both their outer garments with him. "Sit down, Madam. I'm sure no one will mind waiting while you catch your breath."

"Of course we won't," Mrs. Jeffries said. "Take as much time as you need."

"Cor blimey, you musta found out somethin'?" Wiggins grinned at the elderly American.

"Pays to have old friends around the world." Luty laughed as she took her chair. "And I've got a lot of old friends. Come on, Hatchet, quit yer ditherin'. Everyone's waitin' to hear what I've got to say."

"Patience is a virtue, Madam." He hung his hat up and came to the table. "I don't think they'll mind waiting another moment or two. May I have a cup of tea?" He took his seat.

Luty rolled her eyes as Phyllis poured two cups and passed them to the newcomers.

"Right then," Mrs. Goodge demanded. "Tell us what's what."

Luty picked up the top envelope, opened it, and pulled out the telegram. "This is the first one and it's kinda long for a telegram." Clearing her throat, she began to read.

Theodore Stone one of richest men in America. Owns silver mines in Nevada, banking in Nevada & California, property all over both states, ranching both states, manufacturing in Los Angeles. Worth as much as any of the 'Big Four.'

"The Big Four, what's that?" Phyllis asked.

"They're four American men who have acquired vast fortunes in California," Hatchet replied. "C. P. Huntington, Leland Stanford, Mark Hopkins, and Charles Crocker. All of them started out relatively poor, as I believe Mr. Stone did as well. And all of them are now worth millions and millions of dollars."

"Does that mean that this Mr. Stone has more money than Mrs. Andover?" Betsy asked.

"That's exactly what it means," Luty said.

"Harriet Andover's fortune pales in comparison to Theodore Stone's," Hatchet said. "If Stone is being compared to the Big Four, that means his wealth is vast." He looked at Luty. "Read them the other one. That's the important one."

Luty pulled the telegram out of the envelope, opened it, and began to read.

Stone seriously ill but still alive. Not expected to live much longer. No wife, no children. With death of his

last niece, Stone's only family is great-nephew—Daniel
Wheeler. Stone sent Wheeler to Europe a year ago on
business. Wheeler his only heir.

No one said anything for a moment and then everyone
began to speak at once.

"Does this mean that Daniel Wheeler is the killer?" Mrs.
Goodge demanded. "It certainly looks that way." She looked
at Mrs. Jeffries. "Well? Is it Wheeler?"

"I think so." Mrs. Jeffries glanced at the clock. "If I'm
correct, Daniel Wheeler is no more an Episcopal priest than
I am."

"Then what is he?" Ruth asked.

"A very good actor," Mrs. Jeffries said, "and a career criminal. But unless we hear back from Paris, we'll have the devil
of a time proving he's the one who murdered Mrs. Andover."

"We won't be hearing back," the cook complained. "You
asked Mrs. Tyler to reply directly to our inspector at the
Ladbroke Road Station."

"Then we need to get over there and keep an eye on
things." Wiggins pushed away from the table and started to
stand up.

Mrs. Jeffries waved him back to his chair. "Constable
Barnes will send a lad to let us know if they get an answer
to my telegram."

"Alright, I'm confused." Ruth drummed her fingers on
the tabletop. "There are two Daniel Wheelers. Is that right?"

"I think so," Mrs. Jeffries replied. "No, that's not right,
I know so. Luty's telegram confirmed what I only suspected."

"What was that?" Phyllis asked quickly.

"Luty's telegram said Daniel Wheeler worked for his

uncle and that, a year ago, he sent Wheeler to Europe on business. But if he worked for his uncle, he'd know Stone had a vast fortune. I suspect Wheeler began planning a way to get his hands on that fortune quite some time ago."

"What does that have to do with the Reverend Daniel Wheeler? He's the one who's really dead, right?" Phyllis pressed.

"He is. I can't say for certain, but I think Wheeler must have decided to borrow the dead man's occupation." She looked at Luty. "You know the American West. How big is Carson City?"

"It was a boomtown back in the 1880s—there was a lot of silver mining, and by then it was the state capital. But it's lost population and now I'd reckon it was down to three or four thousand people."

"Daniel Wheeler worked for his uncle, and his uncle had lots of business interests in Nevada," Mrs. Jeffries speculated. "Carson City is the state capital. I've a feeling that when Wheeler was there on business, he found out there had once been another Daniel Wheeler, an Episcopal priest."

"I guess he felt really lucky when the other Daniel Wheeler died of scarlet fever," Betsy mused.

"At least we know that this Daniel Wheeler didn't kill the other one," Luty snorted in disgust.

"That's something to be thankful for, I suppose." Mrs. Jeffries shrugged. "Right now let's just hope that I haven't made a monumental mistake."

"What should we do now?" Betsy asked.

Mrs. Jeffries thought for a moment. "I'm not sure we should do anything." She glanced toward the back door.

"Constable Barnes hasn't sent a street lad with a message. Perhaps it's best if we simply stay put."

"Stay put? That ain't no fun," Luty protested. "I say someone should keep watch on the Andover house."

"I agree," Mrs. Goodge added. "I've got one of my feelin's. Something is goin' to happen today."

"There's not anywhere to hide around there," Wiggins warned. "I'm bein' serious. There's not so much as a post box or a shrub."

The cook looked at Mrs. Jeffries. "The reception for Mrs. Andover is today."

"That's right. What of it? I don't think any of us here could talk our way into it."

"No, but if there's a reception goin' on, no one will notice a fancy carriage."

"And I've got one of those," Luty added excitedly. "It's the perfect spot to keep an eye on things. What time does the reception start?"

"The inspector didn't say," Mrs. Jeffries said, "and I didn't think to ask."

Luty turned to Hatchet. "Then you fellers better git to it. We'll wait here and see if we get a message from Constable Barnes. We don't want to miss somethin' important from him."

"Maybe one of them should stay just in case we do hear from him," Ruth suggested.

"Why should one of the men stay?" Phyllis protested. "If we get a message from the constable and it's important, I can go to Princess Gate Gardens. The Andover house isn't very far away."

* * *

The two policemen were in the duty inspector's office. It was furnished with a desk and two straight-backed chairs, a bench along one wall, and a rickety bookcase filled with file boxes. The wood floor was scratched and scuffed by years of wear and tear from the heavy feet of both prisoners and police.

Inspector Witherspoon sat behind the desk reading a letter. He put it to one side and looked at Barnes, who was sitting in one of the straight-backed chairs opposite. "Found anything interesting?"

"I have." Barnes tapped the page in front of him. "This one is family news, but in it, Mrs. Royle comments that her husband and she had had a 'dreadful row' over the money their uncle Teddy sent her as a birthday gift. Apparently Mr. Royle objected to his wife receiving a thousand dollars."

"A thousand dollars? For a birthday gift?"

Barnes nodded and handed him the letter. "Take a look. It's the last two paragraphs."

Witherspoon read it aloud.

"My dear Harriet, as much as I love my husband, he can be a trial at times. It was perhaps very wise of you to have never married. You can then do whatever you please with the lovely money Uncle Teddy sends us every birthday and Christmas. Phillip is trying to convince me to allow him to invest the thousand dollars Uncle Teddy recently sent, but I like having my own money, and thanks to Uncle Teddy, my fortune grows by leaps and bounds."

He put the letter aside. "That's a lot of money."

"Indeed, sir. It was obviously written before Mrs. Andover married her husband. But it's not surprising, sir. Hamish McGraw told us that it was the money this uncle sent her for an engagement present that started her business interests. Yet from what the Andover family said, it seemed to me that she must have had more than just that initial five thousand dollars. This explains how she was able to keep on building her fortune."

"Apparently, that fortune doesn't compare to the one her uncle had."

"Or still has," Barnes quipped.

Witherspoon picked up the next letter. It was dated June 5, 1889. "Finally, a letter from Helen Wheeler. I was beginning to wonder if there was some ill will between Mrs. Andover and her elder sister." He read the first few paragraphs, his eyes squinting at the small handwriting. "Gracious, here's another reason we need to have a word with Daniel Wheeler."

"You mean beside the fact the jewelry we saw in Mrs. Andover's dressing table is an exact match for the jewelry described in that Personal column?" Barnes had shown Witherspoon the paper earlier. He'd also dropped hints about the Pennington Hotel offering storage services to their overseas visitors, especially those like Reverend Wheeler, who were doing research between Paris and London.

"It appears so." He held the page up. "According to this letter, all the Wheelers, including Daniel and his parents, were members of an acting troupe."

"An acting troupe?"

"Yes, the Carlisle Players . . ." His voice trailed off as they heard shouting from the foyer.

"What do you mean, he's busy? I don't care how busy he is, I must see G. Witherspoon," a woman's voice rang out.

"For goodness' sakes, he sent me a telegram. Get me Inspector Witherspoon. I've just spent the last fourteen hours on a mail packet ship and the most uncomfortable train ride of my life."

Barnes leapt up. "I'll see what it's about, sir."

Witherspoon waited a few seconds and then cocked his ear toward the open office door. The shouting stopped and now he could hear voices murmuring and then footsteps.

Barnes and a woman of late middle age appeared in the doorway. "Inspector, this is Mrs. Tyler. She's come from Paris to speak to you." He ushered her into the office and shut the door behind them.

She was tall, slender, and very attractive. There were a few streaks of gray in her black hair and some fine lines around her deep-set hazel eyes. She wore a slightly wrinkled green-and-gray-tweed traveling suit and carried an umbrella in one hand and a small, colorful carpetbag in the other.

"How do you do, ma'am." Witherspoon stood up and bowed slightly. "I'm Inspector Gerald Witherspoon, and this is Constable Barnes."

"I'm Mrs. Jonas Tyler." She acknowledged the introduction with an inclination of her head. "I came as soon as I got your telegram, Inspector."

"My telegram?" His brows drew together in confusion.

"Yes, the one you sent me." She stood her umbrella against the side of the chair, plopped her carpetbag on the edge of the desk, and unlatched the clasp. Opening it, she rummaged inside and pulled out a crumpled telegram. "You are G. Witherspoon"—she held the telegram up—"and this is the Ladbroke Road Station?"

"True, ma'am, but I—"

Barnes interrupted, "The inspector saw the advertisement in the Personal column of *The Times* and realized the description of your missing jewelry matched jewelry we've come across in the course of one of our investigations."

"I posted that notice six weeks ago." She put the telegram back in her bag. "How are you just now seeing it?"

"Again, it was in the course of our investigation that we came across the advertisement and realized you might have some very valuable information for us."

"Please sit down, Mrs. Tyler." Witherspoon gestured to the empty chair and she sat down. Constable Barnes took the other one. The inspector decided he'd worry about who'd sent the telegram later. It was most likely the constable; he'd probably sent it and forgot to mention it. He was very good at thinking ahead and taking action.

"Mrs. Tyler, let's start from the beginning." Witherspoon waited until Constable Barnes had his notebook open to a blank page and his pencil at the ready.

"What is your address, Mrs. Tyler?"

"It was in the newspaper advertisement. Number Seven Avenue Montaigne, Paris," she said impatiently.

"This won't take long," Witherspoon told her. "Please tell me the circumstances of how you lost your jewelry."

"I didn't lose my jewelry. It was stolen from me. That's why I offered such a large reward."

"Yes, a hundred pounds is a great deal of money," Barnes cut in hastily.

"Do you have any idea who took your jewelry?"

"I know exactly who took it," she replied. "It was Daniel Wheeler."

"The Reverend Daniel Wheeler stole your jewelry?" the inspector murmured.

"Reverend?" She laughed. "He's no more a reverend than I'm the Queen of France, Inspector. He's a criminal and I'm a fool for not seeing right through him. The bastard would have taken everything if my maid hadn't walked in before he could stuff the rest of my jewels in his pocket. As it was, he got his dirty little hands on my most valuable piece, my sapphire-and-diamond starburst broach." She broke off and brought herself under control. "I presume the police know where Wheeler is right now?"

"Yes, Mrs. Tyler, we do."

"Then I demand you go and arrest him immediately."

Witherspoon wasn't confused as such, but things were happening so fast, he wanted to be sure of the facts before taking any action. "The man you know as Daniel Wheeler, could you describe him? We wouldn't like to have a case of mistaken identity."

"He's an attractive man in his early forties. He's slender and dark-haired with just a few strands of gray at the temple. He told me he was born in England but grew up in North America."

"What is his occupation?"

"Supposedly he was in Europe looking for investment opportunities for his uncle." She shrugged. "But I suspect that was a lie. Everything the man told me was probably a lie."

"Mrs. Tyler, did you report this to the Paris police?"

"Of course not, Inspector." She looked at him as if he were a half-wit. "That wouldn't have done any good. I knew Wheeler was coming to London so the French police can't arrest him. As I'd had no response to my advertisement, I've hired a private detective, and as it happens, I know Wheeler is living at Number One Princess Gate Gardens. Now, as you've admitted you know his current whereabouts, I demand you go there immediately and arrest him."

"You'll need to identify the jewelry and show proof that you are the true owner," Witherspoon told her.

But she was already rummaging in her carpetbag again. She yanked out a handful of papers and tossed them in front of the inspector. "Will these do? They're receipts for all three of those pieces of jewelry, and as you can plainly see, they are made out to Jonas Tyler, my late husband. He bought them for me and I intend to have them back."

Witherspoon read through them and stood up. "Constable, send Constable Miller and another officer to the Pennington Hotel. We need to know if he's availed himself of their storage service, and if he has, tell the constables to bring whatever they find to the Andover home."

"Yes, sir." Barnes hurried out to give the orders. He'd already obtained the conservatory key from the evidence cupboard.

"Does this mean you're going to arrest Wheeler?" Mrs. Tyler demanded.

"Well, we'll have a word with him," Witherspoon said. "And we'll ask for an explanation if you're able to identify the jewelry."

"I can identify the jewelry and that blackguard." She smiled broadly. "He's a career criminal, you know. When my maid caught him in my bedroom riffling through my jewelry box, he laughed at her, leapt out a window, and was out of the country before I could even raise the alarm. I can't wait to see the expression on his face when he sees me!"

CHAPTER 11

"I'm sorry, Inspector, but you cannot come in right now. They're in the middle of Mrs. Andover's reception." Mrs. Barnard stood in the front door, blocking their entrance. She stared at the small mob on the door stoop and paled. Along with Mrs. Tyler and Constable Barnes, they'd brought Constables Griffiths and Reed along.

"Please, come back later. Mr. Andover is in a terrible state. He's very upset," Mrs. Barnard pleaded.

"Mrs. Barnard, this is most urgent," Witherspoon said. After hearing Mrs. Tyler's description of how Wheeler had escaped with her jewels in Paris, he didn't want to risk losing the man at this point. He didn't quite understand everything as yet, but he realized it was better to err on the side of caution rather than let a possible murderer escape justice. "We must come inside."

"We could put some constables on both the doors," Barnes said quietly.

"Constable Griffiths and Constable Reed are here. They could watch the premises and make sure he doesn't make a run for it."

"Don't be absurd." Mrs. Tyler pushed past the constable. "Wheeler's smarter than that. I told you before, he jumped out a second-floor window in Paris when he was stealing my jewels."

"You didn't tell us he jumped from the second floor," Barnes countered. "That's pertinent information, you know."

"Really, Inspector, you must go." Mrs. Barnard put her arms on each side of the door frame, effectively barring them from entering. "Reverend Wheeler is leading them in the Lord's Prayer."

"Reverend Wheeler!" Mrs. Tyler screamed. "Are you people idiots? He's a flimflam man, a confidence trickster— he's not a reverend. He's a thief and a liar. Now let me in." But she didn't wait for the housekeeper to move; she ducked under the woman's right arm and charged into the house.

"Wait, wait, you can't do that." Mrs. Barnard whirled around and chased after her. "Come back, please, come back."

Witherspoon and Barnes raced into the foyer, but Mrs. Tyler was a determined woman and could move surprisingly fast. She'd already reached the drawing room doors.

"No, no, you can't go in there." Mrs. Barnard lunged forward, her arms outstretched as she tried for the back of Mrs. Tyler's traveling coat. But the doors flew open and Mrs. Tyler, holding her umbrella like a sword, hurtled herself into the drawing room.

Witherspoon, Barnes, and the housekeeper were hot on her heels.

Daniel Wheeler, who'd just finished the prayer, looked up. He wasn't wearing proper church vestments, only a black shirt, coat, and simple white clerical collar. His eyes widened in surprise, his jaw dropped, and he gasped as he took in the spectacle of the advancing woman and the three people racing after her.

"That's him, that's him." She pointed her umbrella at him. "That's the dastardly blackguard who stole my jewelry."

The maids, who'd just come in with canapés on silver trays, stopped in their tracks. The guests' faces were set in expressions of stunned shock, their feet rooted to the spot as they froze in place.

"I'm sorry, Mr. Andover," Mrs. Barnard apologized. "I tried to stop them. But that woman"—she pointed at Mrs. Tyler—"pushed her way inside."

Jacob Andover reacted first. "What is going on here?" he demanded. "Who is this woman? Inspector Witherspoon, this is outrageous. How dare you interrupt my wife's prayer service!"

"Prayer service!" Mrs. Tyler sneered. "You must be as stupid as I was. He's not a priest, he's a crook." She turned to Witherspoon. "What are you waiting for? Arrest him."

"Let's hear what he has to say first," the inspector cautioned. "We want to be sure he's the right person." He knew Wheeler was the one, but he was buying a few seconds so he could think what to do.

"I don't know what you expect me to say, Inspector," Wheeler said calmly. "I've no idea who this woman is or why you're here."

"Don't be an idiot; you stole my jewelry and I want it back." She started toward him, holding her umbrella in front of her like a medieval knight at a jousting tournament.

Barnes grabbed her around the waist and pulled her back. "No, no, Mrs. Tyler, let us handle this."

"Inspector, I've no idea why you've interrupted us with this demented woman," Wheeler began, only to be interrupted by Jacob Andover.

"She claims you stole her jewelry." Jacob stared at him suspiciously.

"He did steal it and I've got the receipts to prove it." Mrs. Tyler squirmed away from the constable.

"We saw the jewelry Mrs. Tyler claims is hers and we saw the sales receipts as well," Witherspoon said. "If you'll send one of the maids upstairs to Mrs. Andover's room, the pieces should be in the top drawer of her dressing table."

"I'll go," Kathleen, one of the upstairs maids, offered.

"This is absurd," Wheeler said, but his voice was shaky. "I'm a priest of the Episcopal Church and an American citizen. You can't treat me like this."

"We're investigating a murder and we have every right to do what's needed to find the truth. We've also sent constables to the Pennington Hotel to take any items you might have left in storage there." He was gambling that Wheeler had taken advantage of that particular service.

"You've no right to do that." Wheeler nervously shoved his hand in his trouser pocket. "You can't search my trunk without a warrant."

"We don't need one, Mr. Wheeler." He looked at Andover. "I suggest you send your guests home, Mr. Andover."

He hesitated for a moment and then turned to the room.

"Perhaps the inspector is right . . ." He broke off as the maid returned and moved quickly to the inspector.

"I've got them, sir. Shall I put them down here?" She stopped by a side table covered with a black fringed mourning runner.

"Thank you, miss, that will be fine." He watched as the three pieces were laid out on the ebony cloth.

"This is ridiculous." Wheeler's eyes narrowed angrily. "I don't know who this demented woman might be, but I assure you, you'll be hearing from my lawyers. I won't tolerate being treated in such a disgusting manner." He glanced at Andover. "I thank you for your hospitality, but under the present circumstances, you'll understand if I leave."

"You're not going anywhere," Witherspoon commanded. He glanced at Griffiths and Reed and they immediately took up positions by the drawing room door.

Mrs. Tyler went to the table and examined the three pieces of jewelry. "These are mine." She looked at Wheeler and smiled. "You're going to prison for a long time, and I assure you, French prisons are dreadful."

"Not so fast, Mrs. Tyler," Witherspoon said. "Daniel Wheeler murdered Harriet Andover. That takes precedence over the theft of your jewelry."

Wheeler gave an ugly bark of a laugh. Gone was the calm demeanor, the sweet expression of the caring priest, the outraged innocence of a wrongly accused man. "Prove it," he challenged.

"We will." Barnes pulled the key out of his pocket and silently prayed that Mrs. Jeffries had it right. "This is the key that was found in Mrs. Andover's pocket when she was murdered. It's been in the evidence cupboard at Ladbroke Road Station. Let's just see if it actually unlocks the conservatory door." He looked at Witherspoon. "Shall I, sir?"

He nodded.

"I don't know what you're trying to do, Inspector," Wheeler snapped. "A key proves nothing."

"A key proves everything if it doesn't fit the lock in the conservatory," the inspector said calmly. "Because it means that Mrs. Andover let her killer in, and after he'd betrayed her, murdered her, he then took the real key out of her pocket and switched it for the one that doesn't work. He then let himself out the door to the garden and locked it."

"Why would anyone do that?" Wheeler scoffed. "Only a fool—"

"You did it because you assumed, quite rightly, that it would be late in the evening by the time her body was discovered and that the police would simply assume the key in her pocket was the one that locked and unlocked the conservatory door."

"That's ridiculous. Why would I murder my aunt?"

Witherspoon ignored his question. The pieces were falling into place but there was still much he didn't understand. "You're one of the few people Mrs. Andover absolutely trusted and you knew she'd let you inside. I think you used the jewelry—the gold bracelet and the pearl broach—as lures. A variation of the Secret Silly Game Mrs. Andover played with her sisters. Once inside, you used the sash you took from Mr. Andover's room, strangled your aunt, switched the key with one that resembled the real one, and then let yourself out the back door."

"I was at the British Museum," he insisted.

"You told Miss Nora Barlow you were going up to one of the galleries to look at the artifacts. You were gone for a long time. We don't know all the details as yet, but I assure you everything will be brought to light during your trial." He nodded at the constables, but before any of them could move, Wheeler shot across the room and grabbed Colleen Murphy, who was standing by the butler's pantry. She screamed and her tray of canapés went flying.

He yanked the girl against him, dislodging her cap as he wrapped one arm around her neck and pulled a revolver out of his pocket. "If any of you move, I'll put a bullet in this girl's brain."

"Let her go," Andover shouted. "She's just a girl."

Wheeler looked at him. "Really, Jacob, you care about your servants now. Dear Lord, before my aunt married you, you half starved them to death."

Several ladies screamed as the guests crowded together on the far side of the room. They watched, wide-eyed and frightened at the spectacle unfolding in front of them.

Mrs. Barnard was staring at Wheeler and Colleen Murphy, her expression one of horror. "Please, she's hardly more than a child. Let her go," she pleaded.

"It'll go easier on you if you let her go," Witherspoon implored him. "She's done nothing to you."

"She's my way out of here, Inspector. That's why people take hostages. It works."

"Don't be ridiculous. If you hurt her, you'll hang."

"You're going to hang me anyway." Wheeler laughed and tightened his arm around her throat. "You people are morons. I've traveled seven thousand miles and murdered two blood relatives to get to this point, but that's gone now. I'm in a bad way, Inspector, and nothing you can say will stop me from killing her."

He moved, dragging her toward the door. But the motion caused the arm around Colleen's throat to shift up, slapping against her jaw. "Get moving, you stupid cow," he snarled.

"Stupid cow!" she screeched. "I'll show you who's a stupid cow, you ruddy bastard." Colleen Murphy dug her heels into the floor and sank her teeth into his wrist.

He yelped in pain as the gun went off. She let go and bit him again, this time hard enough to get blood flowing.

Every policeman in the room charged him.

Enraged, he shouted an obscenity, dropped the gun, and tried to punch her with his other arm, but Colleen, having grown up with three brothers, ducked, kicked the gun away, and fell to her knees.

Witherspoon grabbed Colleen around the waist, pulling her away from Wheeler. Barnes grabbed Wheeler around the neck while Griffiths and Reed leapt toward his flailing arms. It took a few seconds, but they soon had him subdued and on his feet.

The inspector let go of the maid, pushed his spectacles up his nose, straightened his tie, and turned so he could face the man. "Daniel Wheeler, you're under arrest for the murders of Harriet Andover and of Henrietta Royle."

"Once again, prove it," Wheeler sneered.

"You just admitted it, you idiot," Percy Andover shouted. He looked around at his family and friends, all of whom were still standing in stunned silence. "And everyone thinks I'm the stupid one."

*   *   *

"It's about time," Luty scolded as Wiggins, Smythe, and Hatchet came in through the back door. "We've been waitin' to hear something."

"Wheeler's been arrested." Wiggins grinned broadly. "You were right, Mrs. Jeffries. We saw him being taken to the station. Mind you, it was a bit worryin' when we 'eard the gunshot."

"Gunshot! Is everyone alright?" Mrs. Jeffries rose to her feet.

"Really, Wiggins, do be a bit more circumspect. You've frightened the ladies."

"Is everyone alright?" Mrs. Goodge repeated.

"Everyone's right as rain." Smythe slid into the seat next to Betsy. "We stayed in Luty's carriage and kept watch. Then our inspector, Constable Barnes, and Constable Griffiths along with a constable I've never seen before and a woman who I think might be Mrs. Tyler showed up. It looked like they wasn't goin' to be allowed in the Andover house, but the woman shoved her way past the housekeeper, and within ten minutes, all 'ell was breakin' loose. We 'eard the shot, a load of shoutin', and then the inspector and the constables were hustlin' Wheeler into a police van."

Hatchet took his seat next to Luty. "It appears that, once again, you were right, Mrs. Jeffries. Now, how did you figure it out?"

"I almost didn't," she admitted honestly. "All I know is there was one tidbit of information that I couldn't get out of my head. It was the telegram. The one that Angela Evans told Wiggins about. I went over and over it in my mind, but I simply couldn't understand why someone would send a telegram to a person seven thousand miles away and the only information it contained was that 'some old uncle of his was going to Tombstone.' The telegram didn't say anything else so I wondered why it was sent. Why would you just say someone was going somewhere without giving a reason?"

"Maybe it was somethin' Wheeler was expectin' to hear," Smythe said.

"No, I know what Mrs. Jeffries is saying," Betsy argued. "The telegram sounded fake, almost like a code of some sort."

"That was my thought exactly." Mrs. Jeffries smiled approvingly. "And the code in that telegram was that Theodore Stone, Wheeler's great-uncle, was dying. That's why Mrs. Andover had to die immediately."

"He needed her dead first so he could inherit," Hatchet said. "If Theodore Stone died first, his fortune would go to Mrs. Andover."

"Or even possibly to the both of them," Mrs. Jeffries said. "But Daniel Wheeler wanted it all."

"Was that why he might have murdered Henrietta Royle?" Betsy asked. "So he could have it all?"

"That's what I think." She shrugged. "But proving that murder might be even more difficult."

"Poor lady was killed a year ago." Luty pursed her lips in disapproval. "Ain't it awful what some people will do for money."

"Was the telegram the only reason?" Phyllis pressed.

"No, I kept thinking about the 'elderly gentleman' watching the Andover home. Mrs. Pinchon was very sure of what she saw so I knew the man had to be there for a reason, and once we found out Wheeler had been an actor, I understood what he was doing."

"Then why was he there?" Phyllis took a sip of tea.

"Wheeler wasn't looking at the house, he was watching the Andover family. I suspect he did it to learn their secrets."

"And they appear to have a number of secrets," Hatchet added.

"The 'elderly gentleman' was always there at the same time, between ten and half past ten," Mrs. Jeffries continued. "Precisely the time of day that people are out and about."

"But Percy Andover had a job," Wiggins protested.

"True, but Mrs. Swineburn, Mrs. Blakstone, and Jacob Andover didn't work," she pointed out. "Furthermore, I think Wheeler realized that Percy hadn't been working for months."

"He probably only had to follow Percy Andover a time or two to see what he was doin'," Luty added.

"Then of course, there was the Secret Silly Game, the one that Jacob Andover mentioned to our Inspector." She looked at Mrs. Goodge. "You're the one that had me thinking about that. You said that perhaps Mrs. Andover knew her killer, trusted that person, and let them in the conservatory."

"Glad to know I was helpful." The cook chuckled.

"It was very helpful," Mrs. Jeffries replied. "Once I started thinking about that, I remembered the Secret Silly Game and how the three sisters played it."

"What was it again?" Luty asked.

"The sisters would run to their garden shed. Whoever got there first rushed inside, locked the door, and the other two couldn't get in unless they gave the winner a present. Daniel Wheeler would have known about that game from his mother; that's how he got Mrs. Andover to open the door. I finally understood it when I realized that two of the three pieces of jewelry found in her dressing table were the prizes for the Secret Silly Game."

"That's right, he wormed his way into the Andover house with the sapphire-and-diamond broach," Ruth added. "Clever. But if he'd already given her the jewelry, how did he get in on the night of the murder?"

"He didn't need jewelry for that night," Mrs. Jeffries explained. "Simply showing up would have been enough for her to open the door to him. She probably assumed he had something for her."

"Was it just the jewelry then?" Phyllis asked.

She shook her head. "No, there was the gardener's coat and hat being on the wrong peg."

"That was Wheeler's mistake," Phyllis said excitedly, sure she'd figured this part out herself. "I'll bet he used the gardener's clothes to move around the back garden, and if any of the neighbors had seen him, they'd think it was the gardener. But when he put the hat and coat back in the shed, he put them on the wrong peg, not realizing that Mr. Debman always put them in the same spot."

Mrs. Jeffries smiled at the maid. "That's exactly what I thought."

"So the varmint snuck across the garden to the conservatory, rapped on the glass, and probably pretended to have something to give Mrs. Andover, and she let him inside?" Luty frowned. "But why did he need the jewelry in the first place? She liked him from the beginnin'. Wouldn't she have let him in without it?"

"Possibly, but he wasn't taking any chances. He needed the jewelry because of the game," Mrs. Jeffries explained.

"He knew his aunt took her business very seriously and in-sisted on privacy when she worked. I imagine he had the jewelry as insurance, a way to get her to open the door and keep it their Secret Silly Game. But by the time he was ready to murder the poor woman, he was banking on the fact that she'd assume he had something for her and unlock the door.'"

"I wonder what's in that trunk he's got stored at the Pen-nington Hotel," Betsy mused.

"We'll find out when the inspector gets home." Mrs. Goodge got up and began clearing the tea things.

"But that'll be hours from now," Betsy complained.

"Then let's go 'ome and come back later." Smythe got up. "We've a lot to do to get ready for Christmas and there's no sense in us sittin' 'ere wastin' time."

"Excellent idea," Mrs. Jeffries said. "Let's meet back here for a late tea at half past four. I've a feeling we might know something by then."

For once, Mrs. Jeffries was wrong and they were half an hour into afternoon tea when a street lad arrived at the back door to tell them Inspector Witherspoon wouldn't be home till late that evening.

"I don't care what he says, I'm puttin' his supper in the warming oven," Mrs. Goodge said as everyone got up and prepared to leave. "That food at the café across from the station isn't fit to eat."

"You find out all the details," Luty told Mrs. Jeffries, "and we'll be back tomorrow morning to hear everything. The inspector is goin' to work tomorrow, ain't he?"

The housekeeper gathered up the empty tea mugs. "Not to worry, he's on duty so we'll be alright to discuss the case."

Smythe took a very sleepy Amanda out of Betsy's arms. "Right, then, we'll get the little one home." The three of them headed for the back door. Betsy pulled her coat tighter as they crossed the communal garden to the back gate. By the time they'd reached their home, a light rain had begun to fall.

Going inside, Betsy quickly got Amanda, who was now awake and fussing, into her nightdress. Smythe carried her into her room and they tucked her into bed. "She's exhausted." Betsy pulled the door almost closed, leaving it open a half inch in case the little one called out in the night.

They went into the parlor. Smythe flopped onto the blue settee and sighed heavily. "It's too bad we've got to wait until tomorrow to find out what 'appened. But we know the right one got arrested, so I suppose it doesn't matter." He looked at his wife, who was staring out the window at the rain beating against it. "Are you alright, love?"

She turned and smiled at him. "I'm fine, I'm just a bit tired."

"Good." He patted the seat next to him. "Come sit 'ere. You don't mind waitin' a bit longer for your mum and sister's headstone? Blimpey said it might take months to get all the names of the ones buried with 'em."

"I don't mind waiting." She sat down next to him and took his hand. "We've plenty of time. If it's possible, I want the names of every single person buried there. No one should be forgotten in death just because they were poor in life."

"I agree with ya, my love. I just didn't want ya frettin' if the weeks slipped by and we still 'adn't found all of 'em."

"As I said, we've plenty of time. Smythe, I've got something to tell you." She squeezed his hand. "By this time next year, Amanda is going to have a little brother or sister."

"We're 'avin' a baby. Oh Lord, Betsy, that's the best present ya could give me." He pulled her into his arms, squeezing her tight and then immediately releasing his hold. "What am I thinkin'? I don't want to squash ya."

She laughed. "I'm not going to break, Smythe. But once my mum and sister have the headstone, you and I need to have a serious talk about the future."

"I know, love." He looked around the lovely flat that was now their home. He'd provided well for his family: nice furniture, good rugs, and a modern kitchen. But he could give her and their children ten times more than this place. "We've not wanted to talk about it because we don't want to give them up." He knew she understood what he meant. "We want to continue 'elpin' with the inspector's cases and makin' sure that Luty and Mrs. Goodge and the inspector can be part of Amanda's life. We love all of 'em: Mrs. J, Ruth, Phyllis, Wiggins, and Hatchet. They're part of our family as well. But life changes and maybe we've got to change with it. I want our children to 'ave the best of everythin': a fine home and a decent education; I want 'em to travel and see the world and feel the equal of anyone they meet."

"You want them to have everything we didn't have when we grew up." Betsy touched her fingers to his cheeks. "And they will."

"It'll be 'ard to do it without makin' some changes," he warned.

"Change doesn't have to mean giving up who we love." She smiled and touched her fingers to his lips. "We'll find a way to have it all."

"The street lad told us you'd be late." She handed him his drink. "Does that mean what I think it means?"

The inspector had arrived home at half past nine, and he and Mrs. Jeffries were now in his study having their sherry.

"It most certainly does." He took a fast sip. "We've arrested someone for Mrs. Andover's murder. Would you like to guess who?"

"I've no idea," she lied.

"Daniel Wheeler. He's not an Episcopal priest. He's a career criminal, and oddly enough, he's quite proud of himself."

"Gracious, sir, that's stunning news. What happened? Now do be kind, sir, and start at the very beginning. I want to hear everything."

He chuckled. "If Mrs. Tyler hadn't come to the station, we might not have solved this one."

"Mrs. Tyler, who is she?"

"A very determined woman," he quipped. He told her everything, starting with the moment Barnes had shown him the advertisement in the newspapers. He took his time in the telling, making certain to include everything that had happened.

"Well, of course we couldn't let him take Miss Murphy hostage, and I will admit to being alarmed when he held the revolver to the poor girl's head, but I must say, she more than held her own." He drained his glass. "Shall we have another one? I do believe a small celebration is called for, don't you?"

"Of course, sir." Mrs. Jeffries laughed as she got up and poured them another. Both of them knew they *always* had a second sherry.

"The second time she bit Wheeler, it drew enough blood that we had to bandage him up when we got to the station." He nodded his thanks as she put the glass down on the table next to him.

"She sounds a very brave girl," Mrs. Jeffries commented. "What happened then?"

"We took him to the station and charged him with murder." He reached for the drink and tapped his finger on the rim. "That's when the situation became surreal."

"Surreal?" she repeated. "In what way?"

"I'm not sure how to express it, but I think Daniel Wheeler is insane."

"Insane? How so, Inspector?"

"That's the part that's difficult to put into words. Wheeler isn't a raving lunatic or one of those people who imagine they're the King of Naples. It's a different kind of affliction." He stared off into space, his expression thoughtful. "When we got to the station, the constable had brought his trunk from the Pennington Hotel. That's when I began to realize there was something wrong with the man, I mean other than the fact that he's committed several murders."

"What happened?"

"We didn't have to break into the trunk, Wheeler opened it for us. He had the key in his pocket. Then he unlocked it and started taking things out, and as he did it, he gave us a running commentary on his crimes." He took a drink. "It was truly bizarre. The first item that came out was a black top hat and greatcoat. Then he took out a gray wig, mustache, and false beard. He told us how he'd used them as a disguise so he could spy on the Andover family."

Mrs. Jeffries ducked her head to hide the satisfaction she was afraid was written on her face. She'd suspected Wheeler was the one masquerading as an old man. When the inspector had told her about Mrs. Pinchon's observations, she'd known it was true when Ruth reported that Wheeler's father was an actor and not a fisherman. She asked the inspector a question but she was sure she already knew the answer. "Why did he want to spy on them?"

"I asked him that and he looked at me as if I was a fool. He said, 'Knowledge is power, Inspector. Everyone has secrets, and in my profession, learning those secrets is essential.'" He went on to tell us everything we now know about that family."

"You mean about Mrs. Blakstone and Mr. Andover—"

He interrupted, "Not just them. All of the family, including Mrs. Swineburn's predilection for locomotive engines and Percy Andover's shenanigans at the brothel."

"What else did he have in that trunk?'

"Everything, including the key to the conservatory, which was stupid on his part. If he'd just hung the key back on the hook in the kitchen, he might have gotten away with it. There were also six copies of *The Times* newspapers; they were the ones that had Mrs. Tyler's advertisement in them. He'd stolen the papers when they were delivered and then hung about the Andover house to steal the replacement copies provided by the newsagent." He shook his head in disbelief. "Wheeler had been planning these murders for over a year."

"Murders?"

"Oh yes, he killed Henrietta Royle as well as Harriet Andover. His uncle sent him to Europe on business in October of last year. He did the same thing to the Royle household as he did with the Andovers. Disguised himself and found out Phillip Royle was dying. He murdered Mrs. Royle on the day she'd just buried her husband. He shot her as the train she was on pulled into Waterloo Station."

"But surely someone would have seen something?"

Witherspoon gave a negative shake of his head. "He pretended to be an Episcopal priest, leapt onto the first-class compartment she was in when the train left Woking—it was an express so it was the last stop—and then used a derringer to put a bullet in her head. He tossed the gun onto the compartment floor and leapt out before the train came to a stop. It was the busiest hour at the station and no one noticed him. Her death was ruled an accident but most people seemed to think she'd committed suicide."

"This was last year?"

"That's right, then he went to France and once again became Daniel Wheeler, businessman. He made several lucrative deals on his uncle's behalf as well as wooing several wealthy older women. That's where Mrs. Tyler appears. But she wasn't his first victim. Wheeler had several other pieces of jewelry he stole from other women."

"How awful, sir. I'm so glad you've caught him. But I don't understand why he wanted both his aunts dead. Were they his uncle's only heirs? Was that the only way he could inherit himself?"

"As I said earlier, Theodore Stone has a vast fortune, enough to keep a dozen people in luxury for the rest of their lives." He sighed sadly. "Wheeler told us that when his mother died, his uncle told him he was getting her share, a third of his estate. But that wasn't enough for him. He wanted it all, so he set about planning the murders of his mother's two sisters."

"That's dreadfully evil."

"I know, but if you'd seen his demeanor as he told us what he'd done, you'd understand why I think he's insane. It's almost as if he doesn't see other human beings as people, but instead he sees them as objects he can manipulate."

"At least he confessed readily." She put her half-empty glass on the side table.

"He was proud of what he'd done," Witherspoon said. "He insisted we send a message to the American embassy, which we did. He kept saying that, with his money, he can afford the best legal minds in England."

"He thinks money will allow him to escape justice?"

"It's happened before, Mrs. Jeffries," Witherspoon said. "Very few wealthy men actually face the gallows. But what Wheeler didn't realize is that Theodore Stone isn't dead. Ironic, really, because the reason he murdered Mrs. Andover on Monday was because he'd received a telegram with a coded message that implied Stone was at death's door."

"Did he say who sent the telegram?"

Witherspoon nodded. "Apparently, he paid one of Stone's secretaries to keep him posted on his uncle's health. But Mr. Stone made a miraculous recovery, and I don't think he'll be all too pleased when he finds out his great-nephew murdered Stone's nieces." He stood up and yawned. "Gracious, I'm dreadfully tired. But all in all, it's been a good day. The murderer has been apprehended and now we have time to enjoy all our Christmas festivities."

Mrs. Jeffries got up as well. "You should be very proud of yourself, sir. Solving this case was very difficult but I knew you could do it."

He grinned proudly. "Thank you, that's very kind of you to say. Time for bed. I'm sure you're tired as well."

"One more thing, sir. Who sent the telegram to Paris?"

She wanted to be certain that Constable Barnes didn't suffer any negative consequences for her actions. She'd taken a risk by sending that telegram, but luckily, it had been the spark which solved the case.

"It was Constable Barnes. He'd seen the newspaper advertisement yesterday afternoon and noticed the description of the jewelry. It set off enough alarms that he sent the telegram immediately and was going to tell me this morning, but things happened so fast, it slipped his mind. Now you understand why I don't like investigating without him, even though this time it was only for the one evening. I don't know what I'll do if he decides to retire."

"Did you have a pleasant evening, sir?" Mrs. Vickers, housekeeper to Inspector Nigel Nivens, took his overcoat and hung it on the coat tree.

"I did, Mrs. Vickers. Mama always has wonderful parties, especially at this time of the year. The house was beautifully decorated for the season. There were three Christmas trees, some excellent and colorful bunting, as well as holly bushes, ivy, and assorted greenery everywhere."

"You seem to have enjoyed yourself, sir," she said politely.

"Everyone important in London was there. She's quite the hostess, my dear mama."

"I'm glad all went well," she murmured. "Will that be all, sir? Do you require anything else?"

"No, it's late. Go to bed, Mrs. Vickers." Nivens smiled broadly. "I'm not tired. I'm going to have a nightcap in my study."

"Yes, sir. I thought you might so I left the lamps burning. Good night, sir."

"Good night, Mrs. Vickers." Nivens stepped into his study and went to the drinks cabinet. He poured himself a glass of his best whisky and sat down behind his massive desk. "It was a damned good evening," he murmured to himself as he took his first sip. He thought back to the moment when he knew he'd won, the moment when Lord Merton, his mother's latest husband, had pulled him aside.

"Once again, your mother has acquiesced and done what you asked," Merton whispered angrily. "She's convinced the Home Secretary to intervene again. Honestly, wasn't it enough that she got you back on the police force? How many times are you going to impose on her good name and her good nature?"

"As many times as I need to," Nivens had said. "After all, she's my mother. You're merely another husband and she's had many of those." That wasn't quite true. His dear mama had been married only three times. He took another sip, enjoying the sensation as the expensive whisky hit the back of his throat.

At first he'd been grateful just to get back on the force, but upon thinking about it, he wanted more. There was always more for an ambitious man like himself. He wouldn't make the same mistakes he'd made before; not this time. No more wasting his time slaving at an unimportant police station in a miserably poor part of London. This time, he'd be at the heart of things, right in the thick of it. He'd be at the place where important decisions were made, where who you knew mattered, and if one was clever enough, where a career could soar.

He was going to Scotland Yard. He laughed softly. He couldn't wait to see Chief Superintendent Barrows' face when he reported for duty in January. He'd be livid but there was sod all he could do about it. Nivens lifted his glass in a toast. "Thank you, Mama, you came through once again," he muttered. "I don't mind if the best you could get me was the records room. Upon reflection, that's precisely the place I need to be."

He took another drink, put the glass down, and stared at the wooden box on the shelves opposite his desk. The box contained a set of antique dueling pistols. Pistols that had almost cost him the only thing that mattered to him in the world—his career. He'd considered selling them but, during his time away from the Metropolitan Police Force, decided to keep them. They served as a constant reminder to watch your every move and never, ever assume anyone would look out for you except for yourself. Even dear Mama had let him down then, but her marriage to Lord Merton wasn't as happy as she'd hoped and he'd soon have her back in the palm of his hand.

The records room was perfect, and he knew exactly what he was going to do the minute he walked inside. He'd start with the "Horrible Kensington High Street Murders," as the press had dubbed them, and after he'd gone through that case, he'd go through every single case that Gerald Witherspoon had ever solved.

He knocked back the rest of the whisky, put the glass on his desk, and smiled in satisfaction. "I'll prove the man is a fraud if it's the last thing I do."